RECKONING HOUR

ALSO BY PETER O'MAHONEY

The Joe Hennessy Series:

The Southern Lawyer

The Southern Criminal

The Southern Killer

The Southern Trial

The Southern Fraud

The Tex Hunter Series:

Power and Justice

Faith and Justice

Corrupt Justice

Deadly Justice

Saving Justice

Natural Justice

Freedom and Justice

Losing Justice

Failing Justice

Final Justice

The Jack Valentine Series:

Gates of Power

The Hostage

The Shooter

The Thief

The Witness

RECKONING HOUR

A DEAN LINCOLN LEGAL THRILLER

PETER O'MAHONEY

This is a work of fiction. Names, characters, organizations, places, events, and incidents are either products of the author's imagination or are used fictitiously. Any resemblance to actual persons, living or dead, or actual events is purely coincidental.

Text copyright © 2025 by Peter O'Mahoney
All rights reserved.

No part of this book may be reproduced, or stored in a retrieval system, or transmitted in any form or by any means, electronic, mechanical, photocopying, recording, or otherwise, without express written permission of the publisher.

Published by Thomas & Mercer, Seattle

www.apub.com

Amazon, the Amazon logo, and Thomas & Mercer are trademarks of Amazon.com, Inc., or its affiliates.

EU Product Safety contact:
Amazon Publishing, Amazon Media EU S.à r.l.
38, avenue John F. Kennedy, L-1855 Luxembourg
amazonpublishing-gpsr@amazon.com

ISBN-13: 9781662525377
eISBN: 9781662525384

Cover design by Dan Mogford
Cover image: © Douglas Sacha / Getty Images; © Viorel Sima
© Yingjie / Shutterstock

Printed in the United States of America

For Ethan, Chelsea, and Sophie

CHAPTER 1

"Are you sure you're okay coming back here?"

I didn't answer my wife's question. I had heard her, loud and clear, but my eyes were on the road. The South Carolina Lowcountry had presented itself before me and it took my breath away. The Spanish moss danced off the trees, waving in the gusts as we drove underneath the canopies, swaying and twirling and floating to the rhythm of the wind. The scene brought back so many memories of my childhood, running free in the grass, chasing cousins, getting in trouble with nature as my playground.

"Dean?" my wife repeated. "Did you hear me? I asked whether you'd be fine coming back to Beaufort? I know there's a lot of pain here."

Emma was the most beautiful woman I had ever met, from the first day I laid eyes on her to today. She was stunning. The way she moved, the way she smiled, the way she knew me better than I knew myself.

"Earth to Dean? Hello?"

"I heard you." I smiled and tapped my thumb on the steering wheel. "And if this is what you need to do, then this is what we do."

Emma nodded with a knowing look that comes from being married for ten years. Eyebrows raised, chin tucked down, creases in the forehead. I'd seen it many times, and usually it was accompanied by a warning. She allowed the silence to sit between us until a few minutes later, when she added, "Don't cause any trouble."

"Trouble? Me?"

"You can't hide that smile from me. I can see those dimples as clear as day." She grinned. "But I mean it—don't cause any trouble. We've come back to look after my mother, not to disrupt everything. You can be very unwavering in your sense of right and wrong, and it's not always the best thing. Sometimes, you need to compromise."

"I promise I'll—"

Lights flashed behind me. A cop. A country road. No houses nearby. Not a good sign.

Emma looked over her shoulder, then at me, then back over her shoulder, and then exhaled loudly. She knew trouble had a way of following me. I slowed our SUV and parked on the side of the road. I avoided eye contact with Emma, but I could feel her glare on me.

Looking in the rearview mirror, I watched the deputy sheriff exit his car. He was an older man with slicked back brown hair, held in place with too much gel. He walked with a limp, and his stomach hung over the top of his thick belt. His face was round, but not like a new basketball, more like a half-deflated ball that hadn't been used in years, squished and ill-shaped, forgotten in the deep recesses of the garage.

The deputy tapped his hand on the back of the car and approached the open window. "Do you know what I pulled you over for, boy?"

The tone of the word "boy" was laced with arrogance and superiority. I looked at Emma. She squinted, and her expression said more than her mouth ever could—*don't you dare cause any trouble, mister.*

I turned back to the cop. "No, sir."

2

"I pulled you over because you've got Illinois plates and you were going over the speed limit. This is a long drive from Illinois."

"It is."

"It's quicker if you're speeding, I guess. Got your license and registration?"

"Certainly." I turned to reach for the information, but Emma already had it in her hands. She passed it over, still squinting and glaring at me.

"Dean Lincoln, huh?" The man studied my license, then studied me, then studied my license again. "I'll need you to step out of the car."

I grunted, reached for the handle, and flung open the door. I stepped out, towering over the deputy.

"Whoa, you're a big guy," the deputy said as he stepped back. "They didn't tell me you'd be the size of a linebacker."

"Who didn't tell you?"

"Huh? Nobody. It's just a saying," he continued, but it was clear he was lying. "I need you to kneel down."

I chuckled. "Pardon?"

"Are you deaf?"

"No."

"Then I said kneel down."

"I heard what you said."

"Then kneel down."

"No."

"I don't think you understand." The deputy's jaw clenched. He glared at me. His right hand went to his belt, resting on his gun. "I said kneel down."

"*Dean*." It was Emma. Her voice was scolding. She had stepped out of the car and was walking around the back of the vehicle. "I'm sorry, Officer, but my husband has a problem with his knees. He's in his late thirties now, and I guess his body is starting to fall apart. We arrived from Chicago yesterday, and all that driving has been hard on my husband's knees. We've just been out for boiled peanuts, but it's been a while since he got out to stretch his legs. My husband is a defense lawyer, and my mother lives here in Beaufort, off Carteret Street. We're coming back to care for her as she goes through cancer treatment." Emma tried to ease the tension with a story about our local connections. "Can I ask what this is about? Is there a problem with the car?"

The deputy stared at me, before he looked at Emma. He eased his hand off his weapon. "No, ma'am. No problem at all." He smiled, but his tone was patronizing. "Now, why don't you be a good little girl and get back in the car?"

I stepped forward, but Emma held her hand out as a stop sign. "I can get back in the car." Emma smiled her best Southern smile. She leaned forward and read his badge. *"Officer Thomas Grayson."*

Her tone shook him more than my physical presence. The deputy stood up straighter, puffed his chest out, and the tension eased from his face. Emma gave him a friendly smile and returned to her side of the car.

The deputy waited until Emma's car door closed. He grunted, stepped closer and lowered his voice. "I know who you are. I knew as soon as I saw those Illinois plates. Watch your step in this county, lawyer boy."

I didn't respond as he turned and walked away. I had expected a rough welcome to my old hometown, I had expected some feathers would be ruffled, but I hadn't expected it to be so blatant.

As much as Emma didn't want it, as much as I tried to avoid it, there was no doubt about it—trouble had a way of following me.

CHAPTER 2

The landscape of Beaufort County, South Carolina, had an aura that encouraged tenderness and quietness. The semitropical air, the gentle marshes, the smells of azaleas and jasmine and wisterias—there was a seductive quality to the scenery, a softness that drew you in, embraced you, and made you feel calm under its spell.

My return had triggered so many long-forgotten memories, filled with an assortment of pain and joy, of happiness and sadness. I had memories of hot summer days spent with friends by the rivers, of afternoons on boats, of oyster roasts, of heavy August storms, of eerie nights, of festivals, of herons, of sunsets, of the breathtaking magnificence of the Spanish moss. Despite all those wonderful memories, despite all those moments that had shaped me into who I am, returning to the small town still felt like stepping backward in life. The work opportunities weren't here. I had moved to Chicago ten years earlier to make a career, to build something I could be proud of, and until a month ago, I hadn't looked back.

The Law Office of Bruce Hawthorn was in the beating heart of Beaufort, on the main thoroughfare of Carteret Street. The white colonial-styled building stood proudly on a corner block, hiding under the shade of two Southern live oaks. I rolled my SUV over the gravel parking lot and stopped next to a new BMW sedan, recently cleaned, and reflecting the sun's glare like a mirror. I stepped out and took in a lungful of air. It was so thick with humidity I could almost chew it. As I walked across the small parking lot, I wiped my brow with the back of my hand; it was already damp. I was back in South Carolina, there was no doubt about it.

As I entered the building, I was thankful to be hit by a wall of cool air. Natural light flooded through the tall windows, with the white walls and cream-colored carpets only increasing the brightness. All the office classics were there—potted plants tucked into corners, a coffee table with two outdated magazines, and several pieces of landscape art on the walls. The smell was fresh, thanks to a squirt of a nearby air-freshener, and the hum of the air conditioner was constant.

"Hello," I greeted the assistant. "I'm—"

"Dean!" I heard Bruce Hawthorn before I saw him. "Dean Lincoln!"

I smiled as my former mentor appeared out of a nearby room. He was still the same man I had known all those years earlier. He was rounder now, with less hair and more wrinkles, but he still had the same unmistakable grin. We greeted each other with smiles, a solid handshake, and then a hug. We slapped each other's backs hard enough to leave a mark, then pulled away.

Bruce Hawthorn was born in Beaufort, studied in Beaufort, and had been married three times in Beaufort. His children lived in Beaufort, their children lived in Beaufort, and all things going well, their children would live in Beaufort. The area was in his blood. He was a solid man, with shoulders wide enough to be intimidating and hands large enough to double as baseball mitts. His stomach had grown bigger, his hair had grayed, and he seemed shorter than I remembered, barely reaching my shoulder, but his vibrant personality hadn't changed.

"Dean, this is Kayla Smith," Bruce introduced me to his assistant. "The best assistant in the world. I couldn't last a single day without her magic touch. In fact, I'm sure she's an angel sent down to look after me."

Kayla smiled as she walked around her desk. We shook hands firmly. I was impressed—the petite lady had the grip of a rock-climber. Middle-aged, Kayla was well dressed, toned, and had the glow of good health. Her blonde hair was tied back to show off a pair of jade earrings, her red dress hugged her athletic frame, and her red high heels glimmered in the afternoon light.

"I didn't expect you until tomorrow, Dean," Bruce said as he patted me on the back again. "We had everything set up for a big welcome. I've even ordered a Huguenot torte from Charleston. It's one of my favorites—full of fresh pecans and apples."

"I won't say no to that, but I thought it'd be good to drop by for a chat today."

"Absolutely." Bruce held his hand out to point down the hall. "Come into my office."

I followed Bruce into his room, which was spacious and clean, and had a faint smell of sandalwood. I imagined that was Kayla's touch. There was a large mahogany desk to the back, and a tall bookshelf full of old law volumes to the right. They had gathered dust, and it was clear they hadn't been used since the internet had taken over record-keeping duties.

"It's not often you get to work for your mentor," I said as I sat in front of his desk. "It's an honor."

"Work for? Are you kidding me?" Bruce laughed as he sat heavily on the tall leather chair behind his desk. The chair rocked under his weight. "I might have thirty years of practice on you, but you're more experienced than me now. Those ten years in Chicago have given you a world of knowledge that you never would've gained here. I hear you even got your smiling face on the national news a few times. And I tell you, you've got a face for the news, Dean. Those good looks and that thick black hair—you've got the looks of a movie star. Me, well, I've got a face for radio." Bruce chuckled to himself. "Just as well I'm good at law, otherwise I never would've landed my first wife . . . or my second wife, or my third wife." He laughed again. "So, how long are you and Emma planning on staying here?"

"We've rented the house for twelve months."

"Ah, do I sense a hint of reluctance in your voice?"

"Emma needs to care for her mother throughout the cancer treatment, so we're here while that happens, and then we'll head back to Chicago. And listen, I'd do anything for Emma. She could ask me to shave my head, join a moon-worshipping cult, and move to the Appalachian Mountains, and I'd do it." I smiled. "Our life is good up North. My career is booming, but life has a way of throwing things at you. That's why I appreciate you giving me some work while we're here. It'll keep my mind active."

"And your job in Chicago?"

"My firm said my position will still be there when I return. And it's only twelve months. I'm sure the people of Chicago can survive without me for a year."

Kayla brought in two mugs of coffee and placed one in front of me.

"Grab a chair, Kayla." Bruce pointed to the chair next to me.

My granddad, a former defense lawyer, had given Bruce his first job. Bruce, now in his sixties, was determined to repay the favor while I stayed in town. The three of us chatted about nothing in particular for twenty-five minutes, laughing about old law stories and telling well-worn jokes. Bruce was charismatic, charming, and animated, with a deep Southern voice that was perfect for storytelling.

When the stories started getting longer and the laughs getting shorter, I turned the conversation to work. "You mentioned there were a few cases you wanted me to work on?"

"You want to get straight into it? You big-city folk don't mess around."

"After ten years in Chicago, their way of life has rubbed off on me," I agreed, although I thought twenty-five minutes of casual talk was more than enough before moving the discussion to work. It was going to take a while to get used to life in the South again. "I don't like sitting around, Bruce. It gives me too much time in my own head."

"And you're still registered with the bar?"

"All sorted. I passed the bar years ago but set it to inactive status. I paid my membership dues every year, even though I was practicing in Chicago. I worked so hard to pass that exam and I wasn't going to give it away easily."

"Good." Bruce smiled. "So, straight into it then?"

I nodded.

"Okay." Bruce turned to his assistant. "Kayla, can you please bring in Dean's files?"

Kayla hurried out of the room, and returned a minute later carrying two thick files.

"Your timing is excellent. I've got two cases I need help with." Bruce leaned his heavy arms on the table. "One, a murder case that I'll need you to sit second chair on. I've never done a murder case before, so when you said you were coming back, it was a big relief for me. And two." He pushed the other file toward me. "I've taken on an arson case for a guy who did my gardening for years. His son has gotten into trouble, and I said I'd help him out. We're doing it pro bono, as a favor to an old friend, and I thought you could take the lead on that one for me."

"What are you working on?"

"My golf swing." He stood and gave me a live demonstration of an awkward swing that struggled to go past his beer-and-burger-filled stomach. "One thing you'll learn out here is we don't work twenty-four-seven like you city folk. Life is for living, my friend. It's the Lowcountry way."

As Bruce talked me through the breakdown of his golf swing, I flicked through the files and noted the preliminary details. I tried to ask him some questions, but he was more interested in telling me how fast the greens were near his home.

"It's easy work," Bruce said as he practiced his chip shot. "We'll argue with the prosecution about a few points, go back and forth for a while, do a little dance where we dispute the evidence, like we always do, and then the State will give us a great deal and we'll encourage the clients to take it. Then, we'll hit the golf course."

"That's what you're aiming for?"

"Absolutely." Bruce was pretending to watch an imaginary ball sail into the distance. "Everything works smoothly here because everything has its place. We follow the process, and we get results. We'll get both clients a good deal, given their situation, and then move on to the next case. We treat the prosecution well, and they treat our clients well. It's the way things have been done for a hundred years, and it's the way things will be done for a hundred more."

I nodded.

"But listen, I need to give you a heads-up." Bruce stopped after another practice swing. He sighed and then lowered his voice. "There's one thing you should know."

"Go on."

Bruce sat back down, his head dropping a little. Kayla shifted in her chair, uncomfortable in the awkward silence.

"What is it, Bruce?"

"Paul Freeman."

The name sent a shockwave through my system. My fists clenched, as did my jaw. "What about him, Bruce?"

"He was released from prison yesterday. I didn't want to tell you over the phone. I thought it'd be better to tell you face to face."

I stared at Bruce, unable to find the words to express what I was feeling.

"I'm sorry to be the one to tell you, Dean. He got out for good behavior, apparently. After two years of going through the courts, and two months of a trial, he only ended up serving five months of a ten-year sentence."

If one thing was becoming clear, it was that law and order in Beaufort County was far different from what I was used to.

CHAPTER 3

Emma was waiting for me, leaning against the pillar on the front porch of our rental home in the Old Point historic district of Beaufort. I walked up the street, wiping my brow again, strolling under the layers and layers of Spanish moss. The area was filled with mature live oaks that were hundreds of years old, draped in long pieces of the gray-bearded plant, creating a haunting sense of mystery and wonder.

Built in 1855, our colonial-style home was a classic example of Southern architecture, with large windows to take advantage of the breeze off the water, a spacious porch for a shady escape from the blaring sun, and a low-pitched roof that allowed the summer heat to escape. All the houses near us were also Beaufort-style homes—different from the styles of Charleston or Savannah, they had been designed on large plots of land, more akin to smaller versions of plantation-style homes.

Our home was a block down from Emma's mother, who had been diagnosed with cancer five weeks earlier. Only two blocks farther away lived my grandparents, a religious couple in their early eighties who were determined not to let age slow them.

"We've got a porch swing?" I said as I approached.

"It's cute, isn't it?" Emma smiled.

"When I was a teenager in Beaufort, I always wanted one of these." I walked up the steps and sat down, enjoying the gentle swing of the seat. "What girl could resist a porch-swing kiss?"

"Certainly not this one." Emma sat down next to me, gave me a small kiss on the cheek, and then tapped my leg and jumped up. "But that's for another time. I've been cooking all afternoon, and your grandparents have arrived."

I smiled and followed her inside.

I greeted Emma's mother, Jane, with a hug. She was in her early sixties and suddenly frail. She had always been a hard-working and determined woman, a teacher with a good heart and a soft touch, but the cancer had eaten away at her physical health. But while her body appeared fragile, her eyes still sparkled with the joy of someone who had lived a great life. She wore a hat inside, the first time I'd ever seen her do that. Her lovely yellow and white dress flowed behind her as she moved.

My grandparents greeted me next. Grandma Lincoln was first in line. She pulled me down for a hug, holding me close and tight. "I told you you'd come back," she whispered in my ear with a sly tone. Her cheeky smile had never changed. "Just ten years later than I thought."

Then, Granddad Lincoln. He greeted me with a solid hand-shake and a pat on the shoulder. Even in his early eighties, he still had the heavy hands of a hard worker. He was a short man with thick arms and a barrel chest. His shoulders were solid, and he looked fifteen years younger than his age. He was a former Air Force veteran, and in his second career, a defense lawyer in Beaufort. Judging by the photos from their younger years, my grandparents had been quite the good-looking couple.

We sat down to what appeared to be a feast of Southern cooking because, well, it was. Not only did Jane have some of the best recipes in the South, Emma was the best cook I knew. As a duo, they worked well together, with a rhythm only a mother and daughter could have. The décor inside our rental home was dark, but Emma had laid out a white tablecloth, and had already unpacked framed pictures of families, friends, and places we'd visited over the years. Our meal around the dining table was everything a great Southern meal should be—full of chatter, laughter, good wine, and mouth-watering food.

"Heard from your father?" Grandma Lincoln asked me as she finished her serving of Frogmore stew.

"He called yesterday and told me to be careful around here. He thinks I'm going to cause trouble," I grinned. My father, widowed by my mother's heart attack, had moved to Florida almost a decade ago, only months after Emma and I left, and found his second wife there, settling into the retired beach life of Sarasota. "I told him trouble was a genetic trait, and it was all his fault."

Grandma Lincoln slapped my hand while my granddad laughed.

"Well, I, for one, am so glad you're both back," Jane said as she placed her fork down. She reached across and held Emma's hand. "Thank you. It means so much." Emma offered her mother a smile and I could tell she was holding back tears. "I think it's wonderful what you're doing, coming back to help everyone. And you, Dean, this justice system could really do with a shake-up. The same people are doing the same things they've always done."

"I heard Bruce has taken on the murder charge against Caleb Rutledge," Granddad Lincoln said. "Are you helping with that?"

"I am."

"Everyone is talking about it," Jane added. "Do you think he killed his girlfriend?"

"I haven't met him and I've only had a quick look at the case file, so I haven't formed an opinion yet."

"And if he killed that sweet girl, what would you do?" Jane questioned. "Would you still defend him?"

"That's the job."

"An important part of the system," Granddad Lincoln added. "Without defense lawyers, the whole system would be subject to corruption. Defense attorneys play a crucial role in holding up the constitutional rights of the accused. A lynch mob can handle the prosecution of a criminal very well, but lynch mobs are subject to the rules of a few. So how do you verify who's innocent and guilty? By forcing the government to prove it." Granddad Lincoln had always loved a good rant. "And I will add that my old profession reduces the imbalance of power that exists between the government and the governed. Defense lawyers challenge the State to be fairer, to be just and righteous, and to protect the rights of the people. We protect the innocent by forcing the State to be fair and just."

"Hasn't stopped them around here," Jane quipped, despite the convincing speech. "Look at what happened to the Freeman kid. All you need to do is know the right people and all of a sudden you can get out of prison without even serving one tenth of your sentence."

The table paused. In slow motion, Granddad Lincoln's right hand gripped his glass. His knuckles went white. The veins popped out of his skin. The muscles of his forearm pulsed. He took a breath, sucking in deep through his nostrils, the only noise in the room.

He looked at me. "Have you heard?"

"Bruce told me."

Granddad Lincoln punched his left fist on the table. The plates jumped. Nobody said anything. His jaw clenched and then relaxed. After another long breath through his nostrils, he continued, "We were told last night. We were furious that we didn't even get the chance to submit a victim's statement to the parole board. The board called Rhys, but that was it. I was about to go to the prison and shoot him, but your grandmother stopped me." He looked at his wife, and she nodded. "You know why he was released, don't you?"

I didn't respond.

"It's because he's Stephen Freeman's son. It's nothing more than that. We called the solicitor, and he gave us some story about the prison being full, about this and that and budgets and costs, but I know it was all lies." His fist clenched again. "Stephen Freeman is a political lobbyist now, you know. And since he retired as a solicitor, he's been volunteering as a consultant in the circuit solicitor's office. It's a clear conflict of interest, but nobody does anything about it." He didn't raise his eyes from the table. "If you have money and you want something done, you go to Stephen Freeman. He married the daughter of another former circuit solicitor, and his sister married a former sheriff. Now, the whole extended family controls everything. Generations of links and generations of power. There're so many good people in this county, but they're controlled by that puppeteer, and they don't even realize it."

"If everyone knows about it, how does he have so much influence?" Emma asked. "Why doesn't someone stop him?"

"How do you stop a family that controls everything?" Grandma Lincoln said.

"I'll tell you how." Granddad Lincoln raised a finger in the air. "With a bullet between the eyes. That's the only way to stop someone like him."

"Settle down." Grandma Lincoln reached across and rested her hand on his. She looked at us. "It's not good for his blood pressure to get all worked up like this."

The conversation eventually moved on, but tension remained in the air for the rest of the night.

The scars of small-town corruption had left their hard mark on my family, and Grandma Lincoln's words echoed in my head: *"How do you stop a family that controls everything?"*

CHAPTER 4

I wiped a layer of sweat off my brow as I walked toward the Beaufort County Detention Center.

This was a bland, nondescript building, as it should've been. It wasn't a place to draw attention, and it wasn't a place to party. The entrance looked like that of every other office building in the county, but behind the glass doors it was anything but. To the left was a long wall of concrete, topped by barbed wire, and to the right, the Beaufort County Court of General Sessions.

Five days after he was arrested, Caleb Rutledge was denied bond. With new laws governing victims' rights, Caleb's hearing had been pushed back until there had been reasonable attempts to contact all of the victim's family. The sitting judge appeared to be influenced by the victim's family's attendance and stated Caleb was a threat to the community. That didn't appear to be true, but at the instruction of Caleb Rutledge and his father, Gerald Rutledge, Bruce hadn't appealed the decision.

Gerald Rutledge was waiting outside the detention center, sucking on a cigarette, walking back and forth in front of the entrance. In his sixties, he was a good-looking silver fox, with olive skin, brushed back silver hair, and a square jaw. He walked with the arrogant swagger of a man who had experienced years of success and victories, most likely taken and not deserved.

"I've just seen him," Gerald said as Bruce and I approached. "He's doing okay today, and he's feeling good about his chances of getting a good deal." Gerald Rutledge turned to look at me. "You must be the city lawyer?"

"Dean Lincoln," I introduced myself.

Gerald shook my hand like a limp fish. His weak handshake sent a shiver through me. I hated that. Gerald turned back to Bruce. "How's the negotiation coming along?"

"It's going well," Bruce noted. "The prosecution has a few things they want to check out first, but we should be able to get him a deal for manslaughter. Maybe five years, maybe ten. It depends on what else we can find."

"Five years, huh?" Gerald sucked hard on the cigarette, looking back at the entrance to the detention center. "Try to convince Caleb to take the deal. I don't want him to throw his life away because of this silly little mistake. If you can get five years, it'd be much appreciated, Bruce. Everyone said you were the right man for the job, and it looks like they weren't lying. They told me you did your best work behind the scenes, wheeling and dealing, and you'd be able to get a good deal for the kid. That's why I came to you." Gerald patted Bruce on the shoulder. "Good luck in there."

Gerald flicked the cigarette on to the road and walked away.

Bruce waited until he had turned a corner, then leaned close to me.

"I've never trusted that man, so I doubled my retainer for this case." He shook his head. "He's the president of the Beaufort County division of the South Carolina Farm Agency. They're an advisory board, and they have a lot of sway in the state capitol, and he walks around here like he owns the place. But hey, you can't like everyone, right?"

"I don't like him, and I've just met him."

"I always knew you were a good judge of character," Bruce said as he walked toward the front door. "Let's get out of this heat and talk to Caleb about when he might get his freedom back."

We entered the detention center, and once we passed through security, it smelled like every other prison I'd ever been into—a mix of urine, body odor, and sewage. Not the type of place I wanted to stay in for long. An angry scream came from down the hall, and it instantly felt like I was back in the halls of Chicago's infamous Cook County Jail. A correctional officer led us to the meeting room, told us where to sit, and then swung the heavy door shut behind us. It was hot inside. Meltingly hot. There was no air-conditioning, little ventilation, and the dampness was thick on the walls. I loosened my tie and undid the top two buttons of my shirt.

The room was tight, with much of the space taken up by a skinny metal table bolted to the floor in the middle. Four metal chairs were welded to the floor on each side. The chairs were slightly too close to the table, and Bruce had to squeeze his stomach into the small space. I leaned against the side wall, ignoring the dampness against my shirt.

During our wait, Bruce explained that Gerald was not Caleb's natural father but had adopted him when he married Caleb's mother. She had died when he was ten, and it was left to Gerald to raise him. While Bruce was talking, I watched the sweat drip off his forehead. Bruce ignored it, but every time I felt the sweat building, I wiped my brow. It was going to take some time to adapt to the humidity again.

We waited for fifteen minutes before the door opened and Caleb Rutledge was led inside. The prisoner, dressed in an orange jumpsuit, was still handcuffed. Bruce pointed to the cuffs, and the correctional officer removed them as soon as Caleb sat down. Caleb rubbed his wrists the moment they were removed, and the red marks were clear.

Caleb Rutledge was a good-looking Southern kid. Five-ten, solid shoulders, olive skin. The straight white teeth of a movie star. He had a thick mop of dark brown hair, piercing green eyes, and the facial structure of a model. Despite his ten days in prison, his skin still looked moisturized and soft. There was no doubt this twenty-one-year-old kid had been raised with money at his disposal.

The file said Caleb had been a promising baseball player before a shoulder injury stopped his potential career. He now worked part-time at Publix, the supermarket chain, while he was also studying marketing at the University of South Carolina Beaufort. He'd never been arrested, never been investigated by the police, but he did have a few minor indiscretions from his high-school years. He was well liked and everyone spoke highly of his character.

"Caleb, this is Dean Lincoln." Bruce introduced me. "Dean is going to be helping with your case. He'll be sitting second chair, which means he's assisting me with the process. He's a big-time defense lawyer from Chicago who's handled hundreds of murder cases and knows this process inside out. He's gotten more people off murder charges than I've had trials."

Caleb looked at me. "If you're from Chicago, what are you doing here?"

It was an innocent question, and one I expected a lot on my return. "This is my hometown. I grew up here, and my mother-in-law is sick. My wife and I came back to look after her while she goes through cancer treatment."

He nodded, expressionless. "You going to get me out of this place?"

I drew a long breath and looked at Bruce. "From my first read-through of the case notes, I can tell you this isn't going to be easy. There's a lot of circumstantial evidence against you, and the State has built a strong case."

"But it's like I told Bruce—it's all circumstantial," he said. "There's no evidence that I hurt her."

"Most murder trials involve a heavy amount of circumstantial evidence," I replied. "Forget everything you've heard on the internet, this is the real world, and in the real world, circumstantial evidence has the same weight as direct evidence. DNA, fingerprints, hair, blood—that's all circumstantial evidence. It's very rare that there's a direct witness to a murder, and if there is, it's very rare that the case makes it to trial. So, I'll make it clear for you—most murder trials are based on circumstantial evidence. And the circumstantial evidence against you is strong."

"Think of circumstantial evidence as a matter of common sense," Bruce added. "The way I like to explain it is this—you go to bed at night and it's dry outside. When you wake up in the morning, your entire yard is covered in snow, along with the roads, and the buildings, and the trees. You see storm clouds in the distance. You didn't directly witness the snow, but it's clear what the white powder on the ground indicates. That's circumstantial evidence that it snowed while you were asleep."

Caleb threw his hands up in the air. "Circumstantial or not, I didn't do it."

"You've been charged with one count of murder under Section 16-3-10 of the South Carolina Code of Laws for the murder of Millie Aiken." I sat down and opened a file on the metal table. "The minimum sentence for murder in South Carolina is thirty years in prison, as defined by Section 16-3-20."

Caleb shook his head and muttered, more to himself than me, "I can't do that. I can't spend my life in here."

"Millie Aiken, your girlfriend, was found on the kitchen floor of her home with an injury to the side of her skull. The prosecution believes you struck her, and she fell and hit her head. When she fell, she wasn't deceased; however, she later bled. Her mother returned home several hours later to find her on the floor, next to a pool of blood. I'm not going to ask you if you hit her that night, because it can limit what we can say in court, but I need to know if you've ever hit Millie in the past."

"I've never hit her," he whispered.

"But you have gotten into a fight with another guy at a party during high school," Bruce added. "That doesn't look good."

"That was against another guy, and it was self-defense," Caleb complained. "He started it, and I finished it. I was never charged with anything."

"Still won't look good in court, and the prosecution knows this," Bruce said. "So, we're going to do the best we can for you and get you a deal for involuntary manslaughter. That means you'll need to admit you slapped Millie, but you didn't intend to hurt her, and this is all one great big horrible mistake. We'll talk to the prosecution again later this week, and we'll argue you slapped her in a moment of intense passion before she fell and hit her head."

"But I didn't do it," Caleb insisted, staring at the table. "I didn't hit her. Why can't you understand that?"

"You don't need to accept the deal, but it's good for us to negotiate," I noted, but when Bruce coughed twice, I didn't continue.

"I'm going to be honest, Caleb, because that's how I like to work." Bruce paused to allow the words to sink in before he continued. "I won't make baseless claims that everything is going to be alright or dumb things down for you. I'll be honest with you and stand by your side through this whole thing and ensure you have the best possible defense. So let me make it clear—Caleb, you've been charged with murder. Charges don't get more serious than this, and if you don't consider taking the deal, then you might die in here."

22

"Does that mean the death penalty?" The stress was written all over Caleb's face. He looked moments from crying. "I didn't touch her. Why can't you understand that?"

"In South Carolina, for the State to chase the death penalty, there must be one of twelve aggravating factors, as listed under Section 16-3-20 of the South Carolina Code of Laws," I explained. "Among them are murder involving another felony such as rape or torture, the murder of a law enforcement officer, the murder of a witness in a court case, or the murder of a child under the age of eleven. None of your charges falls into those categories. However, the minimum sentence for murder is still thirty years to life."

"Thirty years?" Caleb's eyes pleaded with Bruce. "What about second-degree murder? Why wasn't I charged with that?"

"Unlike other states, there are no levels of murder in South Carolina," I continued. "South Carolina homicide law defines murder as a killing with malice aforethought. That's it. There's no other level. This means either you intended to kill the victim, or you acted with a reckless indifference to their life."

"This is ridiculous," Caleb said, looking away and staring at the wall. "I can't spend thirty years in here."

"That's why we need to talk to the prosecution about reducing your charges to manslaughter," Bruce carried on. "There are two options for that—involuntary or voluntary. Voluntary manslaughter is the unlawful killing in the heat of passion upon sufficient legal provocation. I don't think we can show provocation in this instance, but we can negotiate for involuntary manslaughter. Involuntary manslaughter is an unintentional killing without malice, while displaying a reckless disregard for the safety of others. Slapping someone is not a felony crime, so the slap doesn't fall under the charges for voluntary manslaughter. The penalty for voluntary manslaughter is between two and thirty years in prison, while involuntary manslaughter is between zero and five years in prison. I need you to be open to considering those charges."

"I didn't touch her." Caleb stood, shaking his head, trying to disperse his anxiety. He walked to the far side of the room and leaned his back against the wall. "I didn't hit her."

"The State believes you did." Bruce's tone was firm. "They believe you had the motive, intent, and means to hurt her. The State wants to keep you in here for life. They want to lock you up and keep you back here until you turn fifty-one."

"I get it, alright? I get it." He tapped the back of his head against the concrete. "Why can't I tell the judge that I didn't do it? Can't I go to court and say that?"

"Let's look at the evidence against you, Caleb." Bruce opened the folder in front of him. "We have eyewitnesses who say they saw you arguing with Millie in the days before the incident. You were seen near her place on the night she died, and the gas station attendant says she saw blood on your arm when you went to pay for gas around that time. Your DNA was also present in the kitchen where her body was found. And there are angry text messages between you and her. She even invited you to her house that night. You don't have an alibi, so when it all adds up, the weight of circumstantial evidence looks very solid."

Caleb shook his head. "I didn't hit her. I couldn't hit her."

"The prosecution is running with the theory you did," Bruce continued. "Their theory is you were angry with her, went to her home, argued again inside her house, and then slapped her. She fell and hit her head on the edge of the kitchen bench, and you left her there to die. When her mother arrived home from work a few hours later, Millie was lying in a pool of her own blood and was clearly deceased." Bruce shook his head. "A horrible moment for Mrs. Aiken."

"I didn't hit her," he repeated. "I never laid a hand on her."

"We need to negotiate with the State," Bruce persisted. "Before I try to bargain with the prosecution, I need you to be open to the idea of spending five years in prison for involuntary manslaughter. Are we on the same page about that?"

Caleb didn't answer, staring at the ceiling. It was clear he was struggling with heartache. I'd seen that same look from clients many times—the confusion of grief, the anguish of loss, along with the utter devastation about their newfound situation. For most people, being arrested was a mystifying and bewildering experience.

"You don't need to say yes now," Bruce continued. "But I need you to be open to the idea of a deal. Are you open to the idea, Caleb?"

Caleb took several breaths and then nodded.

"Good," Bruce stated firmly.

He opened a file and began the discussion about the legal terms of a deal. Bruce and I spent another fifty-five minutes with Caleb, but we didn't get much more out of him. He kept whispering to himself, over and over, as the reality of his situation set in. Once we had the information we needed, we left the shell of a young man to return to his prison cell.

Bruce and I walked out of the prison without a word between us.

"What are your first thoughts?" Bruce asked as we stepped outside into the glare of the midday South Carolina sun.

"He should take it to trial." I looked up to the bright sun and wiped my brow. "There's a chance he'll win."

"No, no, no." Bruce shook his head as he walked. "That's not the way we do things around here."

I didn't respond as Bruce walked a step ahead of me. It appeared we had very different goals for our newest case.

CHAPTER 5

The Empty Station was a dive bar across the river from downtown Beaufort. It was a local hangout, tucked away from the tourist hotspots, filled with the same characters as fifteen years ago, seemingly glued to their chairs.

The food was good, the beer was cold, and the view was breathtaking. A former gas station, the Empty Station was where people laughed at well-worn stories, sang old songs badly, and danced even worse. It was where locals whispered rumors and shouted half-truths, where friends fought one day and shared a beer the next, where loves were found, and lifelong friends were made. The Empty Station had received plenty of bad online reviews over the years, but they were from tourists who had high expectations of the dive bar. Locals didn't worry about that. They knew what the place was. And despite the occasional poor review, the seats were almost always full.

I walked in, ordered a beer, and sat outside, staring at the boats docked by the nearby marina.

There were times in Chicago when I missed the sea breeze and the warm weather that wrapped around you here like a wet hug. There were times I missed the rivers; the movement of the tides, the swaying of the marshes, and the wildlife that seemed so free. There was a heartbeat to this land, something bigger than me, bigger than anything I could imagine. But as much as I missed the nature, I didn't miss the slower pace of life in the Lowcountry.

At school, I was determined to be successful. I wanted straight As on every project, and I wanted to be first in every race. For the most part, I succeeded. At college, it was the same. Then, with the lure of the almighty dollar dangling in front of me, I trekked to Chicago to make it big in criminal defense law. Again, I succeeded. It was my career, but more than that, it was my identity. My name was up in lights. I was winning the big cases. I loved it.

I thought I always had to prove myself, to search for ways to test my limits, to go beyond what others considered success. I needed to be the best. I searched for conditions that would show off my abilities, where I could show the world my talents, where I could passionately defend the rights of the disadvantaged. It didn't quite work out like that—most of my clients had more money than morals—but deep down, I accepted this as a part of my success.

My sister, older by two years, was the opposite. Heather had always loved the slower pace of life. She was intelligent and not at all driven. She was athletic and not competitive. She was lively and not stressed. She was comfortable just being and doing and seeing and living. She was everything I didn't know how to be.

Despite our differences, we were very close growing up, and were still close as adults. We talked every week on the phone, often for over an hour, and shared our lives together, despite living in different parts of the country.

When she met Rhys Parker, I welcomed him into the family. They were great for each other. Rhys was hard-working and strong, and Heather was soft and quiet, but their differences fitted like a puzzle coming together. They had two children, a girl, Zoe, now seven, and a boy, Ollie, five. The kids wrestled, they played pranks on each other, and told each other off. They argued, they laughed, and they had each other's backs. They reminded me a lot of Heather and I growing up.

I heard Rhys enter the bar before I saw him. He was a loud man, and he greeted the bartender from the other side of the room. Rhys was wearing a baseball cap on backward. His shirt was grimy, his hands were dirty, and his boots were filthy. When he spotted me outside, he pointed at me and smiled, and I waved back. He ordered a beer and then joined me outside on the deck.

"Rhys," I said as he approached. "It's good to see you."

Rhys smiled and greeted me with a strong hug. He patted me on the back and then sat down, both of us facing the water.

"So, you finally came back for good, eh?" He gripped my shoulder. "Heather was right, you know? She was sure you would one day. She said Emma couldn't leave this place and she'd eventually convince you to come back here. Once the Lowcountry has you, it's in your heart forever."

"If you say so," I responded, not wishing to explain to him that we were only here for a year. "How are the kids?"

"They'll like having you and Emma around more." He looked at the water as a small boat sailed down the river. "But they miss their mother."

I held up my glass and we clinked them together. "We all do."

Grief is a monster of an emotion. It scratches and it aches, and it bleeds and it yearns. It steals your sleep, and it taunts you in the morning. It follows you to work. It's there when you eat lunch, and it's there when you drive home. You begin to make accommodations for it—you allow yourself five minutes to wallow in it, to accept it, to let the emotions wash over you. Then, you need to move on. You need to continue. You need to keep putting one foot in front of the other and convince yourself the memories were joys, were blessings, were moments that shaped you. And over time, it eases. It softens into the background but never leaves. It becomes a part of who you are, always there, always present, lingering, ready to pounce when you least expect it.

When Heather passed away, Emma and I flew down every weekend to help Rhys with the kids. My father did the same, driving up for weeks at a time from Florida. We were all there for them, and we did whatever we could to help.

Life has a way of not stopping, of steamrolling forward, of growing and changing and emerging. Eventually, the children went back to pre-school, Rhys went back to work, and life somehow, someway, in some strange fashion, continued on.

I let the silence sit between Rhys and I for a while, both of us looking out at the water and watching a boat drift into the distance, seemingly in no rush to go anywhere. The silhouette of a woman walked to the front of the boat and stepped up. Her hair blew in the breeze, dancing in a rhythmic pattern behind her.

Once I was sure the pause had lasted long enough, I asked, "How's work?"

"Hard." He lifted his hands to show me the life of a builder. "But I love it. Wouldn't have it any other way."

"Got much on?"

"Lots out at Bluffton. I've got a renovation job there at the moment, but we've been doing lots of new homes out there as well. It's grown so quickly, almost tripled in size in the last twenty years, and that's fine by me. I don't mind the thirty-five-minute drive to the work site. Gives me time to get into the day." He looked at me. "I've heard you're working for Bruce Hawthorn while you're back?"

"Word travels fast."

"Always around here. What cases has Bruce given you?"

"I'm sitting second chair in the Caleb Rutledge case."

"The murder of Millie Aiken?" Rhys whistled in surprise. "That case has everyone talking."

"Did you know either of them?" I expected the answer to be yes, as everyone and everything in small towns was connected by some small degree of separation.

"I've had brief interactions with both their families, and Caleb came and did a few days' laboring for a bricklayer working on the same site, trying to earn some extra cash for summer. When he showed up to the work site, I thought he was too good-looking to actually try to work, but to his credit, he dug in and worked hard. My impression was that he was a good kid." He tapped the bottom of his beer can against the table. "Caleb could've done it, maybe he didn't. It's hard to tell in cases like this. Sometimes people snap. Sometimes, there's something hiding under the surface and that always comes out somehow." He shook his head. "I'm surprised he was charged, though. His father is good friends with every powerful person in town."

"Stepfather."

"Oh? I didn't know that."

"Raised him since he was young, but not his own kid. Gerald couldn't have kids of his own, so when he married Caleb's mother, he legally adopted him. Then Caleb's mother passed away when Caleb was ten, and the stepfather was left to raise him like his own."

"Explains a lot. When he was on the job site, he complained about his old man. From what he said, they didn't get along."

"And do you know the Aikens?"

He sighed. "Like most people around here, I ordered coffee from Millie a few times at the City Latte. She'd always make the kids the best hot chocolate. They loved going there to see her. That's a true tragedy right there—one of the good ones taken too soon."

Another boat drifted down the river before coming to a stop at the nearby pier. One of the occupants jumped off and tied the ropes to the dock, before two more people joined him. They were jovial as they walked along the dock and into the back of the Empty

Station. Rhys stood and greeted one of them, shaking hands solidly, before he came back to sit down next to me.

"That guy was a colleague of Heather's." He sighed again, staring back out at the river. Rhys looked at me for an uncomfortably long moment before he lowered his voice and said, "Have you heard about Paul Freeman?"

I nodded.

"They released Paul after only five months, Dean." Rhys gripped his glass tight. I was surprised it didn't break under the pressure. "Five months of a ten-year sentence for vehicular homicide. That's not right. That's not justice. How could they do that?"

I didn't respond. I didn't know what to say.

"But you know why, don't you? It's because he's Stephen Freeman's son. It's not right, Dean. How could people let that happen? It took two years to get him into court, and he was sentenced to ten years in prison, and he's out in five months? That's not right." Rhys let go of the glass and his fist clenched. He punched down on the table, struggling to control his anger. "The parole board called me and left a message the day before. I was busy. I had work and the kids and all that stuff. I was going to call them back, but by the time I'd gotten round to it, they'd already released him. After five months. Are you kidding me? My wife's life was only worth five months in prison. Paul was extremely drunk, had no license, and was driving an unregistered car. It couldn't be more obvious that the accident was all his fault. It was all his fault, Dean, and he took no responsibility for it. And now, he gets no punishment. He lives his life like nothing happened."

When he turned to me, I could see tears in his eyes. He coughed and then looked away.

"I'm going to kill him," he whispered. I'd heard this before from Rhys. "I'm going to break every bone in his body, and then I'm going to bleed him out. I'm going to show him what real pain is."

"Not today, Rhys." I rested my hand on his shoulder. I gripped it tight. "Your kids need you. You can't abandon them."

"He didn't show any remorse, Dean. Not a second of it. He even smiled at me in court. You remember it, don't you? He was sitting behind the bench and he smiled at me. He knew he wouldn't serve the whole sentence. He's a rich kid who can get away with anything."

The silence hung over us before Rhys stood and went outside. He returned five minutes later smelling of cheap cigarettes.

I hadn't even drunk half the first beer when Rhys ordered two more. I remember five rounds. After that, I'm not so sure.

The remainder of the night disappeared in a blur of beer and bourbon, grief, memories, old stories, and bad singing.

CHAPTER 6

Thursday morning may have existed, but I didn't see it.

I was never drinking with Rhys again. That man was a hardened drinker who could outdrink a fish. In Chicago, it was easy to stay in bed when a hangover snuck up on me. Here, with the bright sun streaming through the window at 6 a.m., it was almost impossible. If I was going to go drinking with Rhys again, I needed to sleep in the basement.

After a long, hot shower, two aspirin, and a gallon of water, I felt normal enough to drive out to the neighborhood of Mossy Oaks to meet my new client, Isaiah Clyburn.

When I pulled up to the house, I stepped out and looked around. The houses in the area all looked the same—run down and in need of care. I locked the car and then double-checked it was locked.

Isaiah Clyburn's house was a small weatherboard home, shaded by a sprawling live oak that hovered over the house like an umbrella. The house needed a paint job. The grass was long, and weeds filled the path. Two plastic chairs sat facing each other on the front porch. Between them was an ashtray with two half-smoked cigarettes. Several empty Coke bottles lay on the ground around the chairs. I walked up to the door and knocked. I didn't knock hard, afraid the door would fall off the hinges with any extra force.

Isaiah Clyburn opened the door. He was a tall and lanky kid, still boyish in his looks. His skin was a dark black, as was his short, cropped hair. He had long arms, and his body appeared mostly skin and bone. His white T-shirt sat loosely on his wide shoulders. His face was expressionless as he answered the door.

"Mr. Clyburn, my name is Dean Lincoln. Bruce Hawthorn has asked me to look after your case."

"Yeah," Isaiah responded and held out his hand. His handshake was firm. His hands were calloused. "Bruce called me and said you were taking over the case. Something about you being a big city lawyer who wants some local cases. I wasn't sure about using someone from off, but he said you were a local at heart."

"Something like that."

Isaiah led me inside the family home to the living room, which was only a step inside the front door. The room was busy, with trinkets on every available surface, and family photos lining the walls. There were two well-used brown couches, and an old television in the corner. The room smelled stale and earthy, with a hint of cigarette smoke hanging in the air.

"This is my father, Eric." Isaiah pointed to a man across the room.

His father rose slightly off the worn couch and offered his hand. I stepped forward, reaching to shake it. Like his son's, the man's handshake was solid, although the effect of years of manual labor had taken its toll on his body. Eric was hunched over, unable to straighten out. He held himself in one position and moved slowly.

"And my mother, Jada."

Jada greeted me with a wide smile, and an offer of sweet tea. I accepted. She was short, with frizzy gray hair, and her warmth radiated across the room.

"Bruce Hawthorn too busy for us then?" Eric asked.

"Bruce has a lot on his plate," I lied. "He was able to handle the bail hearing, and that was good because he got you bail, and now I've taken the lead on the case. I'm working with Bruce, so the case is still pro bono."

"They say you're a big city lawyer," Eric continued. "Got some wins in big criminal cases up there in Chicago. Bruce said you've even been on the national news."

"I was working in Chicago for a criminal defense firm and yes, the firm had some big wins. I can't claim it was all my work."

"But you're here now?" The mother entered the room carrying two glasses of sweet tea. She handed one to me and another to the father. I thanked her, took a sip, and offered her a grateful smile. Jada pointed to the couch, and I sat down, placing my briefcase next to me.

"I've moved back with my wife to be near her mother," I said. "She was diagnosed with cancer and Emma wants to be close to her and help her out."

"Oh, I'm so sorry to hear that, but it's lovely that you've come back for her." Jada paused and smiled. "Got kids?"

"Not yet." It was a touchy subject for me, and I avoided talking about it. I opened my briefcase and removed a file. "We should focus on the case."

"I'll tell you this now, before you go any further, you can't let Isaiah go to prison." Eric raised his finger in the air like he was delivering the gospel. "He's the only one who can work full-time right now, and he's keeping this household afloat. I beat cancer myself last year, but it ruined me. I haven't been able to work a full day since. Luckily, Isaiah won some money on a floating casino, five thousand, and it'll keep us all going for a bit. He's put it in the bank, so it earns interest as well. He's a clever one, our Isaiah. First time he's ever bet on anything, and he wins. Beginner's luck, eh?"

"Gambling on a floating casino?" I looked at Isaiah, but he avoided eye contact. He stood at the side of the room, leaning against the wall with his hands behind his back.

"It's against the law to gamble on poker in South Carolina and Georgia," Jada explained. "But these cruise ships take people from the port in Savannah and sail five miles out into federal waters, and that's where the fun begins. We've been on a few, but years ago. Great fun for a day. Lots of drinks, lots of dancing, and lots of people winning."

A teenage girl entered through the front door, and we all looked up. She was skinny, wearing a white T-shirt two sizes too big and baggy blue jeans. "This is Lana," Jada introduced her. "Isaiah's younger sister."

I nodded hello, gave her a half-smile, and she nodded back before disappearing down the hallway.

I placed a file on the table in the middle of the room, leaning forward and resting my elbows on my knees. "Isaiah, would you like to talk alone, or would you prefer to do it here?"

"You can do it here," Eric stated.

I looked at Isaiah and he nodded his approval.

"I'm sure Bruce told you all this, but I'll go over it for you. As I'm here in my capacity as your lawyer, anything we talk about is covered by client-attorney confidentiality. That means I can't repeat anything you tell me unless the information you tell me is about a future crime. Do you understand that?"

The kid nodded again but didn't provide a verbal response.

"Okay. I've had a good look at your file," I began. "Isaiah, you've been charged with two counts of arson. They've charged you under Section 16-11-140 for the damage to a crop of sweet potatoes. That carries a sentence of up to three years, but no minimum sentence. The second charge is the greater of the two under Section 16-11-110 paragraph B, and this is the charge for the fire in the barn. This section carries a sentence of a minimum of three years and a maximum of twenty-five years in prison. The difference between paragraph B and C is many years in prison. My main focus is going to be arguing that your charges should be reduced to paragraph C, because although the maximum sentence is fifteen years, there's no minimum sentence. If we can change the charges to paragraph C, we may be able to get a suspended sentence without any prison time."

"What's the difference between the paragraphs?" Eric asked.

"The charges under paragraph B claim Isaiah willfully and maliciously caused a fire to a place of business. This is an important point, because we'll argue a barn is not a place of business. Legally, in zoning ordinances, it's an agricultural structure," I noted. "Paragraph C states you set fire to a motor vehicle, which is the tractor and platform header that were damaged during the fire. Both those pieces of equipment were worth $50,000 each and were damaged beyond repair, but we can negotiate with the prosecution about your charges and sentences. Do you understand what I'm trying to do?"

The kid nodded again but didn't answer. I drew a long breath and looked at the notes. His distrust of the system had been ingrained into him from birth, and that distrust seemed to extend to anyone wearing a suit, including me.

The justice system was designed to be a place where fairness ruled supreme, where criminals were convicted, and victims were content. I'd worked long enough within it to know it didn't always work like that.

The criminal justice system was a lot more complicated than, "Do the crime, do the time." There was prejudice in the system, as there was in the human psyche, and that prejudice often affected the most disadvantaged groups in society. The disadvantage created by an imbalance of punishments, by taking parents away from children, taking job opportunities away from those already struggling, created more imbalance, and pushed those groups of people toward more disadvantage.

Crimes of the disadvantaged were punished much more harshly than crimes of the advantaged. A former high-ranking City of Beaufort official was once charged with insider trading, allegedly stealing tens of thousands of dollars, but he never served a single day in prison. Yet, the theft of a television worth no more than two thousand dollars was a felony, punishable by up to five years behind bars.

Good lawyers mattered to outcomes in the system. And since most Americans who faced the criminal justice system were poor, almost four out of five relied on overworked and underfunded public defenders or court-appointed lawyers.

The bias against the disadvantaged was real.

Solving generational disadvantage outside the justice system would solve many of the problems inside it. However, solving that disadvantage would take investment of time, money, and sacrifice, diverting funds away from other services. To do that was not a vote winner for any politician. The solution to ending generational disadvantage was easy, but applying it in practice was not.

"The arson attack was unsolved for several weeks before there was an anonymous tip-off that you were involved," I stated. "Do you know anything about this tip-off?"

He nodded.

"It was his ex-girlfriend," Eric explained. "That's what we think. She got jealous because he won that money on the floating casino, and then she set him up for the charges. But she's the one who knows something about it. She's the one people should be investigating."

I looked down at my notes. "Based on the tip-off, the sheriff's department came here to your home and discovered two of the

38

three gasoline canisters that were used to start the fire. They found the third canister still at the scene of the crime. They state you took the canister from your car and walked up to the barn. You doused the barn in gasoline before you walked back to your car, leaving a trail of gasoline down the middle of the sweet-potato crop. They claim you lit the fire, it burned the crop, and then led to the barn, where the tractors were destroyed. When they arrested you, they took your fingerprints, and found your fingerprints matched the ones found on the canister at the scene. For them, it's an open and shut case. While they have this evidence, what they don't have is a motive. Nobody has been able to list a motive."

Isaiah didn't respond.

"What do you remember about that night? Were you close to the area? Do you have a potential alibi?"

He shrugged his shoulders.

"Oh, come on," Eric exclaimed. "You've got to talk to him. He's on your side."

"I am on your side, but you don't need to tell me anything, as anything you tell me can limit my ability in court. I won't lie for you, but I'll do my best to get you the right outcome. If you tell me you committed the arson, then I can't lie for you in court and say you didn't do it. What I will do, whether you talk to me or not, is get the best outcome for the situation."

"See?" Eric opened his arms wide. "He's on your team. You've got to work with him."

I looked at Eric and then back at Isaiah. Isaiah avoided eye contact.

When I was growing up, my father had used a specific tactic if he wanted to talk to me man to man—we had to be looking outward at something. He said men found it easier to talk if they were looking forward, and not directly at someone. He'd often take me for a drive before he'd ask any difficult questions.

39

"Mr. Clyburn, it might be better if Isaiah and I walk around the block and talk." I closed the file on the table. "Is that okay with you, Isaiah?"

Isaiah chewed his mouth for a moment and then nodded.

I packed my briefcase, thanked Jada for the sweet tea, and thanked Eric for his time. Isaiah led the way outside, and I followed him. I placed my briefcase in my car, locked it again, and then walked next to Isaiah down the street. There was no sidewalk, but it wasn't busy. We walked under the canopy of trees as the birds tweeted around us. I waited until we were out of earshot of the house before I started the conversation. "It must be a lot of pressure supporting the whole family at such a young age."

He shrugged, then began to talk. "It's what I do. Mom works as a cleaner but doesn't make much. And since the cancer, my dad hasn't been able to work a full day. He works here and there but can't do more than an hour before he gets tired. I've got to be able to support Lana while she goes through school. She's got another five years, and I need to help her."

"That's a lot of pressure for a twenty-one-year-old."

Isaiah shrugged again. "I guess so, but it's what I've got to do."

"Tell me about that night, Isaiah. What were you doing? Were you close to the Pearson and Sons farm on Land's End Road?"

"I was around." The tactic was working. He was opening up. "I was drinking nearby with some friends down there. It's quiet and you can sit and drink without much happening."

I didn't feel that was the whole story. "Did you see the fire?"

"Yeah." Isaiah sniffed and brushed the tip of his nose. "Do you think if my skin was white, they'd give me a suspended sentence?"

I thought about the question for a long moment before I answered, "I think if your family were friends with the right people around here, they'd give you a suspended sentence."

"And most of the people in power around here are white."

"True, but that doesn't make the individual racist."

"It's not the individual, it's the system, man." Finally, some emotion from him. "It's not what you know, it's who you know. And everybody who knows anybody powerful around here is white. My uncle was the smartest man I've ever met, but he never had the chance to be anybody because he wasn't born into the right family."

"That's an interesting insight, Isaiah, but it's out of scope for our investigation." I took a deep breath as we turned the corner of the block. "We need to focus on your case, not the system. Right now, you're against a police officer who wants to convict you, and a circuit solicitor who's paid to get results."

"The DA has it wrong. They've all got it wrong."

"There are no district attorneys in South Carolina," I said. "The state has a team of circuit solicitors, which is comparable to a DA or state's attorney in other jurisdictions. We're the only state in the Union to have the title of circuit solicitor. But no matter what their title, they want you to go to prison."

"That's the thing, man. I can't go to prison. You've met my parents. You've seen the situation we're in. I've got to be here for Lana. If I can't work and earn money, how's she going to get by? She's smart, maybe even the smartest in her school. I've got to be able to help her get to college."

"That's very honorable," I said. "Bruce wants me to talk to you about a deal. He wants me to encourage you to consider taking the deal and not risk the case going to trial, because if it does and you're found guilty, you might look at ten to fifteen years in prison."

"Is that what you do in Chicago? Make deals?"

"Sometimes, when the case requires it."

"Does my case require it?"

I drew a breath and decided to go against what Bruce had advised me. "In my eyes, not yet. If we can downgrade the charges to the lower levels of arson, we might be able to negotiate a suspended sentence with no prison time," I explained. "But we need to be able to negotiate with the prosecution."

"That's good," Isaiah said. "I know how this looks. Low-income Black worker who needs a rush, so he lights up a building, but that's not what happened."

"Care to tell me what actually happened?"

"No." He shook his head. "But I'll plead guilty as long as I don't do prison time."

"It's good to know where you stand," I said. "The next step in the process is that we'll head to court in the next few weeks to file several pre-trial motions that will attempt to have the evidence dismissed. The motions aren't likely to win, but we're signaling our intention to the prosecution that they're in for a fight. That may force them to present a better deal."

For the next twenty-five minutes, we walked next to each other, avoiding eye contact, and discussing the case. I took mental notes but kept the conversation light. When we returned to the house, Isaiah asked me to do everything I could to keep him out of prison.

I agreed, but with everything I'd seen of the justice process in Beaufort County, I knew Isaiah Clyburn was probably looking at a long stretch behind bars.

CHAPTER 7

Emma looked comfortable surrounded by family members.

There was a softness to her touch, a calmness to her soul, that had been squashed by the frantic nature of city life. I hadn't noticed it until she moved around our new home.

After graduating from the University of South Carolina, Emma had followed me to Chicago and worked a corporate job, human resources management, for a large multinational company. She was good at it—she was good at everything she did—but I could tell her heart was never in it. We had savings behind us, and she told her bosses she would take a twelve-month break to look after her mother. Seeing her back here, back in her element, I started to doubt if she'd ever return to the city.

On Saturday afternoon, my grandparents, Emma's mother, and several of Emma's cousins, aunties and uncles, had gathered in the living room and spilled out on to the front porch, coming together to welcome us back to the area. Emma was busy in the kitchen with her older cousins Josie and Marie, preparing another feast, when I returned from the store. I greeted everyone with hugs and handshakes, smiles and laughter. Rhys and his children arrived, and I played with Zoe and Ollie for much of the afternoon. There were other little ones running around, squealing with delight as they dashed under the water sprinkler in the yard. While the kids ran free, the adults mingled, speaking of rumors and about the latest issues in the city.

The food was laid out on two trestle tables in the backyard, filling the air with the salivating smells of cooked meats, fish, and fresh bread. A feast was had. People stayed long into the afternoon, chatting and laughing and bonding. When the children began to get tired, when their energy levels started to wane, everyone began their exit. Over the next hour, I thanked the families for coming, for welcoming us back, and then started the clean-up. By the time Emma had said goodbye to almost everyone, I had nearly finished, under the watchful eyes of Jane and Grandma Lincoln, who both liked to tell me what I was doing wrong.

Emma came back into the kitchen and started talking to the ladies. I took a beer out of the fridge, and Emma caught me looking at her. She smiled. I smiled back, popped the top off the beer, and continued into the backyard.

"Good, you're here," Granddad Lincoln said as I stepped on to the back porch. "There're too many women in that kitchen. It scares me when they get together like that. You don't want to be caught up in their line of fire."

"I'm just here to save you, old man."

He held up his beer in a sign of cheers and then leaned back in the rocking chair. I took the seat next to him.

"Ain't nothing beats this," he said, rocking a little. "Look at that. In your backyard, you can watch the sun set over huge live oak trees. And listen." He paused for a few moments. "Hear that? That's the sound of the Lowcountry. Birds and bugs and bugs and birds. There's no more beautiful song in the world."

The evening sun had found a few cracks through the trees. As the day came to an end, the birds were singing, and the bugs were getting louder.

"But you seemed worried?" Granddad Lincoln said. "I could tell you were distracted at times this afternoon."

"I was thinking about what's fair and what isn't," I said, referring to my new cases.

"The world isn't fair. That's why we need the law."

I could feel another rant coming on, and sure enough, he continued. "If the world was fair, we wouldn't need the law. The murderer would get murdered, the thief would be stolen from, and the violent person would be violently beaten. But that's not the way of the world. The world isn't fair. The selfish get rich, the liars get the best jobs, and the corrupt become powerful. There's no natural justice in this world. That's why we need the law. The law ensures justice comes to those who treat others badly, and it ensures fairness applies to all."

I didn't respond, letting the thoughts stew while we sat under the spell of the South for the next fifteen minutes.

The evening was growing dark, the shadows stretching long over the ground, and the moon was making an appearance from behind a slow-moving veil of clouds.

Granddad Lincoln was one of those men who had always understood the wonder of silence, and I didn't want to challenge that. He could sit with the world, staring at the gentle movements of nature and watch and listen and feel and smell. He was a man skilled in the art of passing the time of day.

While he sat and said nothing, my mind wandered. I loved Chicago. I loved the activity, the buzz, the thrill of summer after a dormant winter. The city had so much—great employment, activities, adventure, and such a sense of achievement. Of making it. Of being someone, standing out in the mass of humanity. I loved my career in Chicago. That career had become my identity, a symbol of me as a person. I was the law, I was the lawyer, and I was the suit I wore to work every day.

But here, I was starting to doubt if that mattered at all. The machine still churned on, the system still moved forward, whether I was there or not.

"How could you give this up?" Granddad Lincoln commented after a long silence.

I wasn't sure if it was a rhetorical question, so I allowed a minute before I answered.

"There's not much of a career here," I said.

"Career? What's that worth when you've got all this? The view, the weather, the calmness. The people. The family. Your career has nothing on living in a place like this." He leaned closer to me. "You're at a point in your life where you need to make a choice—do you want to achieve individual success, or do you want to be someone who creates cultural change for the better?"

"That's a big question."

"Then put it this way—do you want to be someone who churns along in the political machine, barely making a difference, or do you want to be someone who makes an impact on his family and his community?"

I didn't want to admit it, but the question hit me hard. It was something I often thought about in Chicago—as much as I tried, I wasn't making a dent in the criminal justice system. There was always another case, always another trial, always another negotiation. There was an endless stream of defendants, an endless stream of cases, and the problems seemed insurmountable. Here, in Beaufort, I could make a difference.

I gazed out at the yard in front of me for a long time before I answered. "I don't know who I am without my career."

The words came out of my mouth without intention, but with truth. It was the first time I'd verbalized anything like that. I didn't look at Granddad Lincoln, but I could feel him staring at me.

"Well, young man, I guess you're about to find out."

We sat in silence for another long moment before my cell buzzed in my pocket. In a desperate attempt to avoid digging any deeper into my suppressed emotions, I took the cell out and looked at the number. I didn't recognize it, but it was local.

I answered. The voice only spoke a few words, but I recognized it. I had been expecting his call.

CHAPTER 8

I arrived at the Safe Harbor marina, a stone's throw from the main shopping strip of Bay Street, at 8:55 a.m. It was a Sunday morning, quiet, with a gentle breeze blowing off the river. The water glistened in the sunshine, the boats clinked against the docks, and the smell of the pluff mud hung heavy in the air. The award-winning marina, known for its great location, had stunning views, excellent amenities, and helpful staff. The workers were always happy to assist any boat owner, armed with a smile and a new joke every time. They were welcoming, jovial, and charismatic.

I spotted *The Captain of the River*, a 2015 Cobalt A25, in a slip space near the end. The twenty-five-foot bowrider was elegant, designed for water sports, fishing, or leisure, complete with leather seats and a swim platform at the rear.

Stephen Freeman leaned over the boat, wiping the windows with a white cloth. He was a tall, slim man, well dressed, with olive skin and unnaturally white teeth. The color of his short-cropped brown hair had faded as he'd aged into his sixties. His shorts were dark black, his boat shoes were brown, and his polo shirt was pink. Even early on a Sunday morning, the smell of his woody cologne was strong.

"Stephen Freeman," I called out as I approached. "You wanted to chat."

Freeman was a Southern old boy through and through. His father was a politician, and his grandfather was a circuit solicitor. His life journey had been paved with wealth and privilege and prestige. If he wasn't a corrupt, dishonest, and self-absorbed man, he might've been tolerable.

"Well, well, well." Freeman turned his focus to me. His Southern drawl was pronounced. "The big-city boy."

"I'm not a boy," I responded.

"No, no. I can see that. I didn't mean any offense by it." He patted the side of the boat. "I need to take her for a quick run. I haven't taken her out for a while, and I have to go every few weeks or the engine gives me some trouble. Come on board and we can have a chat. Fifteen minutes of your time is all I need."

I eyed him for a few long moments before I stepped on board.

"It's so good to have new ideas come into the community, and I can see you're a very smart man." He was clearly trying to charm me with fake compliments. It wasn't working. "And we need to have a little chat about your new role as a defense lawyer in Beaufort. I've been told you're a very good lawyer, won some big cases with some great closing statements in Chicago. That's very impressive for a man your age."

I stood to the side of the boat, resting against the cabin, watching as Freeman loosened the mooring line from the dock. A moment later, he was at the helm, steering us in the Beaufort River.

"I knew your father while he lived in Beaufort, and I know your grandfather," Freeman said as we drifted out of the marina. "The cheeky old fool keeps lodging complaints about me, but they never get anywhere. Your grandfather is an old man stuck in a different time."

I kept my eyes forward, looking out at the horizon. "My grandfather is a great man, and he taught me a great sense of right and wrong."

Freeman pushed the throttle and raced us across the river. The wind blew in my hair, and it was too noisy to talk so he didn't speak, keeping his eyes on the river.

He didn't drive far. We slowed after we crossed the river, approaching Lady's Island, and Freeman pointed forward. "This area here is the Beaufort Sandbar. You can't see it now because it's high tide, but when it's low tide, this whole area is the place to be. And once a year, when the Water Festival is on, there's a concert out here. They bring a barge over for a band and so many boats gather around this place."

"I know the sandbar. I grew up around here."

"Yeah," he said, looking forward as he steered the boat, moving us at a snail's pace over the area where the sandbar appears at low tide. "And you need to remember that this isn't Chicago. You need to remember there's a certain way of doing things in Beaufort County to keep our great sense of right and wrong intact. We have a deep sense of justice here, and a deep commitment to it. Our lives revolve around doing the right thing, living by the words of the Bible, and trusting each other. So, it's important you understand the system you're working in. Can I trust you, Mr. Dean Lincoln?"

I didn't answer.

"Have you forgotten your manners?" he questioned, turning to look at me. "You won't make much of an impact as a defense lawyer if you can't speak."

"Your son served five months of a ten-year sentence."

"Oh." He scoffed, smirked, and then looked back out at the water. "That's what's got you so worked up?"

"Your son murdered my sister."

"Murdered? That's a stretch." Freeman slowed the boat further as we advanced on the shoreline of Lady's Island. When we had stopped, he approached me and put his hand on my shoulder. "Any man with an understanding of the law would know that what Paul did was not murder. Reckless vehicular homicide at best, but not murder."

I brushed his hand off and glared at him, stepping forward to face him eye to eye. He stepped back, daunted by my size.

"Your son murdered my sister. He was drunk and driving an unregistered car. He got into the car knowing the dangers, and he still drove."

"It was an unfortunate accident," Freeman quipped, waving my grief away like it was nothing more than a pesky fly. He moved back to the helm and started the throttle again. He looked down the river, and then behind him, before he turned the boat around, heading back to Beaufort. "And it seems as if the city life has taken away your manners. Here in the South, we don't threaten our friends. We're polite to each other, and we respect our elders."

"You don't get to choose who deserves justice."

Freeman laughed. "That's where you're wrong."

His cell phone rang loudly. He took it out of his pocket, looked at the number, then slowed the boat. When the wind resistance had died down, he answered. "Lance Bateson," he called into the cell. "It's always a pleasure to hear from you."

I recognized the name from his television ads. "The People's Law Man," he called himself. A personal injury lawyer, and one who was known to have very questionable tactics. Freeman talked for a while, telling Bateson that he'd look after him, and he had nothing to worry about. I didn't know what it was all about, and I didn't want to know.

Freeman ended the call a minute later. He turned his attention back to me.

"I don't like that man. Too brash for my liking," he said as he started up the boat again. "But I need his support in certain circles and so I talk to him." Freeman looked around and then used a louder voice as the wind increased. "And he's . . . you know."

"I don't know."

He shook his head. "He likes the company of men when he's in private."

"And what's wrong with that?"

"Well, you know." Freeman shrugged and smiled. "Even an old boy like me can't get away with saying much any more. The world changes so much in a generation, doesn't it?"

"Justice has never changed."

"You're a big fan of justice, aren't you? Like it's some magical notion where the world is fair." He leaned toward me. "I hate to break it to you, but we don't live in some ideal fairyland. The world is a lot harsher than that—it treats the winners well, and it treats the losers poorly. All the poor people of the world, it's their own fault they're in that situation. They're poor because they didn't try hard enough. They're the losers of the world. So, in the game of life, which are you, Dean Lincoln—a winner, or a loser?"

"I don't play your game, Stephen Freeman."

"You stay in Beaufort County long enough, and you'll need to play my game. It's the only way to make things happen. Everything comes through me. I get people elected, I get people deals, and I get things done."

"That's going to change."

He chuckled to himself and shook his head. We didn't speak again until we had crossed the river. Freeman slowed the boat as we approached the marina.

"You really are forward, aren't you?" Freeman waved his finger in the air as we crept toward the dock. "I like that. I really do. It's such a change from the veiled Southern politeness. So, as a sign of my goodwill, let me give you some help. I'll talk to the assistant solicitor and convince him to offer a very good deal for your client, Caleb Rutledge, next week. They were going to offer a deal anyway, but I'll chat to him and make it even better."

"In return for what?"

"Nothing." Freeman navigated the boat against the current, keeping his eyes forward, focused on not hitting the other boats. "Like I said, it's a sign of goodwill between you and me. You help me, and I help you. We're all on the same team—we all want justice. This is how the system works here. You tell me the deals you want, and I can get them for you. I can be very convincing around that office."

"We're not on the same team."

"Maybe you do things differently in Chicago, but here, we have rules, and we have respect for each other." He reached forward and turned the throttle down, slowing to almost a stop as we approached his slip space. "Here, we help each other get the right outcome for justice."

"Is that what happened when my sister's murderer was released?"

Freeman scoffed and then his face lost all expression. He grabbed the mooring line and tossed it on to the dock, looping it around the cleat, and pulling it tight. Once the boat was docked, he looked back at me. "Be a good boy and respect your elders."

I leaned close to him. "If I find out you had any influence on your son's release, then I'll expose you for the corrupt man that you are."

I stepped off the boat and on to the dock. I didn't wait for an answer from Stephen Freeman, and I didn't look back.

Because I knew this wouldn't be the last time we spoke.

CHAPTER 9

The waterways of the Lowcountry had an enchanting and magical power.

Observing the tidal rivers, watching the dreamlike and otherworldly shorelines, a person could become lost under the spell of their haunting and mysterious beauty. Made up of sixty-plus islands, at high tide Beaufort was as much water as it was land. The rivers were surrounded by live oaks and palmetto trees, offering a unique beauty that could only be found in the Lowcountry. Home to eagles, herons, and a variety of other wildlife, the area was also a birdwatchers' paradise.

I drove the roads near the marshes and waterways around the Colleton River, searching for my destination. For many in the county, life was spent on the rivers, by the rivers, or near the rivers. For private investigator Sean Benning, it was all three.

When I checked the address the investigator had provided, it didn't come up on any app I had on my cell phone. I called Sean on his cell, and he gave me directions the old-fashioned way—turn right past the bridge, take your second left, turn right when you see the house painted red, and at the end of that dirt road, you'll find my place.

I followed his directions, and when I pulled up to the end of the dirt road, I realized why I couldn't find it on a map. He lived on a houseboat, which was currently tied to the end of a long wooden pier.

I parked at the end of the dirt road, stepped out of the car, and looked around. Not another soul in sight. Not a hint of another human being. We were alone out here. After years surrounded by traffic, and people, and noise, the lack of anything made me uneasy.

There was a crushing vastness to the emptiness of the landscape.

The air was thick with moisture again. Humidity was the trade-off for living in a place with a perfect winter. The locals knew it, and nobody complained. Occasionally, someone would mention the thickness of the humidity in summer, how it was the worst they could ever remember, and there would be a chorus of agreement, but for the most part, locals accepted the layer of sweat on their skin as a part of everyday living.

Sean Benning's houseboat was tucked into a bay, away from the dangers of the weather, but the boat itself had seen better days. The paint was peeling, the wood was cracked in places, and the name on the front had been faded by the South Carolina sun.

"Sean Benning?" I called out as I approached.

A man stepped out of the cabin, wiping his hands with a towel. Sean Benning looked underfed, like he could do with a good tomahawk steak, or maybe two. He had hungry eyes that seemed to be judging the situation constantly, but he was also an everyman, someone who could blend into the background and disappear without a trace. His white skin looked wearied by the sun, and his brown hair was hidden under a cap, poking out at the sides. His forearms were toned and muscular, although his frame didn't seem to hold much more in this regard.

One of the benefits of living off the road, living in an area missed by many, was the preservation of eccentricity. Outside of the city of Beaufort, away from the tourist hotspots, unconventional characters were commonplace.

"You found the place then?" he called back as I walked down the pier. "This is the best security I know. If I hear someone's looking for me, I can go anywhere and never be found."

"This is where you live?"

"Sure is, and I love it. I could win the Lotto tomorrow and I'd still live on this old thing. She's a part of my family." He patted the side of the boat. "Mind you, I would buy a better truck. I keep my old beast parked on the waterfront in Beaufort, but she struggles to start. Some days, I think it'd be better if I had one of those horse and carriages the tourists use."

There were only two private investigators listed in Beaufort. Sean Benning, who had a decent reputation, and a man named Wayne Cascade, whose reputation was dirtier than the pluff mud. If I had to use one of them, a man who lived on a houseboat it was. And if Bruce trusted this man, then I trusted him too.

I stepped onto the boat, wobbling a little as it rocked, going with the gentle sways of the slow-moving current. Benning opened his hand to indicate I should sit down near the front of the boat. There wasn't much of a breeze to speak of, but I had given up caring about how wet my shirt became with sweat.

"You're from Chicago, I hear." Benning went inside the wooden cabin, but his voice was still loud enough to hear. "And you've come back to Beaufort because your mother-in-law is sick."

"That's right," I called back, not taking my eyes off the view as I sat on the wooden chair. "Not sure how long we'll be back, but it'll be at least a year."

"It'll be longer than that," Benning said with confidence as he came outside holding two large folders. "Once this place gets under your skin, there's no leaving it."

"Not sure about that."

"Wait and see. There's a magic in this place that'll put a spell on you." Benning sat down on the chair opposite, rocking from side to side a little. He placed one folder on the table in front of us and handed me the other one. "It's a bit slow for our young ones, that's why a lot of them take off to Charleston or Savannah or Charlotte, but once you get to an age where you want to slow down in life, there's no better place than here. This landscape will seduce you, hypnotize you, and then, when you think you can leave it all behind, it becomes a part of you."

I nodded, unconvinced by what he was saying. I could smell a faint hint of weed and wondered if he'd spent most of the morning getting high.

"But I can tell you're here to work." He pointed to the folders. "This is what I've got so far on the Millie Aiken murder."

"I've had a look at the files and Bruce's notes, but I'd love to know what you've got." I took the folder, flicked open the cover, and started to read through his information.

"Interesting case, this one," Benning said. "First murder investigation I've ever done, and first one Bruce has done as well. But like Bruce mentioned when he first took the case, it's like all the other cases. We need to look for the right information and we'll find it where nobody else has looked."

"And what are your thoughts?"

"That Caleb Rutledge did it."

I raised my eyebrows.

"All the evidence points to him," Benning continued. "A kid who lost his temper, slapped his girlfriend, and she fell and hit her head. In anger, he walked away. There are witnesses who saw him near the scene, and he was seen pushing her earlier in their relationship. The gas station attendant saw him with a blood smear on his hands on the night of the murder. Sounds pretty solid to me." He shrugged. "Caleb was known to have anger issues after his mother died, and he got in a few fights in high school. He's shouted at people at work, and there are witnesses saying he snapped a couple of times with road rage. He punched another guy at a party years ago, but the charges were dropped, most likely because his stepfather is good friends with Stephen Freeman, but not even Stephen Freeman can sweep Millie Aiken's death under the carpet."

"That doesn't help us."

"I give you the facts, and then we go from there." He looked out to the water. "However, if you're looking for holes in the case, there are a few."

"Go on."

"Firstly, he was seen by a witness driving up the street toward the Aiken household on the night of the murder, but the old lady is blind as a bat. There's absolutely no way her testimony is going to stand up in court."

"Without her testimony, the prosecution's case weakens considerably."

"Absolutely. She's the cornerstone for linking Caleb to the scene." Benning looked at the file. "Next, we have the 'blood' that was seen on his hand by the gas station attendant. She asked him about it, and he didn't know where it was from. She can't confirm it was blood, all she can say is that it looked like a smear of blood on his hand and over his wrist. We can say it's a red pen mark."

"It's a thin straw to clutch at, but I like it." I tapped my finger on the table.

"And the fact his DNA was found at the scene of the crime means nothing. They had been dating for years, so of course his DNA is going to be in her kitchen. His jacket and cap were on the dining room table, but he also had things in Millie's cupboard. He admits he was there in the days before, so that's easily explained."

"That's great." I leaned back in the chair with a smile on my face.

"Well, not really."

"What do you mean?"

"In the big city, all that lawyer talk may work about circumstantial evidence, but not out here. The jury members are going to be locals and if it ain't Caleb, then they'll need another suspect. If you don't give them one, they'll take Caleb as the most likely. I've seen it happen a hundred times in other criminal cases out here. Any jury in these parts is going to convict the best suspect, regardless of reasonable doubt."

"I see."

"And a pretty girl like Millie Aiken? Every person on the jury is going to want justice for her, and they'll convict anyone they think hit her. They'll be after vengeance for her. And you should know the Aiken family is well known and well liked. If her mother starts crying on the witness stand, which she will, then it will tear the hearts out of every member of the jury. The emotion will be enough to convince them to vote guilty."

"You're suggesting that if this goes to trial, we need a third party?"

"That's what I'm saying."

"Any ideas on who that could be? Could it have been a rejected lover? Someone who liked Millie Aiken and she told them no?"

"Possibly. Although Millie and Caleb were dating, she was seen a few times with a young man named Chester Washington." He grimaced as he said the name. "Chester is the son of a successful realtor in Bluffton. They sell a lot of Hilton Head holiday homes to people from off, but their reputation in the local community isn't great."

"Is Chester worth speaking to?"

"I think so, but you'll have to find a way to access him. He won't say a word if you call and tell him that you want to talk about Millie."

I tapped my finger on the side of the table again. "And what do we know about Millie Aiken herself?"

"Millie was very friendly and well loved. She brightened people's day everywhere she went. She worked at the City Latte coffee shop, was studying journalism part time at USCB, and had big ideas of becoming a power-hitting journalist. She had a few nice articles published in the *Gazette* and the *Weekly*, and by all reports, she wanted to be an investigative journalist. She had a way of talking to people that put them at ease, and she could get information out of anyone. I'm a hardened soul, but when I ordered coffee from Millie and chatted with her, even I felt a bit lighter. She would've been great at the job."

"Could she have uncovered anything here that led to her death?"

Benning laughed loudly and then sighed. He shook his head with a smile. "No chance. Every crime in these parts is an open secret. We know who does what and when, and we all know who's who in the zoo. There's nothing to uncover because it's all out in the open."

I closed the file and rested my hand on top of it. "Caleb doesn't have an alibi for the night. He says he was at home the entire time, and it wasn't his car that was seen driving up the street. He said the old lady was wrong about that. Is there anything that proves he was at home the entire night? Cell phone records perhaps?"

"No luck there." Benning shook his head. "There are only two cell towers out in that area, and both have a radius of five miles each. Caleb and Millie's home are only a mile apart, and within the same cell tower range. All that information can tell us is that he was near the cell tower, and whether that was Millie's place or his own place, we don't know."

"GPS on his car?"

"Nope. His car is twenty-five years old. No GPS on that old thing. If he'd been driving his father's new car, we could've had it, but not on Caleb's old truck. The case isn't strong, but it's strong enough."

I hated to admit it, but Benning was right—the evidence might be weak, but the town's need for justice was not. "Bruce is pushing hard for a deal, but Caleb is adamant he didn't do it."

"You don't sound like you think a deal is the right decision."

"I don't like plea deals. I don't like the role they play in our justice system. It's not about taking a better deal to save the courts money—it's about pressuring the vulnerable into taking a deal to avoid thirty years in prison. That's not a deal. That's manipulation."

"I agree with that." Benning nodded.

I looked out at the horizon again. A little blue heron had landed on the water, gently stepping through the marsh, stalking its prey. It was a juvenile. The young ones were completely ghost white before they matured into their deep-blue plumage. It plunged its beak into the shallow water and rose trying to swallow its food. There was no doubt about it, this was a magical spot, and I couldn't find evidence of another soul. I tried to listen for the sounds of modern life, but there were none. Just the birds and the breeze, and the gentle lapping of the water against the boat.

"Did you know I'm an expert on identifying birds?" Benning said, looking out at the heron.

"Really?" I expressed surprise. He didn't strike me as a bird-watcher. I pointed to the distance. "What's that one over there?"

He studied the bird for a while before he leaned back in his chair. "Yep . . . that's a bird, alright."

His delivery was so deadpan that it took me a moment to realize he was joking. I chuckled and nodded. "That was good."

He grinned and winked, happy with his own work.

"How about the arson case?" I pointed at the other file on the table as the heron continued to stalk the waterways. "What do you have on that?"

"Well, this one is as clear as day." He pushed the other file across the table. "Looking at everything, it's clear Isaiah Clyburn lit the fire. After the anonymous tip-off, the deputies searched his home, and found the canisters used in the fire. They know they were the same canisters because he left the third one at the scene of the crime. They matched the canisters as a set. He couldn't explain where he got them, and when they took his fingerprints, they matched them to the fingerprints found on the canister at the scene. He's absolutely guilty of this one."

"I get the same feeling," I admitted. "But I need to do the best for him. He seems like a good guy. He's been dealt a bad hand in life, and he's trying to do the best for his family."

"He is a good guy. I coached Isaiah in junior baseball games when he was younger. I have a son about the same age and they both went to Beaufort High School. I can vouch that Isaiah Clyburn is a good kid with a good heart." Benning looked out to the water again. "But that doesn't mean he's innocent."

"If we think he did it, the question becomes why."

"I don't have a theory on that one, because nothing about it makes sense to me. It's so out of character for him, and the only theory I have is that young boys are known to be impulsive. Maybe he was pressured into lighting the fire by his friends, but even that theory doesn't sit well with me. He was never someone that gave in to peer pressure."

"And why a barn?"

"Like I said, the only theory I've got is that he was pressured into it."

"Maybe he thought the barn was empty? I mean, who keeps a hundred thousand dollars' worth of equipment in a barn? A John Deere tractor and a platform header worth that much should be locked away in a shed. That seems an unusual place to store them."

"Agreed."

"The farm was owned by Pearson and Sons. What do we know about them?"

"Fifth-generation tomato growers, and recently expanded into sweet-potato crops. A few farms around here took on further sweet-potato crops after the quarantine ban was lifted in 2017 and then it was reimposed in 2018. They were preparing for the ban to be lifted this year."

"What was the quarantine ban for?"

"Weevils. Once they start in a crop, there's no turning back. They get into the crop and destroy 95 percent of it. They got into everything in the 1990s and that's when the ban started. The growers could sell the sweet potatoes locally but couldn't ship them out of the county. Couldn't even take the equipment out of the county. Once the ban was lifted, they could sell the crop for so much more. It's a big money crop for North Carolina, but not so much here, even though they grow better here. All thanks to the quarantine."

"Any reason Isaiah might've targeted their property? A personal vendetta perhaps?"

"None that I can see. Pearson and Sons aren't squeaky clean, but they're not criminal. Their insurance claim states there were two tractors in the barn that night and both were damaged beyond repair. Worth 50k each, and the insurance company has already paid out for the replacements, but only to 75 percent of the total cost. The crop of sweet potatoes was worth 25k, and the insurance company will cover that as well, but again only 75 percent of it. The farm took the lower level of insurance cover—lower monthly costs, but lower payouts when things go bad."

"Could Isaiah have burned the barn for them? Maybe an insurance scam?"

"That was my first thought, but there's nothing to connect him to Pearson and Sons. I've checked everything, and there's no link. And Pearson and Sons lose money on the insurance claims, so there's no incentive for them. In the claim, there are mechanical reports about the tractors from two months previous that state they were in good working order."

"75 percent of 125k is a lot when you consider it."

"135k when you factor in the cost of the barn as well."

"How are Pearson and Sons' financials?"

"According to the claim, they're solid. Making a good profit each year, and never had a claim like this in the past. Invested a bit into the sweet-potato crop but were expecting to make a profit."

"And what else does the insurance claim have in it?"

"Not a lot of information. They have a no-fault clause in their fire insurance, but a condition is that they had to lodge a police report. The case would've gone unsolved except for the tip-off."

I sighed. "Isaiah might be guilty, but I still need to do my best for him. I need something to take to the prosecution and scare them. If I can show them that we have a solid defense, they'll give us a better deal."

"I like that." Benning drummed his hands on his lap. "I'll get on it. I'll talk to some contacts and see what we can bring up. I'll call you the second we get any leads."

I closed the file and placed it on top of the other one. As I did so, Benning sucked in a long, loud breath.

"What is it?" I asked.

"Wait here." He stood and walked back into the boat. He returned a moment later with another file. He held it in his hands while he leaned against the edge of the cabin. "When Bruce said you were coming on board, I did some research on you. Call me suspicious, but I need to know who I'm working with."

"I get it."

"And sorry if it's not my place to say, but festering pain has a way of corroding everything. It's best to deal with that sort of pain head-on."

I squinted.

"Heather's death," he continued. "Your sister was killed by Paul Freeman, a drunk driver who only served five months of a ten-year sentence."

"I'm aware of the facts."

"The way I see it, there's two people involved. One—Stephen Freeman."

"I saw him yesterday. We had . . . an interesting discussion."

"Good," Benning said. "But he's almost untouchable, and his actions didn't kill your sister. Person two"—he tossed the file on the table in front of me—"is Paul Freeman."

"What are you saying?"

"I need you to deal with the pain before I work with you. If you don't, it'll corrode everything you touch. This is a small place. You can't escape the past like you can in a city. You can't be anonymous here. You've got to confront your pain first. Deal with it, face it, and then move on."

I sat back, caught off-guard by his blunt approach. "And how do you suggest I deal with the pain?"

"You've got to confront the person who caused it."

CHAPTER 10

I wasn't sold on Sean's theory of unresolved pain.

In the two and a half years since my sister's death, I'd tucked the emotions away, hidden behind a thick wall of stoicism, determined never to confront them again.

But his words resonated with me and here I was, at the bar where Paul Freeman had spent most of his time before going to prison, at least according to the file Sean had amassed.

Being a man in my late thirties, I thought I could trust myself. I thought I had controlled the simmering anger that had consumed me since her death. I thought I could handle it with ease.

But I hadn't counted on his release after only five months of a ten-year sentence.

The sports bar was a home for the broken and lost, those who weren't looking to associate with the world. Located in a strip mall, the pub was covered in sports memorabilia, with several neon signs on the walls. Two older men were playing pool without a word said between them, a patron was staring into his drink trying not to pass out, and the older male bartender, dressed in black and with heavily tattooed arms, was staring at the baseball game. The bartender appeared to have the emotional depth of a rock. As I entered, he looked at me with an expressionless face and then returned his focus to the baseball game. The lighting was dim, the floor was tacky, and the smell of stale beer and fries filled the air.

I spotted Paul Freeman exiting the restroom. He was talking on the phone, jovial and loud, walking back to his seat at the bar. He sat down and clicked his fingers at the bartender while still talking.

Ten feet in front of me, Paul Freeman was making me angry again. I walked across the sticky floor and leaned on the bar beside him. He was drunk on vodka and soda. I could smell it on him. He didn't look at me.

"Hey, bartender," he called out with the phone still next to his ear. He clicked his fingers again. "Beer."

I was surprised the bartender hadn't snapped those fingers clean off, but he most likely knew who Paul's father was.

I could feel the rage bubbling in my limbs. It was simmering in the pit of my stomach, releasing into my arms. The uncontrolled anger was surging through me like an electrical current.

I stopped thinking. I grabbed Paul Freeman by the back of his polo shirt and yanked him off the chair. He fell to the ground. I reached down and grabbed him by the collar. He stood with my assistance, before I pushed him into a nearby bar table. It fell, along with Paul. The look of shock and fear on Paul's face was a great feeling. The other people in the bar stepped closer, but I didn't care. I stood over Paul Freeman with clenched fists.

The unmistakable sound of a shotgun clicked somewhere behind me.

I didn't turn around, keeping my eyes on my sister's killer. The fear in Paul's eyes was real.

"I don't know who you are, pal," a voice called out behind me, "but that ain't happening in here."

I turned to look at the bartender. He held the shotgun in front of him, but not pointed in my direction.

"This man killed my sister," I said.

"You're Heather's brother?"

I nodded.

He lowered the gun behind the bar. "Then I didn't see anything, but it's time to leave. Ain't no relative of Stephen Freeman getting beat up in this bar. I don't need that sort of trouble in here." He looked around and then shook his head. "And I'd make sure you know who you're dealing with before you do anything stupid."

I nodded in a sign of respect. He nodded in return.

I stood over Paul and leaned down. I pressed my finger into his chest. "If you see me walking down the street, you turn around and walk the other way. If you see my car coming in your direction, you pull over and hide. And if you see me in the same room as you, you'd better start looking for the door."

Paul didn't answer, looking like he was on the verge of tears.

I grabbed the bottom of his jaw and made him nod before I shoved his face back to the ground.

I looked back at the bartender. He nodded. I nodded. Walking out of the bar, I didn't look back at Paul Freeman. I hoped to never see him again.

But in a town this small, I knew that wouldn't be the case.

CHAPTER 11

The meeting room was beige.

The walls were beige, the carpet was beige, and the paintings were beige. The furniture was beige, the ceilings were beige, and the window frames were beige. The room even smelled beige, if that were possible. Sitting at the head of the room was Assistant Solicitor Andrew Harley, who appeared to be a human version of beige.

To his left, though, sat Stephen Freeman, who was anything but beige. I could sense the anger rising through him. I had entered the room before Bruce, taking a seat on the right. Bruce entered a moment behind me, holding a glass of water.

"Stephen?" Bruce expressed his surprise as he entered. "I wasn't aware you would sit in on this meeting."

"I didn't want to be here, Bruce." Stephen Freeman's eyes locked on to me. "But it appears someone is making waves where they shouldn't. Dean, I heard you had a chat with my son."

Bruce eyed me as he sat down before placing his laptop on the table.

"Old friends catching up," I replied.

"That's not the way he tells it." Freeman's teeth gritted together. "He says you came into a bar and threw him around."

"If he wants to press charges, he knows where to find me."

Freeman sat back in his chair. "According to the bartender at the dive bar, nobody saw anything. No surveillance footage either. The bartender said he was out of the room when it happened. My son says he's lying." Freeman leaned forward and pointed his index finger at me. "Don't think you can waltz into my town and cause trouble like that."

"Your town? I don't think so."

I kept eye contact with Freeman. Freeman simmered, angry that someone had challenged his authority.

"Andrew Harley, assistant solicitor with the Career Criminal Unit," the lead prosecutor introduced himself, leaning over the table to shake my hand, trying to ease the tension that was threatening to explode. Harley was a plump man with the soft white skin of someone who'd never done a hard day's work in his life. His chin seemed nonexistent, and his light brown hair was slicked back with too much gel. His eyes were shifty, and his blue suit appeared one size too small. "It's good to have another defense lawyer in town. It'll give us new blood to destroy." He chuckled to himself as he loosened his top button. "And it sure is hot out, isn't it? Going to be a scorcher this week. Kelly," he called out to his assistant farther down the hall. She appeared in the room in an instant. "Can you try to get this air conditioner working? It's too hot to be making decisions in here."

Kelly hustled out of the room. We waited for her return, and the tension simmered.

My eyes remained on Freeman. "I'm uncomfortable with a volunteer sitting in on this private meeting."

"He's authorized to be here," Harley replied. "Mr. Freeman's here as a consultant. He helps us with challenging cases. He has no conflict of interest, real or imagined, and his expertise as a former solicitor is invaluable to our work. I feel privileged to be working alongside him."

"He's a political lobbyist."

"It's a small town. Everyone has multiple roles here," Harley scoffed. "And we need all the help we can get. We're a busy team. Last year alone, we prosecuted over five thousand new cases. Mr. Freeman is authorized to assist us in all these cases."

Kelly returned a moment later with a remote control in her hand. She slapped the back of it and pressed several buttons. The air conditioner whirred into life.

"Ah, that's better," Harley stated, not bothering to thank his assistant as she left the room and closed the door behind her. "Let's start with what we know about this case, shall we? We know Caleb Rutledge killed Millie Aiken. We know he went to her house on the night of March 5th, got into an argument with her, and slapped her. She fell, hit her head, and unfortunately, terrible really, Millie Aiken bled out on the floor of her own kitchen."

"He's pleaded not guilty," I stated.

"They all do that to begin with." Harley waved my comment away. "The kid thinks he can get out of the charges because he's watched an episode of a legal drama on television. These young ones think the legal system is open to tricks and trades, and defense lawyers have some sort of magical ability. But as always, they quickly realize that isn't real life. Real life means he needs to face the consequences of his actions. Real life means he needs to face our fair and just legal system, and there are no tricks to it. We see it all the time with these kids."

"This case is not about 'these kids,'" I stated. "Any suggestion this case relates to someone else's is prejudicial."

"Prejudicial?" Freeman laughed and slapped his hand on the table. "You ain't in Chicago now, boy. You're in South Carolina. Home of real people and home of real justice. We're not interested in some fancy law book justice, so don't think you can waltz in here with your Northern morals and try to bully us."

"Justice still applies here."

"Our justice. South Carolina justice. Not your justice. Not the justice you get in a city where 50 percent of murders go unsolved." He turned to Harley. "Did you know that? Every year, 50 percent of murders in Chicago go unsolved. That's such a terrible thing. And this boy wants to bring that sort of justice here? I won't have it. We get justice for victims here." Freeman turned back to me. "We know Caleb was at her house at the time of death. We know he had her blood smeared on his arm. We know his DNA was in her kitchen. All the evidence is there. Caleb Rutledge killed Millie Aiken. That's all there is to it. Take the deal and walk away from it. Don't waste any more of our time."

"All of the evidence is circumstantial," I responded. "None of what you said proves he did it."

"Listen here, you prick." Freeman rose to his feet, pointing his finger at me. "Caleb did it. That's the end of it."

"You're the jury now as well? You really do have a lot of roles in this county," I stated. "Caleb Rutledge has pleaded not guilty because there's no evidence he did it."

"Of course he did it!" Freeman slapped his hand on the table again, harder this time. "All the evidence says he did it! Who else do you think did it?"

"You've got an anger problem. Where were you on the night of March 5th?"

"This isn't a game!" Freeman's fists clenched. "No jury in Beaufort County will believe any story other than the truth. The jury is going to convict him. They want justice for the Aiken family. They want justice for Millie. We all do. And let me tell you this, if you dare take this to court, we'll ask for the harshest penalty available."

"He has a right to take this to a jury of his peers."

"Not in this town! Take the deal, or there'll be consequences."

"Let's not get ahead of ourselves," Harley said, opening his hands wide and trying to ease the tension. He reached across and rested a hand on Freeman's arm. Freeman breathed deeply through his nostrils twice, and then sat down. Harley pushed a piece of paper toward Bruce. "We don't need to take this to trial. The way we see it, Caleb caused her death, one way or the other. We weren't there and for all we know, his intention was not to kill her. This is an offer for manslaughter and we're talking about—"

"No," Freeman snatched the paper off the table. "That offer is gone."

Harley looked at Freeman, whose eyes were directly focused on me. Harley couldn't contain his surprise, his mouth hanging open.

"What's the offer?" Bruce tried. "Voluntary manslaughter?"

"There's a new offer," Freeman stated as he walked toward the door. "Thirty years for an early guilty plea of murder, or we'll be chasing the death penalty for this horrible event. He has five days to decide."

CHAPTER 12

Bruce wasn't in a good mood when we returned to the office.

"I don't know how you do things in the city, but here, we try to be nice to each other. You can't go after Freeman like that." Bruce burst through the door to his office, pushing it with aggression. "We were about to have an offer of manslaughter on the table. I saw the piece of paper; it said, 'Voluntary manslaughter—five years.'"

He slapped his laptop down on the table and walked around the room. Cautiously, I followed him into his office. Kayla came to the door and looked at me.

"The meeting went terribly, Kayla." Bruce slumped into his chair and groaned. "City boy here caused a lot of problems for Stephen Freeman."

"Stephen Freeman was in the meeting?" The shock was written on Kayla's face. "Was that expected?"

"No." Bruce picked up his pen, played with it for a moment, and then tossed it back on the table. "It was supposed to be us and Andrew Harley, but Stephen came to chat with this guy. It didn't go well."

"I think it may have to do with their history," Kayla whispered.

"And that has to be left out of it." Bruce glared at me. "We have unwritten rules here. You don't try and bully the prosecution.

We were there to discuss a good deal for Caleb, but with how you acted, there's no way they'll present a good deal now. You ruined it."

"We need to get the best for the clients," I stated. "That's our job. If we need to take it to court, we take it to court."

Bruce waved me away. "Butting heads with Stephen Freeman is not the way to go about it. You're a fool if you think city tactics will work here. They're not threatened by you. They've seen the likes of you come here a hundred times, and everybody realizes the same thing—this town is about who you know."

"That isn't what the law is about."

"It is here." Bruce rested the back of his head on the top of his chair, and looked up to the ceiling. "Things work here because everyone knows their place. Stephen Freeman knows his place, I know my place, and the client knows their place. You don't disrupt how things are done, because things work."

"We need to do what's best for Caleb, not what's best for the small-town process."

"Don't give me that." Bruce leaned forward. "Right now, what's best for Caleb is to take the deal for five years. He should admit he slapped her, and she fell and hit her head. That's what's best for him. And you've gone and thrown that away. Now, we might face the prospect of the death penalty."

"You know as well as I do, he can't do that. There are no aggravating circumstances."

"Really?" Bruce looked straight at me. "You think they won't find an aggravating circumstance?"

I hated to admit it, but given the situation, Bruce was right. I sucked in a breath and nodded. "Sorry, Bruce."

"Sorry?" he scoffed. "Don't tell *me* that. Tell that to our client who's now facing the death penalty."

"Will they really go after the death penalty?" Kayla remained near the door.

"I don't know," Bruce responded. "Freeman threatened it as he walked out, but hopefully Harley will talk him down."

"Why is Freeman making those decisions?" I questioned. "He's a political lobbyist who works as a volunteer consultant for the prosecution. The choice isn't his to make."

Bruce turned and stared at me. He raised his eyebrows. "You might look smart, but you sure are taking a long time to understand how things are done here." He tilted his head. "Did you really confront Paul and throw him around?"

"On Sean Benning's advice."

"Of course." Bruce threw his hands up in the air. "You listened to the advice of the man who lives on a boat, and not to mine."

I stood. "For what it's worth, Bruce, I'm sorry."

Bruce waved me away, avoiding a response. He swiveled his chair to face the window and stared at the passing traffic.

Kayla indicated it was a good time to leave his office. I stepped out and into the hallway. Kayla followed me a step behind, closing the door behind her.

"He'll be alright." She kept her voice low as we walked down the hall. "He'll need some time to calm down. I suggest you go out for a round of golf with him and lose. He always forgives people if he can beat them over nine holes."

"Got it." I noted her advice and began to walk to my office.

Kayla paused when she arrived at her desk. "And I might be able to help you with the Isaiah Clyburn case."

"What have you got?"

"I was chatting to a friend of mine, Daisy-May, over the weekend. We were talking about the cases, and she said she's got some information about Isaiah that she doesn't want on the record. I didn't ask for specifics, but she said she'd talk to a lawyer, and I think she might be worth hearing out." Kayla turned to her desk and grabbed a pen. She wrote down an address and handed it to me. "She knows you're coming."

I stepped into my office and grabbed my keys. "If Bruce needs me, I'll be on the road."

CHAPTER 13

I rolled through the narrow streets of the Pigeon Point neighborhood and pulled up to a house next to a baseball field, parking in the driveway.

The small weatherboard home was tucked away from the road, behind a row of hedges and large bushes. An oak tree stood over the back, looming over the house, and a large family SUV was parked in the driveway. Flowers lined one side of the yard, and a raised vegetable garden lined the other. Daisy-May was in the garden, a pair of clippers in her hands. She was wearing garden gloves and a large hat covered her head. Her light blue linen shirt was loose on her fit frame, and her blue jeans were dirty at the knees.

"Daisy-May," I greeted her as I stepped out of my car. "My name is Dean Lincoln and I'm a criminal defense attorney. Kayla said you might have some information that can help a case I'm working on."

"Oh, Kayla said you were handsome," Daisy-May greeted me. She was in her early thirties and had the excitement of someone who still had the energy of youth. "But you're a bit too clean-cut for around here."

"Oh?" I smiled as I approached. "Any fashion tips to help me fit in?"

"For starters, you need a little bit of beard growth. A day-old stubble will give you a bit more of a rougher look," she said. "And lose the tie and undo the top button. Nobody out here expects anyone to be wearing a suit. You look too formal to be a local."

I loosened my tie. "Sounds like good advice for this weather."

Daisy-May pointed inside. "Care for some sweet tea?"

"I can't say no to that." I accepted her invitation and followed her up the path, a row of beautiful magnolias lining each edge.

"John, my husband, is working on the farm today. He didn't want to get involved, but I assured him this wouldn't create any problems." She led me into the kitchen. The bright home had a lovely feel to it. There were family portraits on the white walls, fresh flowers on the table, and not a thing out of place. It smelled like vanilla, and I spotted a small candle in a glass jar in the kitchen. I sat at the kitchen counter while she took a pitcher of sweet tea from the fridge. "Mr. Lincoln, this'll be the best sweet tea you've ever had."

"That's a bold claim."

"True though." She smiled. "The pitcher belonged to my great-grandmother, and we've had four generations of our family making sweet tea. The recipe is tried, tested, and infused with love." She took ice from the freezer, dropped it into two tall glasses, and filled each glass with the tea. She placed a slice of lemon on the side and handed me one glass. "So, tell me, are you married?"

"Happily." I raised my hand, showing off my ring.

"Oh, that's a pity. There'll be some disappointed ladies in town."

"Sorry to be a disappointment." I sipped the sweet tea and sat up a little straighter. It was a hit of sugary goodness. "Wow. You were right. This is one of the best sweet teas I've ever tasted." I looked at the glass, condensation already building on the outside. "Don't tell my Grandma Lincoln I said that."

She laughed. "Your secret is safe with me."

A pause hung over us for a moment before I asked, "Daisy-May, what can you tell me about Isaiah Clyburn?"

"All I know are rumors," she began as she placed the pitcher back in the fridge. She walked to the window, checked outside, and then came back to the counter. "And before I tell you anything, I need to say that I'm not going on the record. If you want evidence, you need to figure that out yourself."

"Go on."

She sat next to me but checked the driveway again to ensure nobody else was around. "My husband told me there was talk of people receiving cash for illegal jobs and then running the cash through a floating casino."

"Money laundering through a floating casino?"

"Money laundering has such a bad connotation. It sounds like you're a part of the mafia." She shook her head. "This is more like finding an inventive way of paying someone."

I didn't argue the semantics with her. "And you think Isaiah Clyburn was involved?"

"I just know what I know." She shrugged. "Isaiah is a good kid. Has a heart of gold. Will help anyone." She paused. "But he may have gotten mixed up in the wrong thing."

"Do you know why he was running money through a floating casino?"

She shook her head. "I'm not sure. That's all I've heard."

"Are you able to find out anything more?"

A broad smile drifted across her face. "Are you asking me to snoop into other people's business?"

"If you can."

She moved in her chair, sitting up straight, seeming very pleased with herself. "Then you're asking the right person."

CHAPTER 14

Chester Washington. It surprised me that the police reports on Millie Aiken's death didn't even mention the man from the neighboring town of Bluffton. He'd been arrested twice for sexual assault but never convicted. He was known for his frequent outbursts of aggression on the golf course, in bars, or in the office.

Bruce declined to join me on the fact-finding mission. For one, he didn't like the Washington family. Having sold a home through them two years ago, he described them as fake, dishonest, and deceitful, and those were the nicest things he had to say about them. Also, Bruce still hadn't forgiven me for throwing away a chance at a great deal for Caleb.

A forty-five-minute drive from Beaufort, Bluffton was a gorgeous small town filled with quirky shops, quality restaurants, and eccentric art galleries. Situated on the May River, the town had grown at an incredible rate over the past two decades but still maintained its unconventional core.

I parked outside the real-estate office off Promenade Street, in the heart of the Old Town. In the small parking lot next to the brick building, two spots were reserved for the owners—in one spot was a white 2008 Porsche Cayman and next to that, a red Ferrari 458 Spider. Both cars were spotless.

Stepping out of my car, I looked down the street. Bluffton was prettier than I remembered. Money, care, and good management had gone into making the place look clean, warm, and inviting. I made a mental note to bring Emma down here under better circumstances, and then walked into the offices of Washington Real Estate.

A blonde secretary, no older than twenty-one, greeted me as soon as I opened the door. She introduced herself as Katie and took my details. I spoke to her about my desire to purchase a property in Hilton Head, and that I had heard Chester Washington was the best agent around. Katie was straight on the phone and within minutes, she led me to a private office near the rear of the building. After I sat down, she left the meeting room, returning a moment later with a pitcher of sweet tea and two glasses. I thanked her for her hospitality, and she giggled before exiting the room again.

The spacious meeting room had a large wooden table in the middle, surrounded by ten leather office chairs. There was a large television screen on the left wall, potted plants in each corner, and five real-estate magazines arranged down the middle of the table. A strong smell of lavender circulated the room.

I didn't wait long. Within a minute, Chester Washington burst in, complete with a broad smile and an outstretched hand. He was dressed in black trousers and a white shirt, which was unbuttoned halfway down. I wasn't sure if he waxed his chest, or if he just wasn't old enough to grow chest hair yet.

"Mr. Lincoln, it's a pleasure. My name is Chester Washington," he introduced himself as we shook hands. "I'm going to be the man to find you the perfect home. We're the number one real-estate agency in Bluffton and neighboring Hilton Head. If you've got the money, we've got the home for you."

His spiel was well rehearsed, complete with eyebrow movements and a cheesy smile. No doubt he'd watched an online video about the moves to make, because none of what he said or did seemed genuine. I'm not sure he knew who he was under all the sales talk.

"I'm not here to buy a house."

He squinted as he sat down. "I'm sorry, I must be confused. I was under the impression that's what this meeting was about. It must be my new secretary—she's very pretty but so, so dumb. Women, eh? Can't live with them, can't live without them."

I held my glare on him. "Is that what you told Millie Aiken?"

"Millie?" He sat bolt upright, shocked to hear the name. "Who are you? Like, some sort of cop?"

"I'm a lawyer."

"A lawyer? Who for?"

"Caleb Rutledge."

"Whoa, whoa, whoa." He stood and backed off, holding his hands in front of him. "I had nothing to do with what happened to Millie Aiken."

"I know you were friends. Perhaps you were more than friends."

"Alright, alright." He walked to the door of the meeting room and shut it. He stood there for a long moment, hand resting on the handle, and I could almost see the thoughts ticking over in his head. "But I've got nothing to do with her death."

"I didn't say you did."

He sucked in a deep breath, and then scoffed, laughing a little as he exhaled. "Just . . . keep me out of all this, okay? My father wouldn't like our family name to be associated with that case. It's not good for business."

"Talk to me and we'll see what we can do."

He bit his bottom lip, looking at the floor. "I'll talk if you promise not to tell my father why you're here."

"For now, yes."

He sucked in another deep breath and sat down. "My father would hate our business name to be linked to her death. I'm already in enough trouble with him."

"This is your father's business?"

"He built it from scratch, and it'll all be mine one day. I have two older sisters, but my father doesn't think women can handle the pressure of running a business like this."

I shook my head. "Where were you on the night of March 5th?"

He hesitated, first looking at his hands, then back to the door, and then back at me. "I was . . . with my father."

"Can anyone else verify that?"

"No. But he'd be my alibi."

"Why do you need an alibi?"

He leaned back. "Listen, I don't know what you want to do here, or what you're trying to find out, but like I said, I had nothing to do with it."

"Were you dating Millie?"

"Not dating."

"Sleeping with her?"

He paused and then nodded.

"How many people knew?"

"No one. She wanted to keep it quiet. I didn't mind. I didn't want anything more from her. You know what it's like—use them for what you want and move on."

"I don't know what that's like."

"Then you haven't lived." He smiled. It was a wry smile, one that looked uncomfortable. "You've got to enjoy life."

I ignored the remark. "Have you ever been to Millie's house?"

"No, no, no," he scoffed. "She'd come to my place here, in Bluffton."

"And what would I find, if I looked into your relationship with her?"

"Not much." He eyed me, any sense of friendliness draining from the expression. "She was just another girl who liked The Chester."

"The Chester?" I raised my eyebrows, but it didn't surprise me that he had a name for himself. "And if I investigated 'The Chester's' past, would I find women who were physically abused by you?"

"Don't you dare bring those accusations into this," he snapped, keeping his voice low through gritted teeth. His fists clenched into balls. "They were all lies."

"And if I called those girls to testify, what would you say under oath?"

"This meeting is done." He stood, the chair almost falling backward. He hustled to the meeting room door, opened it, and stood beside it, waiting for me to leave. I sat for a long moment, then slowly rose to my feet, keeping my glare on the immature young man. As I approached the door, I stopped in front of him, studying his face. He didn't make eye contact.

I left the office with an uneasy feeling. Chester Washington was unlikable, quick to anger, and his alibi was flimsy. We had found a new possible suspect.

CHAPTER 15

After Kayla's advice, and what seemed to be Bruce's fiftieth request to walk around the fairways with him, I agreed to play nine holes on Saturday afternoon to ease any tension lingering between us.

Bruce was on to something—the manicured greens and rolling mounds, mature oaks and the nearby rivers made the golf course on Gibbs Island a stunning place to spend a few hours. There was a soft breeze coming off the river, and the air was filled with the smell of freshly cut grass. Thankfully, the humidity had eased. It was the perfect day to spend outside, ruined only by the frustration of golf.

I had planned to listen to Kayla's instructions and let Bruce win, but that didn't appear to be a problem. I hadn't played in years, and it showed on the first drive, ending the hole with a triple-bogey thanks to a wayward tee shot and a three-putt.

As we played through the first few holes, Bruce provided advice on my swing, on where best to place the ball, and how fast the greens were. If it hadn't been for my earlier mistake with the Freeman family, I would've driven the ball straight at him, but I tempered my ego, and moved the conversation on.

While we walked, Bruce and I talked about the weather, the storms, and the threats of tornadoes. Bruce talked about hurricane season, and how he was ready for the "big one." He felt the chill in his bones long before the weather report said a storm was threatening. I talked about the cold of Chicago, the layers and layers and layers of clothes required to go outside, and how I didn't miss the long winter nights. Bruce laughed and reminisced about his holidays north, how his knees and ankles and elbows couldn't handle the chill in the air. We talked about the roads around Beaufort, and the potholes. We talked about the pollution in the river and how the restaurants were dumping their waste straight into the pluff mud. We talked about the fish, and the high levels of mercury in some parts of the river. We talked about boats and how Sean Benning was living the ideal life. We talked about everything and nothing, losing ourselves to the conversation, passing the time with laughs and old stories. Golf was a background activity, serving as nothing more than a reason to spend time together under the wonderful warmth of the South Carolina sun.

"You know, when I was a kid, I wanted to play the electric guitar really badly," Bruce said as I lined up for a putt on the fifth hole. "And I'm proof dreams can come true—I can now play the electric guitar really badly."

I scoffed but missed the putt, before tapping it through in two.

When Bruce started to line up his putt, a few feet farther than mine, I said, "I was doing interviews in Chicago last year, and I asked the applicant, 'How would you describe yourself?' And he said, 'Verbally, but I am prepared to dance.'"

Bruce chuckled and stepped back from his shot. "I hope you hired him."

"Of course."

"Good." He composed himself, and then putted a ten-footer. He picked up his ball, and as we walked to the next hole, he told a story. "I had a couple of clients—both widowed, in their seventies. They'd been dating for five years, and they decided to get married. Before the wedding, they came in to discuss arrangements and they talked about finances, homes, and living arrangements, all that stuff. And then the guy says to his future bride, 'How do you feel about sex?' And she said, 'I would like it infrequently.' He sat there for a moment, thinking, and then he said, 'Was that one word or two?'"

I laughed and we continued trading jokes and old stories for a while, until we reached the seventh hole, where the conversation inevitably turned to work.

"Isaiah seems like a really good kid," I said as I assessed the fairway, looking down it like I expected my ball to go straight. "He's been dealt a bad hand, but he's trying to do something with his life. He wants to help his sister get to college."

"He is a good kid, and that's why nobody can figure out why he torched the barn." Bruce set up his tee, placed his ball down, and not even taking a practice swing, drove his ball down the middle of the wide fairway, avoiding the bunkers. "It's so out of character for him. He was never in any trouble before this."

"Good drive," I noted. "A friend of Kayla's told me that he might be caught up in running money through a floating casino that runs out of Savannah. The theory matches up, because Isaiah's father told me he won some money when I went and talked to them. It seems to be a piece of the puzzle, but I'm not sure how it fits."

"There's been reports about that for years, but nothing has ever been proven. The rumor is that it's drug money, so I don't know how Isaiah would be caught up in that. He doesn't seem like the sort of kid who'd do drugs."

"He doesn't want to spend any time in prison, so I'm trying to build a solid defense, and encourage the prosecution to reduce the charges. It's his best hope."

"If you were nice to Stephen Freeman, you could've asked him to do that for you," Bruce stated. I think there was a sarcastic tone to his voice, but I couldn't tell. "But I trust you'll do what's best for the kid."

I placed my ball down, took two practice swings, and swung hard. I kept my head over the ball, and for the first time that day, I connected sweetly. The ball flew down the middle of the fairway, rolling twenty-five yards in front of Bruce's ball. He didn't seem happy with that.

As a lawyer in Chicago, I'd spent time hitting balls off driving ranges near the city and I felt comfortable swinging the driver. When it connected, when everything came together, a good drive felt magical. My short game, however, left a lot to be desired. After we walked up to our balls, Bruce chipped his on to the green, but mine fell short. Bruce smiled.

"Caleb is a good kid as well," Bruce said as we walked on. "I don't like his stepdad, but Caleb seems to have a good heart."

I agreed. The more I researched Caleb, the more my opinion of him grew. Despite his mother dying when he was ten, despite growing up with an arrogant stepfather, he seemed to be turning out okay. He helped with the kids at the Port Royal YMCA, volunteering there every summer for the past five years, teaching kids in their T-Ball program. The staff there had nothing but praise for him. His classmates at USCB had positive things to say as well. And his colleagues at his part-time job all said Caleb would bend over backward for them. He was young, brash, slightly overconfident, but at his core, he was solid and well meaning.

"It seems everyone also loved Millie Aiken," I mentioned. "She was very popular around these parts."

"Millie was great. Always smiling at the coffee shop and talking about how we'd see her on the TV news one day." Bruce smiled at the memories of her. "How did the meeting with Chester Washington go?"

"As you predicted," I replied. "He was arrogant, entitled, and had an angry streak. As for an alibi, he said he was home alone with his father."

"His father would say anything to keep his boy out of trouble. They're as bad as each other."

"He's a perfect suspect, but we can't use him on the stand without evidence to link him to the scene. Right now, we have nothing to say he was there, and no witnesses place him nearby. And Chester could talk his way out of anything. Without evidence, the jury would see right through that play."

"I agree."

I chipped up on to the green. Bruce putted in two. I putted in three.

"Dean, I know it's not how you're used to doing things, but there's a lot of justice that happens in this town," Bruce quipped as we headed to the start of the next hole. "It's not always court justice. Sometimes, you need to rely on locals dispensing their own version of the law. I'd like to call it community justice."

"I'd call that corruption."

"Call it whatever you like, it works." Bruce groaned as he grabbed his driver and looked down the longest hole on the course. "This town is a great big puzzle and all the pieces fit perfectly in their place."

"That system works for people in power. If you're connected to the right people, life is a dream," I said. "But it doesn't work for everyone."

I stepped out and looked at the course. Par five, 505 yards. A narrow fairway. Trees to the left. Water to the right. Bunkers at 150, 200, and 250 yards. It was a tough one.

"We need to encourage Caleb to take the deal." Bruce was firm as he assessed the hole ahead. "It's his best chance of getting out of prison at a reasonable age."

"That's not the best choice."

"A choice is only a choice if there's a suitable alternative. Otherwise, it's manipulation. Plain and simple."

"It's not that simple."

"It is if you step back and look at it. If someone in authority tells you they've got a world of evidence, that they're convinced you're guilty, and they offer a year in prison, or a life in prison, which one do you take?"

I stabbed my tee into the ground and balanced my ball on top of it. "What if you're innocent and you've been told your whole life that the system hates you? What if the people in authority are so convincing that you don't feel like you've got a choice? What if they convince you there's no other way?"

"It's not manipulation if they're guilty," Bruce grunted. "If we can convince Harley to present five years for manslaughter, it's better than risking the death penalty."

"Even if he's innocent?"

"Innocent? Really? You believe that?"

"There's no evidence to say he did it."

Bruce scoffed. "Sure. If that's what you believe. I'm just out here trying to get the kid the best deal to restart his life at a reasonable age."

"You already think he's guilty, don't you?"

"It's not that. Knowing Beaufort County, and the juries we need to face, I know we won't win at trial. So that's why we deal. And let's say he actually is innocent. Let's say this really is a big mistake. If we take it to trial and lose, an innocent kid spends the next thirty years behind bars. Do you want that on your conscience?"

"That's not right."

"If you don't break the law in Beaufort County, then you won't have a problem in Beaufort County." Bruce leaned on his driver. "Life really is that simple."

I smashed the drive straight down the middle of the fairway. It was a thing of beauty—a sweet, sweet feeling. I turned back to Bruce. "Your version of law and order works for people like Paul Freeman."

Bruce paused. He didn't respond as he placed his tee into the ground, ensuring his ball was perfectly balanced. He stood back and took two practice swings.

"And I bet if I look deep enough," I continued, "I'd find a long list of people who are connected to Stephen Freeman who have gotten off their charges, or worse yet, things have been swept under the carpet. I'm certain that list would go back decades."

"Then I recommend not looking deep enough."

Bruce kept his eyes on the fairway in front of us. He studied it like a pro golfer, as if it would make any difference to his drive. He waited at least a minute before he moved again.

"I looked into Paul Freeman's release for you," he said, still studying the green in the distance. "The report said the prison was overcrowded and ten people were suggested for early release. Five of them were selected. Paul's early release was by the book. He met all the requirements."

"And the five who didn't get released?"

"All violent offenders. One was a wife basher, two were convicted of weapon offenses, and two were convicted of violently assaulting other people. So, who would you rather have back in the community—a violent offender or an idiot kid who made a stupid decision to get behind the wheel when he was drunk?"

"Neither."

"Unfortunately, this state doesn't have endless funds to keep people locked up. They had to be released."

Bruce didn't continue the conversation and lined up his drive. He swung hard and cracked the ball. The ball started straight but then curved deep into the trees.

"Don't like the pressure, Bruce?" I smiled.

"No, I don't," Bruce grunted. "That's why I have you."

He looked to the right of the fairway and saw a pickup parked behind the tall chain-link fence. I'd seen the same pickup follow my car earlier that day.

"Friends of yours?" I questioned.

"Not mine." There was a hint of fear in Bruce's voice. "But I hope he's not there because you've dug too deep."

I looked out at the truck. Its windows were tinted, and I could feel someone's eyes on us.

I had the feeling I might soon discover how trouble was handled in South Carolina.

CHAPTER 16

As I loaded my clubs into the car, the sunset was starting to drift over the horizon.

Bruce thanked me for the game and for allowing him to win by five strokes. He said he knew Kayla had asked me to lose, but I assured him it was because of rusty play-making, rather than emotional blackmail. He laughed and told me he didn't believe me, but it was the truth. I'd three-putted four times in nine holes. I had no chance to win if I played like that.

Bruce left the parking lot with a spring in his step, jovial and joyous, happy to have defeated a much younger man in an athletic endeavor.

The evening sky was awash with colors as I drove out of the golf course. Relaxed, and without a need to rush anywhere, I drove off the main road to catch a better view of the sunset and snap a picture to send back to my colleagues in Chicago. I parked off the main road, stopped in a clearing where I could see the river, and got out. Adjusting my cell phone, I tried many different ways to take the photo, but my cell couldn't capture the calm beauty of the moment.

As I put the phone back in my pocket, I caught sight of a set of lights coming up the road. I could tell it was a pickup. It came nearer. An F-250, at least fifteen years old. It grumbled to a halt behind my car.

A young man, no older than twenty-five, stepped out. He was a big guy. Rough. Had the face of someone who had seen more than his fair share of bar fights and the knuckles of someone who had won most of them. Wearing jeans, boots, an old T-shirt, and a baseball cap. It seemed to be the uniform around here.

"I got lots of problems, mister," he called out. "And you've been added to my list."

"What's that supposed to mean?"

He didn't bother to elaborate. As soon as he was close enough, he swung with a heavy right. Having spent years in a boxing gym, I could see it coming a mile away, and I slipped out of his direction.

"A smart guy, uh?" he said, and swung again.

I stepped back, leaning out of his range.

His third swing was the heaviest, and he loaded all his force into it. I slipped to the left, and he fell forward, his shoulder coming past my nose. I shoved him to the ground, and he slammed into the back door of my SUV.

"You prick," he said as he collected himself. He paused with one knee on the ground, puffing hard.

I stepped forward. "Want to tell me what this is about?"

He wiped his nose and grunted. He stood, held his eyes on me for a long moment, and then pointed his finger at me.

"Don't touch Paul Freeman again," he growled in his most threatening tone. "Or next time, I'll bring some friends."

"I'll invite you all to dinner if you give me your number."

He spat on the ground and walked back to his truck. He roared it to life and spun his tires out of the dirt.

It appeared the waves I was creating were becoming bigger.

CHAPTER 17

Kayla looked at her watch as I walked into the office on Monday morning.

"I know, Kayla." I shook my head as I placed my briefcase down. I handed her a takeaway coffee. "Emma and I went out for a morning walk on Hunting Island Beach but got caught up in the traffic on the way back. The whole place shuts down when the Woods Memorial Bridge swings open. Traffic was terrible out there. We were stuck over on the other side for at least twenty-five minutes."

"Thanks for the coffee." Kayla smiled. "They said they weren't going to open the bridge during rush hour any more. It must've been a special occasion."

"Yeah—to start my week off on the wrong foot."

"But you have to admit, there are worse places to be stuck in traffic."

I sighed and then conceded. "True. We had a nice view of the river while we sat there doing nothing. It was . . . nice."

"Nice? Really? Maybe you're starting to slow down?"

"No chance." I smiled. "Bruce in?"

"No." Kayla leaned across her desk and checked the schedule. "He's playing a round of golf with the mayor this morning. Networking, he calls it."

"I'm starting to understand that's how business is done around here."

"Sure right about that," Kayla said. The daughter of an accountant and a schoolteacher, Kayla's organizational skills were second to none. She had a sweet charm about her. Mother to two boys, both in high school, and wife to a realtor, she had dreams of one day studying art history. *"When the boys move out,"* she'd told me last week. I had told her to follow her heart, but reality often isn't that easy. "Settling in yet?" she asked.

"I think so. For Emma, this was always home. She looks like she's never left. She's got family around every corner, already knows all the neighbors' names, and knows everyone at the grocery store. She looks more relaxed than I've seen her in years."

"And you?"

I looked at my office door, and then back to Kayla. I offered her a small smile. "There's a lot of greenery here."

"You didn't have that in Chicago?"

"Everything is gray there. The buildings, the clouds, the sidewalks, but there's a comfort to the grayness. There's a sense of anonymity. You can be anybody or nobody. A ghost among the buildings, or a hero for a day. Here, well, you can only be who people expect you to be."

"Is that not enough?"

I shrugged and started to turn away, then paused.

The families of Beaufort were connected by hundreds of years of stories, filled with tales of woe and triumphs, creating the history that helped form a nation. The stories were repeated often, passed down from one generation to the next, with each generation adding its own layer of complexity to the city. It was a place where people knew each other's families, where neighbors waved good morning, and where rumors spread like wildfire. The sense of community was strong, and the sense of pride was stronger. Everyone knew everyone and everyone knew everyone's problems.

"Kayla." I sat in front of her desk on one of the office chairs. "Considering Bruce isn't here, what can you tell me about the Rutledge family?"

"What do you need to know?"

"What's their reputation?"

"The kid? Caleb? I don't really know him, but from what other people have said, he's like his mother. She passed away ten or eleven years ago, but I remember her as very kind and helpful. She volunteered at the Arts Council and was a docent at the visitors' center. She loved the history of Beaufort, and everybody knew her. I'd met her a few times, here and there, and she was so lovely. A truly good heart."

"And the father?"

"The stepfather."

"Yes, stepfather. What do you know about him?"

She squinted. "I know wild horses couldn't drag me to his house for dinner."

If there was one thing that was prevalent in the locals of the Lowcountry, it was that straightforwardness was not in their nature.

"Pretend you're in Chicago for a moment." I smiled. "And give it to me straight."

"Ah." She shrugged. "Okay. Right, well, Gerald Rutledge is a terrible man."

"That's better. It makes me feel like I'm back in Chicago." I laughed. "Anything else?"

"Rumored to have beaten his wife for their entire marriage and will rip people off at the drop of a hat. Has no real friends, and most people are wary of dealing with him. Is related to Stephen Freeman by marriage, and that seems to be about the only thing that keeps him in power with the South Carolina Farm Agency.

He's got some sway with the politicians in the state capitol because of the advisory board, but he's got no respect back here."

"Do you trust him?"

"Well, I wouldn't walk across the street to ask for his advice."

I smiled. "Okay. So, the direct way of talking doesn't last long here." I leaned back in the chair. "And why would someone like Gerald Rutledge come to Bruce to defend his stepson? In his whole career, Bruce has never taken on a murder trial before, but Rutledge came specifically to him. Why?"

"I have a theory."

"Go on."

"Because Gerald Rutledge hates Caleb. He always resented Caleb and never wanted to raise him, but he can't be seen as doing nothing about these charges. His reputation would be completely destroyed if he hung the kid out to dry. It's not the Southern way to abandon your family. So, he hires a reputable lawyer who has never handled a murder. He hires a lawyer who has a reputation for never taking anything to trial and always taking the deal. Nobody knew you were coming on board with this case. Gerald Rutledge chose Bruce because he thought Bruce would force Caleb to take a deal." She leaned forward. "My theory is Gerald Rutledge has no interest in winning. He wants Caleb out of his life and saw this trial as an easy way to do it."

CHAPTER 18

The media had gathered outside the front doors of the Beaufort County General Sessions Courthouse.

Five vans were parked outside, each with a cameraman and a reporter. They peppered us with questions as we walked toward the building, and Bruce ignored them until he found the right position. He strategically stopped in front of the American flag, framing himself in the picture. He answered numerous questions, and then gave a pre-planned soundbite for the media: "The great state of South Carolina has afforded Caleb Rutledge the right to be innocent until proven guilty."

After he delivered his piece, Bruce walked into the solid two-story structure of the courthouse, tucked away from the road, behind a row of thick trees. Redesigned in 2008, the building was modern, solid, and imposing. I followed Bruce through security before he leaned in close and said, "I think that went well. They'll use that soundbite on the news, and it'll look good for us."

"Your pretty face is going to be everywhere tonight."

Bruce nodded with a broad smile across his face. "My wife will like that. She'll think I'm a television star."

He led the way through the foyer, filled with people awaiting their chance in court, and up the narrow stairs to the courtroom at the end of the hallway.

The courtroom had two contrasting colors—cream for the walls, ceiling, and carpet, and brown for everything else. The room smelled freshly cleaned, with a hint of pine in the air, and the seats were spotless.

I followed Bruce to the defense table, and Kayla moved into the first row of pews behind us. I opened my briefcase and sat down on the brown leather chair. Bruce and I reviewed the case files for the next twenty-five minutes, reading over our options. At 9:55 a.m., Assistant Solicitor Andrew Harley entered the room with two female assistants. They were followed by Stephen Freeman and two associates I didn't know. Their faces were stern as they sat in the row behind the prosecutor's desk.

Caleb Rutledge, still in his orange prison uniform, was escorted into the room by the bailiff and seated next to me. The clerk at the front of the room read the case number in an expressive fashion, and then asked the room to rise for Judge Gregory Grant.

Judge Grant moved deliberately and with purpose. His black hair was cut short, his skin had a healthy glow, and at fifty-five, he had a distinct lack of wrinkles. "Good genetics," he claimed to anyone who asked, but Kayla had explained the local rumor was Botox. I couldn't tell if Botox was also the cause of his lack of facial expressions or if it was his lack of personality.

As Judge Grant walked into the room, he didn't give Bruce or I the privilege of eye contact. He sat down, adjusted his robe, opened his laptop, and studied the file in front of him. He then looked up to the courtroom. He welcomed us, and we introduced ourselves.

"Begin, counsel." Judge Grant was still reading the brief as he talked in a slow drawl. "And make it sharp."

"Thank you, Your Honor." Bruce stood at the defense table. "The defense has two motions to lodge. The first is to compel discovery. We haven't received a complete witness list from the prosecution and it's more than five weeks since Caleb's arrest. We've made numerous requests and—"

"Your Honor." Harley stood, interrupting Bruce. He held a piece of paper in his hands. "We sincerely apologize to the defense for the delay in the witness list, but there were factors outside our control. We've had numerous administration staff leave the office over the last few weeks, and we haven't been able to clear our backlog of tasks. However, we have the complete witness list in question here. We have the completed witness statements available as well."

"Very well," Judge Grant responded and indicated that Harley should hand over the list.

Harley turned and handed the five sheets of paper to Bruce. Bruce thanked him, glanced briefly at the pieces of paper, and then handed them to me. I took the files and scanned the fifty names on the preliminary witness list. I was sure the prosecution would add more in time, but this was at least a starting point.

As I ran my eye down the first four pages, there were no surprises—the medical examiner, the Sheriff's Department's investigator, the witness who claimed she saw Caleb drive past that evening. On the fifth page, I saw a name I wasn't expecting to see—private investigator Wayne Cascade. I underlined the name and then pointed it out to Bruce. Bruce looked over my shoulder and expressed his surprise as well.

"I'm glad that's sorted," Judge Grant stated. "And the second motion?"

Bruce adjusted his tie. "The defense would like to enter a motion for the jury to be selected from another county, pursuant to the Section 17-21-85 Order for jury selection in a criminal case to be conducted in another county. We've filed this motion because it's clear the jury pool in this county will be prejudiced against the defendant."

"Prejudiced against the defendant?" Judge Grant looked over his reading glasses at Bruce. Still, there were no creases on his forehead. "You need to provide further context to your reasoning, Mr. Hawthorn."

"Of course." Bruce adjusted his tie again. "It's impossible for the defendant to receive a fair jury trial in this county. This entire county is aware of the death of Millie Aiken, and everyone has a personal opinion on this matter."

"Interesting argument." Judge Grant looked to Harley. "Does the State have any objections to this motion?"

"Absolutely, Your Honor." Harley stood and buttoned his blue suit jacket. "The prosecution is opposed to selecting the jury from another county. This murder happened in Beaufort County, the victim lived in Beaufort County, and the accused deserves to be judged by his peers in Beaufort County. Moving the selection of this jury to another venue would be a slap in the face to the fair and just residents of this county."

"Agreed," Judge Grant said. "Response?"

Bruce looked at his notes and fiddled with his tie again. He must've put it on too tight. "We, ah." Bruce took a deep breath. "We just don't think the jury pool in Beaufort County would enable the defendant to have a fair trial."

"That's ridiculous, Your Honor," Harley responded. "That's why we have *voir dire*. It's the very purpose of the process, to ensure a fair trial."

"Again, I agree," Judge Grant responded. "Do you have anything more to add to the argument, Mr. Hawthorn?"

"Your Honor," Bruce said and read the notes before him. He wasn't strong in court. His strength was in negotiating behind closed doors, discussing and conferring and deliberating until he landed the best deal for a defendant. Bruce looked at me, then leaned closer. "I'm drowning here. Want to have a turn?"

I nodded and then stood. "Your Honor, my name is Dean Lincoln, and I'm the assisting counsel on this trial."

"I know who you are," Judge Grant groaned. "Do you have anything to add?"

"Yes, Your Honor, the defendant is afforded the right to a fair trial by the South Carolina Code of Laws. This Code provides the discretion to approve this motion if there's a substantial risk to the fairness of this trial."

"I'm well aware of the law," Judge Grant grunted. "And this trial is on the docket for May?"

"That's correct, Your Honor," Harley replied. "And there's no reason to move it."

"Your Honor," I argued, "if the trial is to continue in the county, it would severely weaken the defense's ability for a fair trial, and the defense would be at a major disadvantage if the case was to remain here. The jury pool within Beaufort County is tainted by the extensive media coverage of this situation, including widespread coverage in the newspapers, in news bulletins, and online social media channels. Continuing the trial here would severely prejudice the case against the defendant."

"You don't think my court is capable of being objective?" The condescension in Judge Grant's voice was unmistakable.

"It's not the court I'm concerned about, Your Honor. It's the jury pool."

"And that's why we have *voir dire*," Harley bit back. "The people of Beaufort County are very capable of being impartial. It's a misleading and offensive accusation to suggest they're not. We're not some backwater country town as the defense suggests."

"The defense has made no such suggestion," I responded.

"And there have been many studies to show exposure to publicity isn't enough to influence bias," Harley continued. "Potential jurors don't need to be ignorant of the facts to be able to sit in the jury box. And during *voir dire*, if a potential juror proves to be incapable of fairly judging the evidence against a defendant, he or she is dismissed. It's a complete process and the residents of Beaufort County should be the peers who judge the actions of the defendant."

"I'm inclined to agree." Judge Grant looked at Harley over the top of his glasses.

"Thank you, Your Honor." Harley tried to hide his smirk, but it was obvious. "And as you can understand, the office of the circuit solicitor doesn't have endless resources. We have a limited budget, and as this trial may take many months to resolve, bringing the jury from another jurisdiction may unfairly limit the prosecution's ability."

"Your Honor, that's a very inflammatory argument," I argued. "The cost to the state should not be an influence on the decision for this motion."

"Unfortunately, it is, as stated in the Code of Laws." Judge Grant waved my argument away. "I completely understand the prosecution's apprehension about bringing in a jury from another county. The motion for jury selection to be conducted from another county is denied, pursuant to Section 17-21-85 of the South Carolina Code of Laws. However, to appease the defense as I'm sure there'll be further arguments, the court will provide the option to refile this motion if *voir dire* proves the bias this motion alleges."

"Thank you, Your Honor." Harley grinned like a schoolboy who's been patted on his head by his favorite teacher.

I didn't respond as Judge Grant asked if there were any further motions, and when he confirmed there were not, he moved out of the courtroom. Bruce looked at me and shrugged. I expected the loss, but it gave us grounds for an appeal if bias did occur later in jury selection.

After Judge Grant had exited, I sat down and wrote several notes on my legal pad, trying to ignore the cheerful buzz from the prosecution team as they left the courtroom. I overheard one say they were happy the city lawyer had been beaten in the local court. A fair trial seemed nothing more than a joke to them. They needed it to be a carnival of revenge. A parade of reprisal. A chance to destroy the man they thought had killed innocent Millie Aiken.

Bruce, Kayla, and I waited until Caleb Rutledge had been taken back to his cell before we packed up and left the courtroom.

"Unlucky, champ." Freeman had waited for me outside the doors. He was leaning against the wall opposite the courtroom. He had his hands in his pockets and a sly grin on his face. "But you should get used to it. That's how we do justice here."

I stepped toward Freeman. "Caleb Rutledge deserves a fair trial."

"He killed an innocent girl, Dean. This community needs justice for that aggressive act."

"He claims he didn't touch her."

"They all say that." Freeman scoffed. "Now, I could understand if he said it was an accident, or if they got in a fight and he didn't mean to kill her. That would be a sound legal argument. But innocent? No chance. Look at the evidence. Nobody wants your type of justice here. Go back to the city and leave us alone."

My breathing was short, my heart thumping against the walls of my chest. I could handle the smugness, I could handle the arrogance, but I couldn't handle his sense of justice.

I decided not to engage Freeman further. I turned and walked away from him without another word.

"You're out of your depth, Dean," Freeman called after me. "You won't be able to save Caleb Rutledge."

CHAPTER 19

Found Local was a taco bar and restaurant in the center of Bay Street, downtown Beaufort. The staff were funny and energetic, the room buzzed with liveliness, and the music was upbeat. It had a delicious food menu, great seating, and a drinks menu full of local favorites. A bar ran along the left side of the room, with tables and chairs along the right. The smells of lime, cooked meats, and freshly poured margaritas filled the air. From opening to closing, the place was full.

The true splendor of Beaufort County went deeper than the seductive marshes and historic streets. It went deeper than the tourist activities and the grace of the Spanish moss. Beaufort's real splendor was in its local places, its festivals, its restaurants, its bars, in its cafes and shops. It was in the smiling faces of the locals, their welcoming attitude, and willingness to socialize with anyone. It was the buzz of the small town, the greeting of old friends, and the echoes of laughter that radiated through most buildings.

But for all its splendor and magnificence, there was a dark side to Beaufort, one born of a tragic past. The locals knew it, the tourists knew it, and the history books knew it. There was no escaping the fact Beaufort was once at the heart of the slave trade. There was no escaping the racism that had many layers. There was no escaping the prejudice that still existed in some streets.

Isaiah's case was running through my head as I entered the restaurant. Isaiah seemed to be a hard-working, honest kid, with a great set of morals, and I couldn't understand why he had conducted the arson attack. It was troubling me.

Sean Benning waved at me from the far end of the bar. He was in conversation with the bartender as I approached.

"You've got to try the carnitas taco," Benning said with a mouth full of food. "Beautiful."

I shook my head, ordered a Coke, and sat down.

The male bartender leaned across as a pregnant woman walked past. "You know, they say childbirth is the most painful thing in the world, and listen, maybe I was too young to remember, but I don't remember it hurting much."

I chuckled slightly, and Benning laughed loudly. The pregnant woman also heard the joke and she turned around, smiled, and gave the bartender a little clap.

"You like that one?" The bartender nodded to Benning. "Well, my roommate knocked on my door at 2 a.m. last night. Can you believe that? It was lucky I was still up playing the drums."

Benning laughed heartily as the bartender moved to help someone else.

"Can't get this in Chicago," Sean said. "Local people, local conversation, local food. This is the life, my friend."

"The jokes are newer in Chicago," I said.

Benning shoved the rest of the taco in his mouth before it fell apart. "Don't tell me you still miss that place?"

"I miss the activity, the hustle and bustle. You feel like you're in the middle of the action. There's a buzz to a big city that you don't get here." I thanked the bartender as he placed the Coke in front of me. "You're on the cutting edge of innovation and you can almost touch the future."

"You can only have so much of it. The human body wasn't designed to live in concrete towers. We were made to live out here, in the open air, surrounded by greenery," Benning stated with a sense of great authority, even though he didn't have it. "I went to New York once, and another time I went to LA. Spent a week in each of them. That was enough of the city for a lifetime. There's no way you'd catch me in one of those places again."

When I was little, I felt the same. My world had been full. Playing under the Spanish moss, jumping in the river to cool off, running with my cousins. What else could I want? I grew up in a world where children wandered free, away from the worries of modernity, gaining their independence by running in packs. It was where groups of kids raised each other, always led by the eldest and with the group looking out for the youngest, until the call for supper rang through the neighborhood. It was the freedom to explore, to be an adventurer, to be a climber of trees. It was where you invented games out of boredom, where you threw rocks into the river, where you fought with sticks and pretend guns. And then, when you were old enough, it was where you learned to fish, where you learned the respect for hunting, and where you gathered oysters from the rivers.

But when I grew into a young adult, I discovered there was so much more I wanted. While some of my peers were being praised for their sporting talents, I was praised for my academic ability. It gave me confidence, but more than that, it gave me an identity. My academic skills made me somebody. I was sporting, but I always felt there was more to me than that. I felt I had to leave Beaufort to fulfill my potential.

I waited until the bartender had moved to the other end of the bar before I asked Benning my question. "Wayne Cascade's name has been added to the witness list of the murder trial. Any idea why?"

"Private investigator Wayne Cascade?" Sean groaned. I nodded my response. "That dirty man's name has a way of showing up in just about everything. He's an arrogant prick. He thinks the sun comes up just to hear him crow."

"Thoughts on why he would've been added to the list?"

"Any witness statement attached to his name?"

"None. He's the only witness that doesn't have one."

"I'd say they've added him as a decoy."

"A decoy? That's a cheap tactic."

Benning shrugged. "I've seen it happen before. You chase this lead, wasting valuable hours and money, only to find it leads nowhere. The prosecution will say it was an administrative error, but really, they want to lead you down the wrong path. Did you ask them about it?"

"Bruce put in an official request this morning for his full statement, and their response was that they'll look into it. I imagine they'll take weeks to get back to us."

"Wayne Cascade is the right name to make trouble. If you start investigating him, he'll get angry." Benning shook his head. "Freeman probably added him, and because there's no witness statement, he knows you'll go out there and talk to him. It's a trap. Cascade is dangerous and not the sort of man you want to cross."

"I'm not afraid of him."

"You should be." Benning wiped his mouth with a napkin, and then his hands. "Cascade is a loose cannon with deep connections to Stephen Freeman. He knows a lot of secrets around here, and people don't like making him angry. Everything he does is an open secret, but nobody will say anything."

"Sounds like I should meet with him."

"I wouldn't recommend it."

"You got an address?"

Benning looked at me, then grabbed another napkin from the table. The bartender passed Benning a pen. Benning wrote the address down and then pushed the napkin toward me. "But don't go there at nighttime. Wait until the morning before you drive out to his property."

"Why?"

"Because he'll shoot you if he can't see who you are. And that man doesn't miss."

CHAPTER 20

In small towns, everything is connected. Everyone knows a lot of secrets; however, some know more than others.

I took Benning's advice and waited until morning to see Wayne Cascade. Up a long dirt driveway halfway between Beaufort and Bluffton, I found the shed and caravan that Cascade called home. Past an old wooden fence that was falling apart, past a large field with shot-out tin cans in the distance, I came to a clearing. The shed was large and new, no older than five years. It was big enough to park a semi, maybe two, and the roller door was open.

Although there wasn't much on the property, I was sure Cascade had more than enough money stashed away somewhere. He seemed to have little use for it. From what I'd heard, his life revolved around hunting.

He walked out of his shed as my SUV rolled into view. His camouflage pants were dirty, as were his hands. He was wearing a black T-shirt and military-style boots. In his forties, he looked like a shifty man who would sell his family secrets for a piece of gum. He was toned and muscular, with a lack of body fat. His face was gaunt, and his eyes bulged out, creeping out anyone who looked at him for too long.

Cascade was pulling back on the lead of a black pit bull, struggling to hold back the muscular dog. It was snarling as it growled in my direction, desperate for a feed. Its mouth was salivating, and its eyes were hungry. The dog looked like he hadn't been fed in days.

"Big-city guy going to try and talk to us locals, eh?" Cascade called out as soon as I stepped out of my car.

"You know who I am then?" I didn't get close. I didn't want to tempt the pit bull.

"I know everyone in this town. It's my business to know everyone."

The dog continued to snarl at me, growling louder each second.

"Your name was mentioned in court this week," I shouted to him, keeping my distance. "I came out here to speak to you about that."

"Court? Why was my name mentioned in court?"

"The prosecution added your name to the witness list in the trial of Caleb Rutledge. I hadn't seen your name mentioned on the other court documents."

"Caleb Rutledge? The murder of Millie Aiken?" He shook his head and pulled hard at the lead. The pit bull was almost dragging him with it. "I know nothing about it."

"It was the first time I heard your name connected with that case. It's not in any of the other files."

"And I suppose they put my address on those files as well?"

"No."

"Then how'd you find me?"

"I asked around."

He expressed his surprise and yanked hard on the dog's lead again. The dog settled for a moment. "And what do you want?"

"I need to know why your name is on the witness list."

"Like I said." Cascade shook his head. "I have no idea. I'd say it was an error. I testified in a previous trial about my investigations, and they probably transferred my name to the new files."

"Where were you on the night of March 5th?"

"Why?"

"Because I'd like to know."

"I can't remember."

"I need you to try really hard and remember where you were."

His eyes narrowed and he kept his focus solely on me. "What are you accusing me of?"

"I'm not accusing you of anything. What I want to know is where you were on the night Millie Aiken was murdered."

"Enough questions." He stepped forward, and the dog strained against the collar. "It's time for you to leave, Lincoln."

I nodded. My message had been received.

I was watching Wayne Cascade.

CHAPTER 21

I followed Kayla out of our office building and on to the street as the sun began to dip. The humidity hadn't eased. Menacing gray clouds were gathering in the distance.

"It's going to be a big storm season." Kayla pointed to the skyline. "I can feel it in the air. With all this humidity, there'll be a powerful storm behind it."

I looked out at the horizon, studying the clouds. I loved the charged feeling of a spring storm. There was something about the electricity in the air that made me feel alive.

Out of the corner of my eye, I spotted an old white pickup truck farther down the road. It was crawling at a snail's pace, rolling forward in the empty parking spaces on the side of the road. It slowed to a stop near the intersection. The windows were tinted. They were too dark to see inside.

"There's bound to be a storm in the justice system as well," I said. I stood at the edge of the parking lot, studying the vehicle. "I'm not going to let Freeman influence how it should operate. I'm not going to back down from his threats."

"He won't like that." Kayla stood next to me. "He's not a very nice person if he gets angry."

I looked across the street. I spotted Wayne Cascade parked in a truck on the other side of Carteret Street. When he saw me looking at him, he stepped out and lit a cigarette. He walked around the back of his truck, leaned against the tray, and looked down the street.

I turned to see where his vision was focused. The lights on the next block were red. Stopped at the front of the line was the beaten-up pickup truck. I squinted to get a better look at the driver.

The light turned green. The truck edged toward us.

Closer.

"Dean, you need to be careful. You'll make people angry if you keep trying to do things the Chicago way. Listen to Bruce's advice, just a little bit," Kayla said. "If you try to fight the prosecution on everything, you'll never win anything. If you can show them you're willing to compromise, perhaps they'll also compromise a little. Meet them in the middle."

"That's not how I work." I stared at the beaten-up truck. There were no plates.

"I know, but this isn't Chicago. We're just a little city trying to survive. It might be time to play their game. There's still a lot of anger out here about Millie's murder, and by taking it easy, you might make things easier on yourself."

I didn't respond. I watched the truck, tires rolling forward, then turned my attention to Kayla.

Something didn't feel right.

"Dean?" Kayla questioned. "Are you listening?"

The tinted window of the truck rolled down. It was only a second before I saw the rifle, pushed out of the window.

I looked at Kayla.

"Move!" I screamed. "Get down!"

The first gunshot rang out. It was unmistakable, echoing down the street.

I grabbed Kayla and pushed her toward the edge of the building, my back to the road, protecting her.

The second shot came quickly after the first.

My arms were wrapped around Kayla as we huddled next to a bush at the side of the parking lot.

The tires of the truck squealed forward.

I turned and watched the truck race around the corner and down the next street. People rushed out of the nearby buildings to check on us.

I turned back to Kayla. "Are you okay?"

"I'm fine." Kayla stood, dusted off her dress, and then straightened it. "But whoever fired the gun won't be when I'm through with them."

I turned back to the street, looking for clues about the shooter.

And still there, leaning against the back of his truck, unmoved by the gunshots, was Wayne Cascade.

CHAPTER 22

Two days after the apparent shooting, I stood on the front porch of my home.

The police report stated there was no evidence of any shots fired. Wayne Cascade gave a witness statement, saying he believed the noise of the gunshots was actually just the backfire from the old truck. The police report agreed, concluding we had most likely heard a truck backfiring. I didn't see the gun clearly, but I also didn't buy the idea that Wayne Cascade was there by coincidence.

Emma stepped out of the house, leaving the door unlocked, and began to walk down the street. I pointed back at the door.

"It'll be fine," she said with a smile. "We'll be back soon. We're just going over yonder. Come on. Leave it."

Nervously, I stepped away from the unlocked door.

We walked through the historic district to downtown for the local 'First Friday' event. In downtown Beaufort, on the first Friday of every month, the main street was closed for one event or another. This month, it was classic cars. The cars were dotted along Bay Street, parked in the middle of the road, with people mingling around them, telling well-worn stories of adventures in their pride and joys. Shops opened later, residents boated in from down the river, and the bars were packed. Tourists smiled and chatted, telling everyone what a beautiful town it was, and locals greeted each other with solid handshakes for men and gentle kisses on the cheek for women. There was a live band, and several people dancing. The street was full of joy and laughter, and the sound of children playing on the nearby playground carried on the wind. It was a community here, and that meant something.

The sun reached the horizon, causing everyone to squint if they looked west, and the sky became a flame of orange and pink and yellow and red.

After looking at the cars, we mingled in the bars, said hello to more of Emma's cousins, and were introduced to many new friends. I heard too many names to remember them all.

Two hours later, with a drink, some tacos, and enough socialization under our belt, we drove out to Hunting Island State Park. It was Emma's idea. "I haven't seen the stars in years," she said.

I agreed and we hit the road for twenty-five minutes. Emma reinforced all the new names of the people I had met earlier. I still didn't take them all in.

We arrived at the park and stopped on the side of the road. We sneaked past the signs that told us the park was closed and made our way to the beach. There was no light pollution, and no city to see in the distance. Looking out to the Atlantic, with dense trees behind us, there was no evidence of human civilization at all. We walked along the sand, hand in hand and alone. A light breeze blew, and the ocean gently lapped at the shore.

We were at the edge of the world, and the night sky seemed naked, exposed in all its beauty. It was a wonder, a dazzling display of twinkling holes in the sky, a spectacular moment of nothing more than the universe continuing to exist.

I looked up and could see so many stars that it felt like a revelation. The blanket of stars made me feel small on the ground but enormous in my soul. I felt connected to the heartbeat of something greater than myself.

"It's so beautiful here," Emma whispered as she snuggled into my arm. "And so quiet."

A shooting star shot across the sky and Emma gasped. I smiled.

"Make a wish," she said, and we were both silent for a moment as our wishes were sent into the far reaches of the galaxy.

"If you look at one patch of clear night sky for fifteen minutes with no light pollution, you'll see a shooting star," I said. "They're very common, but usually, our eyes aren't adjusted to the night sky enough to see them."

"Thanks, Mr. Science."

"Just laying down the facts." I laughed and pulled her in close. "You want another fact? I discovered what a phobia of people chasing you with a chainsaw is called."

"What is it?"

"Common sense."

She giggled and punched me lightly in the stomach. "But here's a real fact—cats don't meow to other cats."

"What's the punchline?"

"No punchline. They hiss at other cats, and meow at humans because it mimics a baby's cry." I could tell she was smiling. "Just laying down the facts for Mr. Science."

We strolled, arm in arm, bodies pressing against each other, and I wondered if this was how all married couples felt—like they were inventing something new, creating depths of emotions never felt before, having waded into untested waters and finding paradise lay just beyond the breaking waves.

"I love being back here, amongst all the nature," Emma whispered. "And I have so many good memories here. Do you remember the Castle?"

"Of course," I said as the memories came back into focus. "The large mansion off Craven Street that was once used as a hospital during the Civil War."

"Ever try to jump the fence as a kid?"

I laughed. "There wouldn't be a ten-year-old in Beaufort who hadn't tried to jump the fence. We wanted to get close to the haunted house."

I remembered it well. It was a game we all used to play around these parts. The challenge was to jump the fence, run forward, and touch the side of the house without being seen by the owner.

"Ever see the ghost?"

"There was no ghost." I shook my head. "It's an old story to scare little kids."

"No, no, it's true. The place is haunted. My friend said she saw him when we were little. The story was the ghost was a jester brought to the area by a French explorer in the 1500s, and he's been residing in the area ever since."

"Sounds legit." I laughed.

"And the woman who used to live there was lovely," Emma said. "She caught one of our school friends one day, and she invited him into the house. Being a good Southern kid, he had to say yes, and they shared a sweet tea on the front porch while we hid in the bushes."

"Manners are the Southern way."

"I love that having nice manners is more important than having a nice handbag here."

"How so?"

"A woman came into the hospital today and she was clearly a Yankee. She talked down to everyone and demanded the staff help her find her friend who was being cared for in the ward. All the nurses said they were too busy, and she needed to wait. Nobody wanted to help her. And about five minutes later, a younger woman comes in, not well-dressed, her clothes creased, but she was so polite, and everyone bent over backward to help her."

"I see what you mean."

We chatted for a while longer until my thoughts drifted back to work. Emma sensed it and tried to pull me out of the daze. "I was thinking of trying to boil some okra. The advice I got was to boil it beyond all recognition and it'll taste a thousand times better."

"That'll be great."

"And I was going to try and cook some hush puppies."

"Fantastic."

"And some she-crab soup."

"Great."

"And another Frogmore stew."

"Yep."

"Oh, Dean Lincoln." Emma used her best condescending tone. "Bless your little heart."

I stopped walking and smiled. "Really? You've become that Southern overnight, huh?"

"You bet." She laughed and snuggled into my chest. "But I can tell when you're distracted. Even in all this beauty, you're still thinking about work, aren't you?"

I sighed and then nodded. She knew me too well. "It's the two kids. One rich, one poor, and they're both facing a system that's against them."

"Both guilty?"

I shrugged as we continued walking. "Maybe one kid is, and maybe one isn't. Maybe they both are. I don't know."

"And you think it's connected to the shooting this week?"

I nodded again.

"Things are escalating, Dean. First, we get pulled over on the way into town, then some guy tries to jump you, and now a shooting. What's next?"

"These people aren't a threat. They're just great big dumb men whose mothers didn't hug them enough."

"I thought we agreed you would stay out of trouble?"

"I'm trying."

We continued to wander along the beach, and I did my best to forget about work, trying to lose myself under the blanket of stars.

The waves crashed on the shore, gently and sometimes aggressively, and Emma took her shoes off, dipping her feet into the coolness of the Atlantic Ocean. When I didn't do the same, she kicked up the water and splashed me. Reluctantly, I took off my shoes and socks and walked next to her, feeling the coolness of the ocean on my feet.

Hand in hand, with our feet in the ocean, we chatted about everything and nothing, about the town, about the people we'd met, about the nature surrounding us. We chatted about buying a boat, docking it at the marina, and having weekend adventures. Emma talked about the people she'd met at the hospital, about her mother, about the high quality of care she was receiving from the doctors and nurses. I talked about the house prices, about the new developments around town, and about the best bars and restaurants. We talked about Chicago and how we missed our friends. We talked about our car and how it was time for an upgrade. With smiles on our faces and water on our feet, we lost ourselves in the moment.

The drive back to our home was quiet. Emma turned off the music, letting her mind wander, staring out of the window as I drove. There was something about the calmness that did that.

Maybe, just slightly, the beauty of the Lowcountry was getting to me.

CHAPTER 23

We arrived home after our night out and noticed the car parked outside our house. I looked at Emma and she raised her eyebrows at me. I raised my hands in surrender, not knowing why someone would be at the edge of our property on a Friday night. I didn't want to scare Emma, so I left my Glock in the glove box. I parked the car in our driveway and stepped out.

"Dean Lincoln," a man called out as he walked toward me. "It's been a long time."

I squinted as I tried to place the face. "Terry Wallace?"

"You bet," he responded. "I'm impressed you recognized me."

"It's been a while since I hit your pitches over the fence."

"You weren't that good," he said. "Maybe you hit one or two pitches over the fence, but I remember striking you out a few times. I must've been throwing those pitches at eighty-five miles an hour." He rolled his arm over his shoulder. "I could've been a champion except for this shoulder injury."

"The older we get, the better we were."

He laughed and we shook hands. He looked good. He was fit, healthy, and had a good head of hair. He was well dressed in slacks and a polo shirt, and his shoes were polished. A strong cologne wafted in the air around him.

"Hello, Emma," he greeted my wife. "You look amazing. You haven't aged a day since high school."

"Thanks, Terry." She smiled and greeted him with a hug and a kiss on the cheek. "It's been a long, long time."

"Can I get you a beer?" I pointed inside.

"No, Dean." He leaned against his car. He folded his arms across his chest. "This is a work visit."

"A work visit?"

"There was a call from one of your neighbors about a man lurking around here." Wallace looked up at our house. "I work with the Beaufort Police Department these days. I've had a look around, and I couldn't see anything."

Emma gasped. "We left the front door open."

She raced inside. Wallace and I were quiet until she came out a few moments later. "It doesn't look like anyone has been in, and all our valuables are still here."

I nodded my response, as did Wallace. Emma eyed me for a long moment. Her eyes clearly said, *"No trouble."* I nodded and she folded her arms across her chest and returned inside.

Wallace pulled a cigarette box from his back pocket. He lit one, took a long drag, then looked around the street. He held the cigarette between his middle finger and thumb, a throwback to his teenage years when he wanted to look cool. When he was satisfied there was nobody else around, he looked back at me.

"You're making a lot of waves, Dean. People are talking. I've been an investigator in the Beaufort Police Department for the past decade, and word is you're causing a lot of trouble here. I've been out to dinner tonight, and a lot of people were talking about the city lawyer who's trying to tear up a close-knit community and make it into a version of Chicago. When I heard it was you, I thought I owed it to you to come down and chat. The call from your neighbor was the perfect excuse."

125

"I've got the whole place talking. That's got to be encouraging."

"The wrong people are talking." He took a long drag of his cigarette. "And I don't think you understand how dangerous these people can be."

"What are you saying?"

"As an old friend, I'm giving you some advice. I'm telling you to keep your head down for a few weeks. Folks around here don't appreciate being harassed by a city boy."

"We grew up together. You know I'm not a city boy."

"To them, you are."

"And to you?"

"To me, you're an old friend." He took another drag of his cigarette and blew a large puff of smoke. "And as an old friend, I'll give you a heads-up." He looked up and down the empty street. "I shouldn't tell you this, but it's my way of keeping the peace. I'd hate to hear you've been found in a shallow grave somewhere."

"Go on."

"You didn't hear it from me, but if I were you, I'd look into the footage at the Marine Repair Store on Lady's Island."

I squinted again. "What am I looking for?"

"The facts. The prosecution wanted to hold off on this, but if you're anything like the kid I remember, you won't stop until you find it. The way I see it, I'm saving everyone a lot of trouble," he said. "But you've been warned, Dean. Be careful where you step."

CHAPTER 24

The following Monday morning, I walked the ten minutes into the office slowly.

The morning was heavy with jungle-like humidity. The air was heavier than I'd experienced in years. By the time I reached the office, I was exhausted, almost requiring a good lie-down to recover.

When I stepped inside the thankfully air-conditioned office, Kayla greeted me with a confused look. "You're growing a beard?"

"Growing some stubble," I called back, wiping my hand over my chin. "Trying to fit in."

"Well, you'd better go in there." She pointed to Bruce's office. "It's about the murder case."

I heard Sean Benning's voice in Bruce's office. I walked in. Sean had his feet up on the desk, and Bruce was standing by the window, watching the traffic slowly crawl past.

I looked at my watch. "I thought I was early."

"You are," Bruce grunted, "but this guy called me up at 5 a.m. this morning."

"5:55 a.m. It was practically six." Sean smiled. "Stop your complaining."

"And I was supposed to be out on the course at nine." Bruce shook his head. "But I'm not making it there today."

"What's the problem?"

"Two things." Bruce held up two fingers. "First things first, Wayne Cascade's name has been removed from the prosecution's witness list for Caleb Rutledge's case."

"Like I said," said Benning. "He was a decoy. They put him on the list to waste your time and get you chasing your tail."

"Maybe." Bruce shrugged. "The prosecution has stated his name was added to the list in error. They've had a high staff turnover in recent months, and some of the files have been mixed up. A simple administrative error."

"They're trying to scare you, Dean," Benning told me.

"It didn't work."

"I'm not sure it's that complex," Bruce stated. "They said it was an error, and I believe them."

"It wasn't unexpected," I said. "What's the second issue?"

"After getting your call on Saturday morning"—Sean tapped the space bar on the laptop before him—"I spent all weekend researching the lead you got on the murder case. Your tip-off about the Marine Repair Store was right."

He turned the laptop toward me and hit play.

"What am I looking at?" I asked.

"There, as clear as day, is Caleb's car driving toward the scene of the crime."

I sighed and sat down.

"How did you get this?" Bruce asked.

"Dean called me Friday night and said there was a lead at the Marine Repair Store on Lady's Island, which is about half a mile from the Aiken household. It's also about half a mile from Caleb's place. Right in between the two homes, along Little Capers Road. This footage places Caleb driving toward the scene of the crime at 9:05 p.m., which fits with the time of Millie's death." Benning turned the laptop back toward him and typed a few more lines, then turned it back to us. "And this is the second piece of footage."

The footage played and this time, the timestamp in the bottom corner read 9:35 p.m.

"He was logged as arriving at the gas station at 9:25 p.m. From my calculations, it's a two-minute drive from the Marine Repair Store to the gas station. That leaves an eighteen-minute window where his location is unexplained. He could've easily gone to the Aiken household in that time, and then to the gas station after that. The missing eighteen minutes convicts him."

"If the footage is real." Bruce grunted. He paced the floor for a few moments before looking at me. "Do you think the prosecution has this already?"

"The prosecution has had this all along. That's why they were so certain about this case." I leaned my head against the wall and looked at the ceiling. "They would've been 'verifying' the footage from the start. They would've received it before they arrested him, but it's taken them weeks to verify it. Of course, they can't put it in discovery if they haven't done that."

"Why would they do that to us?"

"They wanted us to spend time trying to disprove the old lady's ability to see, wasting hours and hours, but they had this in their back pocket the whole time."

"All these games. I'm not used to it." Bruce shook his head. "We're straight up and down here. If they've got something, they give it to us. That's the way we do things."

"You've never had a murder case either," Sean quipped. "I've heard these tactics are common."

"He's right."

Bruce sat with a heavy thump, leaned back, and looked out the window. "All this because Caleb hasn't accepted the deal yet. If he'd taken it, none of this would be happening."

"Where does this leave us?" Sean asked.

I looked at Bruce with raised eyebrows.

"We need to convince Caleb to sign a deal," Bruce repeated. "Because if that footage is real, there's no way he's winning this trial."

CHAPTER 25

Bruce stopped outside the entrance to the Detention Center. He looked up at the flag on the street, hanging off one of the streetlamps.

"This sign bothers me." Bruce pointed up at it.

"What's wrong with it?" I squinted as I looked up into the sun.

"It says, 'Welcome to Historic Beaufort. Discovered in 1514 and founded in 1711.'"

"And?"

"And there were twenty-nine indigenous tribes or nations in this area before the colonial period. They're a part of the history of this land, and we should acknowledge that. Beaufort isn't just the town, it's the whole area. All this land, the rivers and marsh. I'm not saying give the land back to the indigenous peoples, but we should acknowledge their history here. The sign should say, 'Settled by indigenous tribes 4,500 years ago, discovered by the Spanish in 1514, and founded by the English in 1711.' We should celebrate all the history of this land."

"That's a very modern take on it, Bruce."

"My forefathers have been in this state for two hundred and fifty years, and not one of us has traveled back to England. Not one. I have no connection with the British. The land I'm standing on is my home. The dirt beneath my feet is my home. All this, all this beautiful land, is my home. And part of the history of this land is the indigenous tribes who lived here. This state, all of this, is my home, not some far-off country I've never been to. I couldn't care less about the English and their settlements. My forefathers fought to get them off this land."

"I didn't take you for a woke progressive."

"I'm not woke," he grunted. He shook his head so much that his chin wobbled. "And don't you dare paint me with that brush. I'm all for common sense and fairness for all, but I'm not for some new-wave political ideal."

I raised my hands and smiled. "Hey, forget I mentioned it."

We started the walk into the detention center, but Bruce paused again, watching as an F-35 fighter jet flew overhead, returning to the Marine Corps Air Station, three miles northwest of Beaufort. The noise was deafening. I could hardly hear myself think.

"That was a loud one," I said as the sound dissipated. "He was flying low."

"And that, my friend, is the beautiful, beautiful sound of freedom." Bruce placed a hand on my shoulder. "Now, let's go and talk to Caleb about how he's about to lose his."

Fifteen minutes later, we were waiting in another meeting room, deep within the thick concrete walls of the detention center. It was a different meeting room this time. Luckily, this one had ventilation.

Caleb was led into the room five minutes later. He was looking worse than he had before. He was skinnier. Gaunt. His skin looked drier, and his hair had matted together and looked like it hadn't been washed in weeks.

"How are you holding up, Caleb?"

"Okay." He nodded, but it wasn't the truth. "I'm okay."

"Thank you for meeting with us again. We—" Bruce began, but Caleb interrupted.

"I've got nothing else to do."

Bruce shrugged. "You might have to get used to that for a few years."

"Why?" He squinted.

"While we could've doubted the lady's eyesight who stated she saw you drive toward Millie's house on the night of the murder, the prosecution has new evidence of you heading toward the crime scene that night."

"What do you mean?"

I put the laptop in front of Caleb and hit the space bar. The footage of his car passing the Marine Repair Store began to play.

"What's this?" he asked.

"It's evidence of you driving up Little Capers Road around the time Millie was killed," I said. "And the footage shows you returning after her estimated time of death. This footage places you directly near the scene of the crime around that time."

"I . . ." Caleb fumbled over his words. "I don't know what to say."

"You better start with the truth," Bruce grunted. "Enough games. Enough lies. Give us the truth. If I have the truth, I can take your case to the prosecution and discuss voluntary or involuntary manslaughter charges." Bruce leaned closer to Caleb. "I'm very good at negotiations, Caleb. I can get you a great deal. One that will see you out of prison in half a decade, but I need you to work with me. You're a good kid. I know that. Everyone knows that. Maybe you made a mistake. We all have moments of anger. Work with me. Please."

Caleb leaned back in his chair and rubbed his hand over his head. The shock on his face was evident. He shook his head and then looked up to the ceiling.

"The truth isn't up there," Bruce said. "If you've got another reason to have been driving in that direction, we need to hear it now. This is your last chance to explain it, and where you were for the eighteen minutes between driving past the Marine Repair Store and walking into the gas station."

"Alright, alright." Caleb stood and paced the floor. "But I wasn't home that night."

"Then where were you?"

"Argh," Caleb grunted and then slumped back into the chair. "I was with someone else."

"Who?"

"Ava."

"And who is Ava?"

Caleb shook his head.

"Who, Caleb? Who is she?"

"Ava Healy," he whispered. "She lives two doors down."

"And why were you with Ava Healy?"

"Because I was sleeping with her."

Bruce and I threw our heads back at the same time, and we both made the same groan of disappointment.

"I didn't say anything because I didn't want her to get in trouble. I wanted to keep her out of it. I wanted to protect her, you know?" He shook his head. "Millie and I were breaking up. Millie wanted to see other people, and so did I. We'd been together since we were fifteen and we wanted to explore other options. We'd ended it between us, but other than Ava, nobody else knew about that. It was the next stage of our lives."

"How did Millie take the breakup?"

"She's the one who suggested it."

"That's not good," I noted. "Don't tell anyone else that. The prosecution could say that it gives you a motive to hit Millie. You weren't happy with the breakup, and you got angry. That won't look good in court, so don't repeat it."

Caleb bit his lip. "Okay."

"Was Millie dating anyone else?" Bruce had his pen prepared, hovering over his legal pad, ready to take notes.

"Not that I know of. She had a brief fling with some guy from Bluffton, but that was all I knew. That was the start of the breakup, but really, we were drifting apart anyway. The actual breakup was her idea, and I agreed to it—it was time to move on. But our lives were so linked that it was taking time to break up fully. Our families knew each other, all our friends were the same, and our whole world revolved around each other. Our lives were so deeply intertwined."

"And you became intertwined with Ava Healy before everyone knew you'd ended things with Millie?" Bruce asked.

"Yeah." Caleb shrugged. "Ava lived two doors down and moved in about five or six months ago. We hit it off and we were always flirting. It seemed natural we get together after Millie broke it off. I loved Millie, I really did, but we were never going to be together forever." Caleb shook his head. "I was with Ava a few hours until I left. I guess I was at her place between 7.30ish and 9 p.m. I left to get gas and a chocolate bar at around 9 p.m."

"Two houses down from you?" Bruce repeated. "So, before you reach the Marine Repair Store?"

"Yeah."

"Then there's still a missing eighteen minutes," I stated. "The footage from the Marine Repair Store places you driving away from Ava's house toward Millie's at 9:05 p.m. You then buy gas on Fairfield Road at 9:25 p.m. It's a two-minute drive from the Marine Repair Store to the gas station. Where were you for the remaining eighteen minutes?"

He sighed. "I pulled over on the side of Fairfield Road and Alumni Road and smoked a joint. Ava and I had a really good time, and I wanted to get high. I wanted the buzz to continue."

"Did anyone see you?"

"No. I parked off the road. There's a marsh there, and I parked under a tree, sat on the hood of my car, and listened to the bugs." He shook his head. "I'd had a few drinks and then got high, and when I was getting back into my truck, I cut myself. There was a sharp bit of metal near the door handle, and I caught myself on it. I was so high and drunk that I didn't even realize what I'd done until the gas station attendant said something. It was all my own blood on my hand. I was stupid, but I was high. I didn't even notice the cut."

I looked at Bruce, and he was shaking his head in a rhythmic pattern like he could've been listening to techno music.

"You know how this looks, don't you, Caleb?" I said. "It looks like you were sleeping with Ava, Millie found out, broke up with you, and in a jealous rage, you slapped her, and she fell and hit her head, you tried to pick her up, got blood on your hand, and then raced from the scene. This missing eighteen minutes is enough to convict you."

"That's not what happened," Caleb whispered. "I was smoking a joint."

"But this could be good," Bruce suggested. "If you left Ava's place at 9:05 p.m., we might have another suspect. Did Ava Healy get along with Millie? Were they friends?"

Caleb avoided eye contact.

"Caleb?"

"No." He shook his head slightly. "Ava hated Millie."

CHAPTER 26

Located on the edge of the Beaufort Town Center shopping mall, the Wilderness Grill was a family restaurant known for its large, and cheap, meals. With the ambiance of a Texas steakhouse, complete with leather booths and décor that reflected all things Texas, the space had a wooden ceiling, dim lighting, and a large menu. When we stepped inside, we were confronted by a wall of steakhouse smells.

I had argued with Bruce for fifteen minutes in the parking lot outside the detention center about our next steps. Bruce wanted to go straight in and question Ava Healy about what had happened on the night of March 5th. I'd told him to wait. It wasn't a good idea. We needed to settle, refocus, and assess the situation. We had new information and we had to evaluate it first.

Bruce disagreed. After fifteen minutes of arguing, he pulled the "I'm the boss" card. With that, I got into his car and we drove to the steakhouse.

"Good afternoon, gentlemen," a voice said from behind us. "How can I help you today?"

I turned to face Ava Healy. She was slim and healthy with distinctive blue eyes. She had multiple highlights through her brown hair. She held herself with the confidence of someone who was youthful and attractive—and she was both. Her smile was easy, and her manner was friendly.

"Miss Healy, my name is Bruce Hawthorn, and this is Dean Lincoln." Bruce offered her his most charming smile. "We'd like to talk with you."

"To me?"

"That's right."

"What about?"

"We're lawyers and—"

"Lawyers? Why would a lawyer be looking for me?" The panic on her face was clear. "Is everyone alright?"

"Yes, yes, of course," Bruce assured her and looked around. "Can we chat somewhere privately?"

"Can you tell me what this is about first?"

"We'd rather do that in private," Bruce continued. "It's a delicate matter."

"No, no." Her eyebrows sprang up, and her tone lost any friendliness. "Are you representing Caleb?"

Bruce nodded and the silence hung heavy between them as she decided her next move.

"That lying prick," she whispered under her breath. She looked around to ensure no one was watching, then pointed to a door near the back of the room. "I'll take a break in five minutes, and we can talk out back. If you walk out this door, turn right. I'll meet you in the parking lot."

We headed back out the door, turned right as instructed and walked to the parking lot where five cars were parked. All were older. All had paint damage from the Carolina sun.

"I'll do the talking," Bruce said. "She'll react better to me than you."

I agreed.

The paved parking lot at the rear of the restaurant backed on to a reserve, and the bugs were loud as the evening started to take over. Ava Healy walked out a few minutes later, but instead of stopping, she gestured for us to follow. Not even the back parking lot was private enough for her. She led us toward the far corner of the lot, near a small brick fence that stood around hip height. Judging by the cigarette butts lying on the ground, I reasoned this was where the staff came to escape for a few moments of calm. A giant live oak stood near us, and the Spanish moss blew gently in the breeze.

"Before you start," Ava said as she stopped and turned to face us. She crossed her arms over her chest and ensured there was a safe distance between us. "I want to say it's horrible what happened to Millie. Nobody wants that to happen to anyone."

"Agreed," Bruce stated. "Ava, what can you tell us about your relationship with Caleb Rutledge?"

"What did Caleb say?"

"We'd rather hear your version of events first."

She bit her lip and looked around. She blinked back tears. "I don't know what to say."

Bruce raised his hands. "We want to hear the truth, that's all. No pressure."

She shook her head. "Caleb and I . . . well, we got together a couple of times."

"Including the night of March 5th?"

She bit her lip. "Maybe."

"What time did he leave?"

She waved her open palm at us. "I was told to keep my mouth shut, and Caleb would keep me out of it. I wanted nothing to do with any of this."

"Unfortunately, Ava, this is a criminal case. The truth has a way of finding its way to the surface," Bruce explained as he stepped closer. "Can you please tell us what time Caleb left that night?"

"I don't know. Maybe 9 p.m."

Bruce nodded. "And he was at your house before that?"

She shifted, uncomfortable with the questions. "Do I really need to be a part of this?"

"I'm afraid so," Bruce told her. "This case might go to court, and if that happens, everything will be out on the table. It's best to talk to us now. What was your relationship with Caleb? Were you boyfriend and girlfriend?"

"Nothing like that. We'd . . . we'd seen each other a few times."

"And were you aware he was single?"

"That's what he said. He said Millie had dumped him, and he was a single man for the first time in his adult life. I don't know." She shrugged. "Caleb was cute and fun and lived two doors down. That's why we got together."

"Did anyone else know about your relationship?"

"No. Not a soul. Caleb wanted to keep it under wraps and so did I. He didn't want anyone else to know he and Millie had broken up yet. We met up at my house a few times. Had some fun, that's all."

"Did your friends approve of your relationship?"

"They didn't know."

"Not even your closest friend?"

"No. I only moved to Beaufort last year and I'm not really that close with anyone yet. I called my sister in Atlanta, and she knew I was seeing someone, but I never told her his name."

"When you and Caleb were together, what did you do?"

"Wow, man." Ava snapped. She looked up and met Bruce's gaze. It was like a different person had taken over. "What do you think we did, you old creep? We got together."

"So, you slept with him?"

Her mouth hung open for a few moments before she folded her arms again and looked away.

140

"Do you know Chester Washington?" Bruce continued.

"Yeah, I know him. So what?"

"Did you sleep with him as well?"

"Really?" Ava took a moment and contemplated her thoughts. Her tone was no longer pleasant. "What is this? Some sort of interrogation?"

"All we want is the truth," Bruce explained further. "A horrible thing has happened, and we need to get to the truth."

"The truth?" She stepped back. "Are you saying Caleb didn't kill her?"

"We need to follow all avenues, at this point," Bruce replied.

"You've got the truth." Ava's voice rose to a higher pitch. "I don't know what you're doing, but you'd better be careful."

"Why's that, Ava?"

She moved nervously, unable to stand still, rocking from one foot to the other, and then she tried to walk past me.

I stepped to my right, blocking her path.

Ava looked up at my size and then turned back to Bruce. She pointed her finger at him. "Listen to me, I don't want to get messed up in this. I want nothing to do with it."

"I'm afraid that's not an option now, Ava," Bruce said. "What was your relationship with Millie like?"

She stood up straighter, shocked by the question. "What are you suggesting?"

"We're not suggesting anything." Bruce tried to calm her down. "But we need to know the details. Did you like Millie? Would you consider her a friend?"

"Uh-uh." She began waving her finger in the air. "No way, mister. You're not bringing me into this. I'm not going to be the fall guy for you."

"We're not doing anything," Bruce explained further. "We just need to know about your relationship with Millie."

"No, no, no," Ava repeated. "I'm not going to be a part of this. I had nothing to do with her death and I don't want to talk about it. I didn't touch her."

"Can anyone verify your whereabouts after Caleb left?"

"Are you accusing me of hurting her?"

"We're trying to get to the truth," Bruce said.

"I've kept my mouth shut because of Caleb, and this is how he repays me?" she snapped. Her fists clenched. "No way am I taking the fall for this. I'll say anything to keep my name out of it."

"Ava—"

"Do I have to talk to you?" she questioned.

"It's best if we talk now," Bruce continued. "That's all."

"I'm done." Ava's face tensed as she pointed her finger at Bruce. "I wanted to stay out of it, and Caleb said he'd keep me out of it. I'm done talking to you."

She turned and stormed off.

I looked at Bruce and he grimaced. The chat hadn't gone to plan, but one thing was clear—Ava Healy had an angry streak.

CHAPTER 27

Prosecutor Andrew Harley called and asked for a meeting.

Bruce agreed as quickly as he could. He hoped Harley had convinced Freeman to put the offer of manslaughter back on the table.

"If we don't get the deal we want, should we reveal we might be going for third-party culpability?" Bruce asked as we drove toward the courthouse. "Do we suggest Ava Healy might be a suspect?"

"It's not wise to play our full hand yet," I said. "It'd be best to give them a hint, and they'll say we're bluffing. We'll give them a slight clue and see what they say. If they bite, we might get an even better deal for Caleb. If not, then we can surprise them in the week before the trial. It'll send them scampering. Confidence is the key to this discussion."

Bruce nodded. "All this murder trial stuff is too intense. This'll be the last one I ever take on. I'm not going to take any more after this."

"Why'd you do this one anyway?"

"Gerald convinced me. He's a good talker, and when he talked about how I was the best in town and the only one that could save Caleb, I couldn't say no."

I didn't respond.

I stepped inside the building at Ribaut Road, next to the courthouse. Inside the entrance, the title of the fourteenth circuit solicitor was displayed proudly on the wall beneath the Seal of South Carolina. The American flag stood on one side of the entrance, and the South Carolina state flag on the other.

Assistant Solicitor Andrew Harley was waiting near the entrance, talking to another staff member. When he saw us, he welcomed us a little bit too confidently for my liking. It set alarms bells off in my head. Harley shook hands with Bruce and I, made a few comments about the heat and humidity, and then led us through the halls to his private office.

I was cautious as I entered. The room was spacious and modern. There was a clean white desk with a computer monitor, a leather couch, and a plain white bookshelf filled with red-colored law books. An artist's picture of Beaufort hung on the far wall and an indoor plant sat in the corner. The air conditioner was working overtime, and the room felt cool, a great relief from the outdoors.

"Can I get you anything?" Harley asked as he sat down behind his desk and indicated that we should take a seat on the other side. "Hot drink? Cold drink?"

"No, thank you," Bruce said as he sat down. "I'm fine."

"How's life in Beaufort?" Harley turned to me. "Feeling at home now?"

"We're doing well."

"That's nice. My wife and I met your wife last week at the coffee shop. She's so lovely. Very genuine, and both my wife and I said she seemed like a good Beaufort person." Harley leaned back in his seat. "And then we started discussing you."

I said nothing. I had no interest in his opinion of me.

Harley waited a few moments and when I still stayed quiet, he continued anyway.

"It seems like the locals here all have the same impression of you, Dean. A big-city man who hasn't got used to our way of life yet. My wife thinks you'll settle down, learn the ropes and how things work around here, and become a local. Me, well, I'm not so sure. I don't think you'll last in a place like this."

"Andrew, we're here for business," I said. "We should discuss the case."

"We had another defense lawyer like you," he carried on. "Came down from Columbia a few years back. Thought he could shake up the whole system and tell us how to do our work here. He was working fifty-five-hour weeks and didn't have time for a game of golf. He only lasted five months before he went back. He couldn't take the way of life."

"You really are a talker, aren't you, Andrew?"

"I love to chat. I'm—"

"About to tell us about the new offer for Caleb Rutledge's case," I interrupted. "We're busy people, Andrew. We need to move it along."

"Alright, alright." Harley smiled and looked to Bruce. Bruce smiled and shrugged as if to say, "What can you do?"

"Down to business then," Harley said. "Caleb Rutledge murdered Millie Aiken. Those are the facts as we know them. He slapped her in a jealous rage, and she fell and hit her head. Unfortunately, she died."

"Those aren't the facts. We're—"

Bruce reached out his hand to stop me continuing. He gave me a nod and said, "Let's allow Andrew to finish what he was saying."

"Thank you, Bruce. At least somebody here understands how things are done in these parts." Harley smiled and then drew in a long breath. "What's interesting is that we've had someone come forward overnight to provide a witness statement about Caleb's whereabouts on the night of the murder."

I squinted. "Who?"

"A young lady named Ava Healy." Harley chuckled a little. "Apparently, she was trying to keep out of the case but had a visit from two defense lawyers, and she found the older one quite rude." Harley looked at Bruce with a broad grin on his face. "She then came to us. And let me tell you, it doesn't look good for your client."

Bruce leaned forward. "And what exactly did Miss Healy say?"

"That she'd been sleeping with Caleb Rutledge for several weeks, including on the night of the murder. Caleb left her home, only half a mile from Millie's place, at around 9 p.m. She wasn't sure where he went after that, but she knew he was angry with Millie. In fact, she said"—Harley opened the folder in front of him and read off the page—"'Caleb was angry with Millie. He was upset that she was seeing someone from Bluffton. I didn't like it when he was angry. It frightened me.'"

Bruce groaned and sat back in the chair. He ran one of his hands over the top of his head, until he said, "That doesn't sound good for Caleb."

I turned and looked at him. Bruce had laid his feelings out on the table. It wasn't how I was used to negotiating.

"There's still no evidence Caleb visited Millie after he left Ava's place," I said.

"There doesn't need to be. Ava is unsure where he went, but he was angry. What jury isn't going to believe that?"

"Ava didn't say he was angry when we talked to her."

"Well, it's in her official statement." Harley tossed a piece of paper across the table. "Have a read."

Bruce reached forward, picked it up, and opened it. He began reading over the lines of the statement, mumbling to himself.

"And I need to thank you for finding her," Harley continued, the grin never leaving his face. "She never would've come forward otherwise. She felt threatened by you and didn't want to get caught up in the wrong thing. She only wants the truth to come out, and she felt we could protect her from those nasty defense lawyers."

Bruce drew in a breath and sat up straighter when he had finished reading the file. He caught my eye. His look said it all—her statement wasn't good.

"And by the look between the two of you"—Harley chuckled again—"I'm going to guess you were going to come here and suggest you've got someone to apply third-party culpability to."

"Ava Healy doesn't have an alibi after Caleb left," Bruce said. "And we know she's got an angry streak. Maybe she wanted Caleb all to herself?"

"She doesn't need an alibi." Harley struggled to hold back his smile. He seemed to be finding the whole situation hilarious. "We've got the killer, and if you even suggest Ava Healy as a suspect, we'll paint her as an angel. No jury will ever convict her after we're through."

"Go on, then," Bruce sighed. "Is there an offer on the table?"

"Well, there's something else we need to discuss first."

"Go on."

Harley turned his monitor around to face us. He clicked his mousepad several times and a video came on the screen. "This is video footage from the Marine Repair Store. The location is about half a mile from the Rutledge household in one direction and about half a mile from the Aiken household in the other. As you can see, Caleb's car drives past at 9:05 p.m. and he doesn't arrive at the gas station on Fairfield Road until 9:25 p.m." The smile broadened on Harley's face. "That's enough time for Caleb to drive to the Aiken household, have an argument with Millie, slap her, and then leave."

"You had the footage from the start, didn't you?" Bruce stated. "It's why you've been so certain on this case."

Harley tilted his head to the side. "You don't seem shocked by the footage, Bruce."

"We came across it yesterday."

Harley expressed his surprise with several nods. "We couldn't submit a video into discovery without verifying it. We had no control over the time it took to verify the information."

"Is there a deal?" Bruce pressed.

"Well, as a sign of goodwill between us, yes, there is. Everyone in this office understands taking this case to trial will be costly for the state, and we wish to avoid that, if possible."

"And Stephen Freeman?"

"Stephen has relaxed his stance. So, we're willing to put an offer on the table for voluntary manslaughter under Section 16-3-50, and we'll note this crime was under intense passion and sufficient legal provocation. He does fifteen years and then gets out. He'll only be thirty-six by the time he's released. That's still young enough to make something of his life."

"Fifteen years?"

"With Ava Healy's testimony, it's about as good as it's going to get. You won't receive an offer for less than that." Harley looked at me. "And that directive has come from the top."

I held my stare on Harley for a long moment, and when he didn't flinch, I stood and offered my hand. "We'll take it to our client."

Harley stood and shook hands with Bruce first, then with me. "Gentlemen, a word of advice—you don't want to take this to court. There'll be a lot of upset people if this one makes it into the courtroom. The whole community is hurting from the murder, and to have that played out publicly will hurt everyone even more. And if you do take it to court, we'll push for the maximum penalty possible. We'll be under pressure to appease the Aiken family, and we won't have a choice. But if we do it behind closed doors, we can negotiate down. So please, encourage your client to take the deal. It's best for everyone."

"We'll take it to the client."

"Bruce." Harley's tone was firm. "Maybe you've forgotten how things work around here. We all help each other out. We're connected one way or another, and we all listen to each other's advice. Don't forget where we are."

Bruce didn't respond.

He picked up his briefcase, turned, and left the office. He walked through the halls, said goodbye to the secretary, and stepped out into the bright sunlight covering the parking lot.

"That prick," he mumbled as I stood next to him. "Threatening me like that."

"Threatening?" I questioned.

"He said, 'Don't forget where we are.' That's as clear a threat as any in these parts." Bruce shook his head. "And I don't take kindly to threats."

CHAPTER 28

There was always more than one case, always more than one place to put my focus. Even in a small town, that was the life of a defense lawyer. Another file, another motion, another witness to talk to.

Isaiah Clyburn's case was progressing, but at a snail's pace.

I engaged the services of a retired firefighter from Charleston, now a fire investigator. He reviewed the files and the evidence and found that Isaiah most likely lit the fire. That didn't help.

I called a farm mechanic. He confirmed the details in the insurance report, and stated the tractor and platform header were most likely in very good working condition. That didn't help.

I filed a request with the insurance company and spoke to their assessors. I arrived at the offices and entered a meeting with five of their lawyers. They certainly didn't help.

The farm on Land's End Road on St. Helena Island was hidden behind a thick row of trees. Passing motorists only got a glimpse at the scale of the operation through the gaps in the trees. When I drove in, I was stunned by the endless fields of tomatoes. Under directions from the staff, I traveled the dirt road toward the sweet-potato field, where I found it was already dug up. The remnants of the burned-out barn were at one end, closest to the road, and a large metal shed stood at the other. I headed toward the shed.

Pearson and Sons seemed to have a clean record. Locally, there were rumors about dodgy dealings, about selling crops to local buyers to avoid tax, but nothing was ever taken to court.

I saw John Pearson, the owner, standing at the entrance to the shed. I pulled the car up and a cloud of dust followed me. I had called John numerous times, and he had finally agreed to meet, as long as I came out to the farm. He was a tall, skinny man, with layers of dirt seemingly replacing his skin. His flannel shirt was dirty, his skin was dusty, and his boots were scuffed. His jeans were loose, blackened by hours of hard work. His belt buckle was shining in the light. His cap, however, was spotless. He was a proud Clemson supporter, that much was clear.

"Thank you for meeting with me, John. I appreciate it," I said as I stepped out of the car. I was met with the strong musky smell of tomato plants. John approached and shook my hand. It was a workman's hand, almost as rough and dry as concrete. "I'm trying to work with Isaiah Clyburn on this case and I understand if you're angry with him."

"I'm not angry. I'd met Isaiah before, and he seemed like a good kid," he responded, but he was cautious. "Tell me, is he pleading not guilty?"

"At this point, yes. He'd like to avoid prison time."

John looked around and scrunched his face up. "Listen, I don't want to see a kid go to prison if he doesn't need to. Maybe they were just having fun out here. We all did stupid things at that age. I would've been locked up for years if the police knew what I was getting up to. Smoking weed, doing burnouts on fields, graffiti. One night, a guy got his hands on some LSD and we popped the tablets. But you know what? I grew out of it. By twenty-five, I was working full-time, had a wife, and a baby on the way. I'm sure glad the past didn't catch up with me."

"I hear you. We all did stupid things back then."

"What I'm saying is if you need me to say something to the judge or the courts or whoever, I'll help him out. I don't want him to go to prison. The only reason I filed a police report was for the insurance claim, but I can't withdraw it, or the claim goes out the window."

"Those tractors were worth a lot of money."

"A John Deere 4520. 2005 model, worth about fifty grand, along with a platform header for one of our other machines, which was also worth about fifty grand. They were reliable workers."

"And the insurance claim was all paid?"

"It was."

"And you bought new ones?"

He grimaced a little. "Replacements. Not new ones. They work well enough."

"And the crop was destroyed as well?"

"Yep. The sweet-potato crop."

"Not the tomato crop?"

"No, but our sweet-potato crop was worth around 25K. That hurt."

"And you've dug it up already?"

"That's right."

"No problems with weevils?"

"Terrible blight on the farming industry here." He spat on the ground. "We're close to getting the quarantine ban lifted on the county, if no more weevils are found in the next five months. It's been a three-year process trying to get the ban lifted."

"And if the weevils were found again?"

"That'd destroy a lot of family farms who were investing for when the ban is lifted. We don't want a repeat of the quarantine."

"But the insurance paid out on your crop as well?"

"That's right."

I nodded. I wasn't really sure what I'd hoped to see or find out, just some clue to help Isaiah's case. "Can you show me how the fire ran through the place?"

"When he lit the fire, he ran a line of gasoline down the middle of the crop to the barn." John pointed his long arm toward the road. "He lit it, and the middle of the field went up, until it hit the barn. The smoke damage meant we had to pull out all the sweet potatoes and destroy them." He shrugged. "What did you hope to see out here?"

I looked at the barn in the distance, five pieces of lumber still standing, although heavily burned. "I'm trying to figure out why your farm was doused in petrol and then set alight."

"Your guess is as good as mine."

A farmhand called out from the paddock nearby. To me, the call was indistinguishable, but John seemed to know what the man was saying. "Sorry, Mr. Lincoln, but I've got to go and help the young'un, but can I ask you something first?"

"Go on."

He rubbed his chin and grimaced. "What if I was involved in something that led to something else and I feel guilty about it? I don't want to be charged with anything criminal. Any criminal convictions would mean I could lose the farm, and my family's had this farm for five generations. I can't be the one to lose it."

"Was your involvement criminal?"

He nodded.

"It depends on the situation. I'd need more information."

"What if I didn't do anything wrong, but the person I talked to did something criminal?"

"Again, I'd need more details."

He wiped his nose a few times with a handkerchief and sniffed. "That's what I thought." He grunted and then held out his hand. We shook hands solidly again. "Thanks, Mr. Lincoln."

I squinted at him as he walked away to help the man.

There was more to his story, more to the story of the farm, but I didn't know how to get it.

CHAPTER 29

Isaiah Clyburn was waiting for me outside the shed he worked at when I arrived a little after 7 p.m. He'd pulled another ten-hour shift, and instead of making him come to the office, I agreed to meet him in the parking lot. Other workers were also leaving, joking with each other despite another heavy day's work on the tools with the concreting firm.

Isaiah climbed into my SUV. He smelled like work—a mixture of body odor, dirt, and concrete. His knuckles were scarred, and he had a cut up his right arm. His clothes were dirty, as was his cap.

"Hello, Isaiah," I greeted him. "How was work today?"

"Same as always. Hard, long hours, not much pay. We're preparing some concrete for the road crews. Good people, though. They look after me. What else can I say?"

I nodded. "At least it's a job."

"I'm not complaining," he agreed. "How's the case?"

"Isaiah, I'm not going to dance around the point, because you're a smart man. You know how it looks. There aren't many options left for your case. I don't know what else to tell you. All the evidence is against you, and while there are no guarantees in court, you're unlikely to win at trial."

"Any chance?"

"There's always a chance. Every jury trial is open to how people feel about the law. We can harp on at them about the evidence, but in the end, it comes down to twelve people making a choice."

Isaiah nodded, looking off into the distance. "You've met my parents. I can't go to prison. They can't support Lana if I'm not around. If you can get me a deal without prison time, then I'll take it. Otherwise, I need to chance it at a trial. If you put me on the stand, I'll tell the jury whatever they need to hear."

"If we go to trial, the prosecution will push for a harder sentence."

"So, I get punished for trying to make it to trial?"

"That's one way to look at it. Or you can see it as being rewarded for saving the state time and money by taking an early plea."

"That's screwed up, man." Isaiah shook his head. "I can't do prison time. That's it. It doesn't matter if it's one month, or two years. I can't do time."

"I get that, but it may be your best option."

"I'll plead guilty if they suspend the sentence, but I can't go to prison." He rubbed his hand along the back of his neck. "My best friend died in prison, and I can't go back there. He was innocent, and they forced him to take a deal, and then he died. I don't want that to happen to me."

I let the pause sit between us for a while.

I wanted to tell him that he shouldn't have set the barn on fire, but I resisted. It wasn't for me to judge. "How did you win the money on the floating casino, Isaiah?"

"What?"

"Your father said you won money at the floating casino off Savannah. What game did you win it on?"

"Poker."

"I've heard a rumor some people were winning money on the floating casino and their luck might not be legitimate."

"Whatever." He shook his head. "I got lucky."

"That's not what I heard. I heard you won money through a dealer who runs drug money through the casino to clean it."

"Not drug money. I'd never do drugs." Isaiah rested his hand on the door handle of my car. "But you can't repeat that to anyone. Don't say that in court."

"Why not?" I eyed him. "Has someone been talking to you?"

He avoided eye contact, flicking the handle.

"Isaiah? Why shouldn't I talk about it?"

He didn't answer.

"Isaiah?"

"A few people are scared about what might come out in court, and they want this case gone," he whispered, staring out the window. "But I can't leave my parents behind."

"Who's pressuring you?"

He shook his head. "Listen, get me a suspended sentence. If you can get me a suspended sentence and keep me out of prison, I'll plead guilty. Otherwise, I've got to take a chance at a trial."

I nodded. "We go to court tomorrow to try and have some evidence thrown out. This will be our chance to pressure them to make a better offer. You don't need to attend the pre-trial motions, but you can, if you wish."

"I want to be there. I want to see what it's like." He looked at me. "Do your best. Please."

He stepped out of the SUV. I liked the guy, he was honest and hard-working, but I didn't like his chances in court.

When Isaiah entered his car nearby, I started the engine and drove to a place I'd avoided since I had returned to Beaufort.

CHAPTER 30

It was a small intersection. Nothing outstanding. Nothing unusual.

The oak tree was still there, still standing strong, still standing firm. The skid marks had long faded, washed away by rain and time. My memories were beginning to fade as well. That broke my heart. The memories of someone who I had spent every day with for the first eighteen years of my life was fading into history.

When you're in the midst of it, living can seem ordinary and plain and every day. It can seem nothing worthwhile, passing moments to be forgotten. Through the lens of time, looking back at those moments gives them meaning and worth. The ordinary becomes extraordinary, the plain things become the memories you hold on to the most. The long conversations about nothing, the smile during a game of cards, the jokes and the pranks. The moments that meant nothing mean everything during the long stages of grief.

I rested my hand against the tree.

Heather had been driving home after a dinner with friends when her car was struck by Paul Freeman's, who was racing through the intersection without a second glance. He hit the front end of her car and she slammed into the tree. I had forced myself to look at five photos of the crash scene, although I hadn't been able to look at any more.

I was living in Chicago at the time. When my father called, I was on the next plane home. The next week had been a blur. I remember barely keeping it together for Heather's funeral, but I refused to cry in church. I held it together until I had a private moment in my car.

Zoe's speech at the funeral was heartbreaking. Only five at the time, her little voice had echoed around the church. She ended her speech with, "I love you, Mommy," and there wasn't a dry eye left in the audience.

It seemed a strange place to remember someone, an intersection, a tree, a quiet road, but it was where she had last been alive, and it was where I felt her presence the most. I returned to my car, took out a bunch of carnations held together by a white piece of paper, and placed the flowers at the foot of the tree as a few drops of rain fell.

"I've seen your kids a few times," I said into the air, almost like she was next to me. "They're well. Growing up big. They're a lot like us, you know. Emma invited them around yesterday, and we had dinner. Zoe loves mac and cheese, like you did. Zoe . . ." I drew a breath and sighed. "She still insists on setting a place for you at the dinner table. She says it's so you can have dinner at the same time in heaven."

Even after two and a half years, Zoe still insisted on setting a plate for her mommy. Rhys didn't argue with her. While she was doing it, he gave me a knowing look. I nodded my approval. As hard as it was for him, it was confusing for Zoe.

Rhys and his children had planted an elm tree behind the oak, and it was growing strong.

A few minutes later, when I heard another car in the distance, I resettled myself and sucked it up. I had had a moment of grief, a moment where I let my walls down, and that was all I ever allowed myself.

When I walked away, thinking of her beautiful children, thinking of the lost moments they could've shared together, the memories that never were, the moments that could never be, my heart broke a little more.

CHAPTER 31

"It's intimidating," Isaiah Clyburn said as he approached me in the parking lot of the judicial center. He looked up while another F-35 fighter jet flew overhead. Once the deafening roar of the jet had started to ease, he turned back to me. "Is this when I get to tell the judge I can't go to prison because I've got to support my little sister?"

"Not yet," I responded, shaking his hand solidly. I wiped my brow with the back of my hand as we began the walk into the building. "Today is an evidentiary hearing on a motion to suppress."

"What does that mean?"

"The motion is trying to have evidence presented by the prosecution thrown out. We're trying to weaken the prosecution's case by saying their evidence doesn't meet the standards of evidence gathering as set out by the court. The prosecution has the burden of showing it has been lawfully obtained and meets the high standard required. Our motion is to suppress the evidence given in the tip-off against you."

"What will that do?"

"If we can get the tip-off thrown out, it means all the evidence gathered after that was unlawful. If that happens, the prosecution doesn't have a case."

"Really?" Isaiah said. "It could all be over today?"

"It's not likely, but it's worth a shot." I was honest with him. "What we're also doing is showing the prosecution this won't be an easy fight. We're saying to them that we're going to fight hard against these charges, and we're trying to get them a little scared. If the judge gives them a signal that we have a strong argument, then they'll present a better deal to prevent losing in court at a later time."

"No jail time," Isaiah said again. "If you can get me a deal with no jail time, I'll say whatever they want me to say."

"I understand." I nodded to the deputy as I reached the security checkpoint. I placed my keys and briefcase on the conveyor belt and then stepped through the metal detector. The deputy asked me to step aside and waved his security wand over me, then let me go. He did the same to Isaiah, and soon we were walking inside the foyer of the courthouse.

The foyer was subdued, almost like a library, with a few groups of people sitting around, waiting for their turn in the courts. Their discussions were whispered, and the tones were hushed.

Isaiah saw the sign for the bathrooms and turned left. He didn't bother to tell me where he was going, and I decided to wait for him. I leaned against the wall in the foyer, looking up at the flags, the American flag and the flag of South Carolina hung proudly in the middle, flanked by the Union Jack, and the Scottish flag. A stylish woman approached me. She held herself well, dressed in a gray skirt and white shirt. Her brown hair was tied up, and her red glasses showed a touch of flamboyance.

"Mr. Lincoln?" She smiled as she asked my name. I nodded my response, and she offered her hand. "Assistant Solicitor Stacey Casey."

"Stacey Casey?" I raised my eyebrows. "That's a great name."

"My maiden name is Smith, and I still decided to take my husband's name, even though it rhymed." I shook her hand. She had an effortless charm that made me feel at ease, and a soft smell of jasmine floated around her.

"I'm the prosecutor in the case against Mr. Clyburn," Casey stated in a hushed tone. "It should be an interesting hearing today. It'll give us a chance to understand where we both stand."

"I hope it is interesting," I quipped.

"It will be." She smiled, nodded, and when she saw Isaiah returning, she stepped back. She greeted him briefly and then moved away. I waited until she was out of earshot and then explained the process in more detail to Isaiah. Five minutes later, I led him into the courtroom on the first level.

Without an audience, and we didn't expect one for the hearing, the courtroom felt cold and lifeless. I drew a breath and sat down at the defense table. Isaiah sat next to me. I opened the file and reviewed my notes. At 10:55 a.m., Casey entered the room, followed by a junior assistant. Five minutes later, the clerk at the front of the room read the case number, and then asked the room to rise for Judge Joan Connery.

Judge Connery was in her early seventies, but she maintained her sharp wit. She had a reputation built on years of hard work, seeing thousands of cases and thousands of defendants. Judge Connery took a few moments to become settled and then looked out to the courtroom. She greeted us all and then made sure Isaiah was comfortable. She explained he wasn't required to be there, and when she was sure he understood, she began.

"We have one motion today, lodged by the defense," she said. "Mr. Lincoln, can you please start with the motion to suppress evidence of the tip-off?"

"Certainly, Your Honor." I stood behind the defense table. "We believe the anonymous tip-off came from someone who had a grudge against the defendant, and without the right to confront them, the defendant is being denied his constitutional rights.

161

Pursuant to the South Carolina Code of Laws, Section 17-30-110, supported by an affidavit, we have lodged a motion to strike the evidence of the tip-off, and subsequently all the evidence that was taken as a result. The anonymous tip-off violates Mr. Clyburn's Sixth Amendment right to be able to confront the witness who provided the evidence. His rights to confront the witness are written in the constitution. This tip-off was purposely made to directly accuse Mr. Clyburn of a crime. The Confrontation Clause ensures Mr. Clyburn must be afforded the same rights as everyone else. He has a right to cross-examine the person who accused him of such actions."

"That's a strong argument, Mr. Lincoln," Judge Connery agreed. "Where was the tip-off given?"

"In an anonymous telephone call to the Beaufort County Sheriff's Department."

"And that call was recorded?"

"It was." I opened the file on my desk and read over the notes. "There are recent precedents for this in this county, Your Honor. In the State v. Goldner, 2015, information from an anonymous tip-off led to the arrest of the defendant for drug possession charges at his home. On appeal, the Supreme Court overturned the conviction, stating the officers had no reasonable grounds to search the home, because the anonymous caller did not place their credibility at risk and could lie with impunity. The Supreme Court ruled that because the defense could not call into question the credibility of the caller, the risk of evidence fabrication became unacceptable." I turned a page in the file. "Adding to this, because we cannot possibly determine probable cause by questioning the caller, the defendant's Fourth Amendment rights are clearly violated. The constitution protects individuals' rights from unreasonable searches, and without the identity of the caller, we cannot even begin to establish if this has happened."

"Interesting, Mr. Lincoln." Judge Connery wrote several lines on her notepad. "Have you prepared a response, Mrs. Casey?"

"We have, Your Honor." Casey stood. "The recording of the tip-off has been included in the discovery material, and it's clear a reasonable basis for the search was established. The caller wished to protect themselves from reprisal by the defendant but also wished to tell the truth. They are not on trial here."

"Their concerns should not replace the defendant's constitutional rights. Without this anonymous tip-off, the prosecution cannot prove the chain of evidence," I argued. "If this evidence is admitted into court, it's a clear violation of the defendant's constitutional rights."

"Anything further from the State?"

"We've lodged our written argument in the affidavit, Your Honor."

"Thank you, Mrs. Casey." Judge Connery checked the files on her desk. "These are very strong arguments, Mr. Lincoln, and I will need to consider them further. And because of the complex nature of this evidence, and its impact on the case, I will take some time to consider these arguments and reserve my decision for a later time."

"Thank you, Your Honor," I replied, and looked at the prosecutor's desk.

Casey kept her eyes down, clearly feeling defeated.

After Judge Connery confirmed there were no further motions, she adjourned the hearing and left the room. Once she had gone, Casey stepped close to me.

"That was a good argument, Mr. Lincoln. A very strong legal case," Casey said. "But those sorts of arguments won't win you any friends around here."

CHAPTER 32

Judge Connery delivered her decision five days later. She dismissed the motion based on the good faith exception, a legal principle that allows evidence to be used in court if the law enforcement officers performed their duties with a reasonable belief that they were acting within the law. Her decision was grounds for a possible appeal, but that didn't help us now.

My focus turned to Caleb's case, and the following weeks of trial preparation flew past.

Hours upon hours disappeared under stacks of paperwork and strategy discussions about Caleb Rutledge's best defense. Bruce, Kayla, and I discussed plea deals, new witnesses, and new tactics. We argued about the best strategies, how to structure the witness list, and the best way to influence the jury. We talked about the State's witnesses and the best way to discredit them. We discussed further motions for the case. We drafted our best questions, picking apart the witness statements. We talked about the potential for appeals. We discussed plea deals. We lodged several motions to dismiss more of the prosecution's evidence; however, every motion was rejected. None of it seemed to matter. Bruce was certain we'd lose at trial with a third-party culpability defense.

We checked the entire night's footage from the Marine Repair Store. Caleb's car was clear as day. Also on the footage was Mrs.

Aiken driving home before midnight, Gerald Rutledge coming home after dinner in town, and numerous other cars driving up and down the road. None of them were solid leads, and all had alibis.

Caleb was holding on. Every time I saw him, he looked worse, as if descending into the life of a criminal. Prison was often called "Crime University." The sharing of information between criminals was rife behind bars—the best way to break into a house, the best way to steal a car, the best way to mug someone without getting caught. Prisoners shared information about how to avoid getting arrested, what to say to prove their innocence, how to treat police when they conducted searches. A person could walk into prison with little knowledge of wrongdoing and walk out five weeks later with a degree in criminal activity.

During the weeks of trial preparation, Bruce and I discussed Chester Washington at length. He was a good candidate for the third-party culpability, but nothing linked him to the night in question. Sean Benning had worked hard to connect him to the scene of the crime but had found nothing. If we called on him to testify, Chester would be asked about Millie and Caleb's relationship. We had no idea what he would say, but we were sure it wouldn't be favorable to Caleb. Chester was a skilled liar, and he would say anything to protect himself. We added his name to the witness list in an attempt to bait the prosecution, but we had no intention of calling him. He was too much of a risk.

As the Friday morning sun bathed Beaufort in humidity, I sat on a bench in the Henry C. Chambers Waterfront Park, taking shelter in the shade of an oak tree. The sun was hot, but the breeze off the water was refreshing.

Daisy-May approached, walking next to Kayla, who had a coffee cup in each hand. She handed one to me, and I thanked her. We walked along the waterfront, performing the Southern dance of beginning each discussion with a few minutes of small talk before turning to work.

"You know how you said local knowledge would solve Isaiah's case?" Kayla said, ready to move the conversation into work. "Well, this is it."

Daisy-May looked pleased with herself. She had a bounce in her step.

"I'd love to hear it," I said.

"After you came over and we talked about the money being won on the floating casino, I did a bit of digging." She smiled. "I asked several people what they knew about it. There were a few rumors floating around, so I dug deeper. It was all so fascinating. I felt like a detective in a mystery, and I was thinking about it all the time. I haven't been this excited in years."

"I hope you didn't get yourself into trouble," I said. "I don't want you going around the wrong places and finding yourself in with the wrong people."

"I tell you, if someone wanted to find trouble here, and they wanted to bring it my way, then they don't know me well enough. My cousin used to run with the Rebel Sons, a motorcycle gang. They're a one-percenter gang that runs drugs through the state. Mostly small-time stuff, but you wouldn't want to cross them."

"And?"

She looked around the park. There were tourists wandering the streets, a group of students throwing a frisbee, and children playing in the nearby playground. Two teenagers were throwing a baseball between them, trying to outthrow each other each time. When she was sure there was nobody interested in what she had to say, Daisy-May continued.

"After a little convincing, my cousin took me to a biker bar in North Charleston. Entry into the bar is by invite only," she beamed, happy to have a little excitement in her life. "And that place was rough. I never knew places like that existed."

"They would've liked you," Kayla quipped. "A new hot young woman in the bar."

"I didn't have to buy one drink," Daisy-May gushed. "And I never felt threatened once. They were all very respectful and were true Southern gentlemen. One guy was telling another about how he beat up a guy in Myrtle Beach last week for bumping into a woman at a bar."

"Real gentlemanly." I smiled. "So, what did they tell you?"

"After a few hours of talking and drinking and getting to know them, I asked some questions about the floating casino. And they were so honest. Just straight up with the facts."

"And what did they say?"

"The guys confirmed the floating casino was a way to launder money," Daisy-May continued. "I was told there were two ways they were doing it—a simple cash-in, cash-out scheme, and collusion between players. The cash-in, cash-out scheme worked by the players taking dirty money into the casino, exchanging that money for chips, playing for a while, and then cashing out by legitimately transferring the money to their bank accounts."

"You're saying Isaiah got biker money using this scheme?"

"No, no, no." She shook her head. "Not at all. Isaiah isn't messed up with all that. Isaiah was involved in the second way they clean the cash—through the player collusion method."

"Go on."

"I was told this method works by taking dirty money into the casino and deliberately losing it to another player. In poker, they set it up that one player plays an accomplice, and the dealer is in on it as well. The dealer makes sure the two players have lined up against one another, and when the time is right, they bet big, and the accomplice cashes out their winnings. It all looks legitimate, and nobody asks any questions if the winnings are below ten grand. The winner then legitimately asks the casino to transfer the money to their bank account."

"Any names?"

"Wayne Cascade is the dealer who cleans the cash. He deals in poker. He deals a suspect hand, and when he's ready, he taps the table, and the two players battle it out until one loses big time."

"And this is where it gets interesting." Kayla leaned forward. "Go on. Tell him."

"Do you know Gerald Rutledge?"

"I do." I nodded.

"One of the guys at the bar recognized him. He'd worked for Rutledge years earlier, and said he was a real prick. He said the pompous old man walks on board and bets five grand on one poker hand. Loses it all. And guess who he was playing poker with?"

"Isaiah," I whispered.

"Now, I'm not saying I have any evidence this is true, and I sure wouldn't testify about what I heard at a biker bar," Daisy-May said, "but I'd bet my house they're linked."

CHAPTER 33

The drive from Beaufort to Gannet Point Road, twenty minutes out of town, was a sea of green.

Gerald Rutledge had invested in a horse stable, sharing the property with five other investors. From what I could gather, he did it out of love, not money, which seemed unusual for a man like him. The property was large, flat, and so, so green. As I drove across it, beautiful horses were grazing on the grass behind wooden fences, framed by dense bushland behind them.

I had considered confronting Wayne Cascade again but decided it would lead nowhere but trouble. He wouldn't give me any information, and stirring him up would only likely lead to more gunshots. Instead, I called Gerald, and told him we needed to meet. He told me he was spending the day on the farm, and I'd have to come to him.

I parked at the end of the long gravel driveway, next to a tall red barn on the other side of the property from the homestead. Next to the barn was a new Mercedes sedan. It was a beautiful car—slick, modern, and stylish.

"New car?" I called out as I approached.

"Had it almost a year." Gerald was wearing jeans and boots, with a loose blue shirt. His hands looked dirty, but his clothes were still clean. "It's reliable."

"I hope so," I said. "With the amount these things cost, I'm sure it'd come with every piece of modern technology available."

"I wouldn't know about that. I don't pay attention to those types of things."

"Really? Did you know these cars are constantly monitoring your GPS location?"

He shook his head. "I've got nothing to hide."

"Expensive though."

"I make good investments, which means I can afford nice things."

"Farming?" I stood shoulder to shoulder with him, staring out at the fields.

"Yeah. Farming," he said. "I've invested a lot of money around here. The five families who own this place are all farmers, or former farmers, like me. We invest in local farms and do our best to keep the industries going. Our latest investment is about to pay dividends and go big. We might even look at expanding this place."

"Sounds like a good investment. What is it?"

"It's none of your business, is what it is," he said, and began to walk back into the darkness of the barn, obviously upset by my presence. "Why come all the way out here to ask me some questions? Couldn't you have asked the questions on the phone?"

"I wanted to talk to you off the books," I said as I leaned against the barn door. "And here seemed like as good a place as any."

Gerald stopped and looked back at me. He picked up a rag, cleaned his hands, and then sighed. "Spit it out then. Has there been a development in my stepson's case?"

"It's progressing." I put my hands in my pockets. "But I need to know why you lost five thousand on a floating casino earlier this year?"

"What?"

"You took five thousand on to the floating casino earlier this year and lost it all within an hour."

"How would you know that?"

"It's a small town. Word gets around."

"What can I say?" He shrugged. "It wasn't my day."

"Ever done that before?"

He paused. "I didn't realize my financial habits were on trial here."

"They aren't. But if your son's case goes to trial, the prosecution will dig deep into his family's connections. Everything will be uncovered and put into the open. We need to be prepared."

"You can keep my name out of Caleb's trial."

"Not my choice," I responded. "I need to know so I'm prepared. Why did you lose five thousand in one day?"

He stared at me for a long moment before he answered. "I was there to have fun. That's what the floating casino is for. A way to blow off steam," he said. "I bet it all on poker. There'd be a video of me going to the boat and placing the bets. It's all legitimate and above board."

"Did you win at all?"

"Not that day. Lost every single dollar." He turned and picked up a horse brush. "I like the thought of the long shot winning. I always back the outsider. Unfortunately, it never works for me. But like I said, if you want to check it out, I'm sure there's video of me betting it all through the dealer."

"Wayne Cascade."

"What?"

"Wayne Cascade was the dealer."

"I can't remember his name," Gerald quipped. "But if you say so." He was being deliberately evasive.

"Do you know Isaiah Clyburn?"

For a split second, his mouth dropped open, and he hastily closed it again. Once he had managed to compose himself, he continued. "Only in passing. Don't really know the kid."

"Did he ever do some work for you?"

"Like I said, I only know Isaiah in passing."

"That's not what I asked."

"I'm not sure what you're asking." His jaw clenched. "You come here and accuse me of . . . I don't know what you're accusing me of, but I don't like your tone."

"What work did Isaiah do for you?" I watched him closely. "Did you have a problem with John Pearson?"

"We're done." He glared at me and then stepped forward. "Don't be asking any more questions about it or you might find yourself in trouble."

I held his gaze. He fiddled with the horse brush, then flung it down and walked away. I watched him reach one of the fields in the distance before I turned and left, knowing that I'd bet my house on the link as well.

CHAPTER 34

Two days after I met with Gerald Rutledge, I searched for further details about the dealer Daisy-May had mentioned. Wayne Cascade seemed to be involved in everything.

I made a few calls and found that Cascade was known to run money for the biker gangs and clean the cash through the floating casino. He would set up the cards in poker, and when the time was right, he would tap the table, and the designated players would sit down. One player would lose the money, and the other player would win the same amount of money. The winners would then cash out legitimately. Every cash out was through the floating casino's outlet and transferred into the designated bank accounts.

If they kept the winning amount under ten thousand per transaction, they didn't gather the attention of the authorities, and if it was done in house, it didn't attract any trouble. Some days, as much as two hundred thousand was won and lost on the same table, all registered in separate transactions under ten thousand dollars. There were no news articles about it, no police reports, nor any federal investigations. As long as there was no trouble, nobody was interested.

I was sitting at my desk, searching for further information on Isaiah's case, when Bruce and Kayla walked in with donuts and coffee. The expressions on their faces were clear.

"I don't like the look of this," I said.

"Donut?" Kayla offered. "We've got glazed, cinnamon, or jam."

"No, thank you." I shook my head. "What is it?"

"It's about Isaiah." Bruce sat in front of my desk but wouldn't make eye contact.

"I've been thinking a lot about him," I replied. "I've been wondering why he didn't just take the five grand in cash and store it under his bed. But then I looked at the family's police files—they've had five break-ins over the last two years. If Isaiah had left the money in the house, it might've been stolen. He needed an excuse to put the money in the bank, and the casino winnings were the perfect way to do it. Nobody would ask any questions if it came from there."

Bruce didn't answer. I waited for him to respond, but he still wouldn't meet my eye. I looked at Kayla but she wouldn't look at me either.

"Bruce." I leaned forward. "What is it?"

"It's Isaiah," Kayla said. "He's disappeared."

"What do you mean, 'disappeared'?"

"Nobody can locate him." Bruce sighed. "It's been two days since anyone has heard from him. His father notified me when he didn't come home from work, but I thought I'd wait before I told you. I wanted to see if he showed up somewhere. But . . ."

"But he hasn't." I tossed my pen on to the table. "Two days? The last time I spoke to him, he seemed positive. We were in a good position. Why would he run now?"

I stood and walked over to the window. I could sense Kayla in the background holding her breath.

"What is it, Kayla?"

"Well," she said, "you also spoke with Gerald Rutledge two days ago."

I leaned my back against the wall, looking up at the ceiling as the realization hit.

"Think they're connected?" Bruce questioned. "Do you think Gerald spoke with Isaiah, and that's why he ran?"

"It's more than a coincidence," I said. "Did you ask Isaiah's father what he thought?"

"I did. He said he didn't know anything about it," Bruce said. "He said Isaiah left some money on the table two days ago and hasn't been seen since."

I closed my eyes. As soon as I got a lead, everything seemed to fall apart.

CHAPTER 35

The Port Royal Farmers' Market was filled with an abundance of delicious smells—the smell of baking bread, of barbeque, of freshly cut onions, of collard greens, of fresh oysters. It was filled with the smell of damp rain, of smoky wood, of freshly cut grass. When the wind blew through, there was the strong odor of pluff mud, a salty goodness that hung heavy in the air. The produce in the market was abundant, and with South Carolina's mild winters, many fruits and vegetables were available almost year-round.

It was the perfect way to spend a quiet Saturday morning. A heavy storm was predicted in the afternoon, and everyone wanted to get out before it arrived.

Emma, being outgoing and vibrant, talked to the stallholders. Some talked with passion about their products, while others were indifferent to the sales of their wares. The honey seller talked about his bees, and how he only used the best bees to make his honey. The coffee-van owner talked with anyone who would listen. The fruit seller yelled to everyone about the price of his apples and the book seller was happily sitting in her camp chair, ignoring everyone as she was engrossed in her dog-eared book. Throughout the market, locals greeted each other, families tried to wrangle with sugar-filled kids, and tourists took photos at every turn.

Emma and I wandered around the market, bought some trinkets for the house, followed by a tasty croissant and another coffee. Our morning disappeared in the gentle bustle of the market. It was a welcome escape from the stress that had been building over the past weeks.

As we drove home, my thoughts drifted back to work. Nobody had heard from Isaiah.

His family hadn't heard from him, his friends hadn't heard from him, and there were no reported sightings of him. His family didn't report him missing, because if they did, his bail conditions would be revoked.

We asked Sean to follow it up, but in the two weeks since his disappearance, there had been no further leads. He'd either chosen to vanish, or someone had made him vanish, either by way of a plane ticket or a hole in the ground. I didn't know which was more likely.

Emma and I arrived home as the storm clouds rolled in. The first drops of rain fell, and Emma nodded to the horizon. "It's going to be heavy."

She was right. She always was. Within five minutes, the storm had started.

With a glass of sweet tea each, we sat under the shelter of the front porch and watched the storm arrive, getting splashed by rain but in awe of the power of nature.

As the heavens opened, the rain came down vertical and sideways, frontward, backward, and any other way but up. It came in whispers, it came in sprays, it came in heavy downpours. It came with the smells of the ocean, of salt and seaweed and shellfish. It came with thunder and lightning, threatening the lands underneath. The storm had moved in off the great Atlantic Ocean, and it threw itself against the land with aggression. The lightning cracked, the thunder roared, and the electricity in the air buzzed. The storm was an event, something to behold, something to wonder at, something to make you feel small under the great beauty of nature. The winds howled and the trees creaked. The storm lashed the land for an hour, threatening to become worse with each passing moment, until it was done, passing over us and leaving nothing but a small flooded front yard and an air thick with humidity.

"Caleb's trial starts on Monday," Emma said as the skies cleared. "How do you think it'll go?"

"Not a great chance of winning."

"He didn't take the new deal?"

"No." I shook my head. "And even I think he's going to find it tough in court."

"What does it hinge on?"

"Getting the right jury. All I need is to convince one person there's enough reasonable doubt. A hung jury in a case like this is likely not to be retried, because it would cost the state too much time and money and there would be no guarantee of a different result. I need a leader in the courtroom, someone with strong opinions, and a good understanding of the law."

"Think you'll find that?"

"I hope so," I said. "For Caleb's sake, I hope so."

CHAPTER 36

Standing in front of the courthouse, I took a deep breath and let a bead of sweat run down the side of my face. I watched as Bruce and Kayla rolled into the parking lot in Bruce's BMW, parked, and then jogged toward me.

"Never be late for Judge Gregory Grant," Bruce said as he approached. "He hates two things—out-of-towners, and late people. You're already one of those things, don't make it two."

We hustled into the courthouse and through security, where the deputy sheriff talked about the heat as he scanned our items. He hadn't seen it this hot in May in years, he said. After all our items were scanned, he waved Bruce closer. Bruce stepped in to listen and the deputy explained there were a lot of people interested in the start time of the trial, more than he'd ever had before. There was interest from all over the state. There was even a reporter there from Columbia, he said, already waiting in the foyer.

I avoided eye contact with everyone lingering in the foyer and walked up the first flight of stairs, and down the hall to the courtroom. Stepping through the wooden doors, I took a moment in the empty room.

The judge's seat was raised at the front of the room, in front of the Great Seal of the State of South Carolina. The American flag sat on one side of the seal, the South Carolina flag on the other. There was a monitor on the wall to the left that would soon come alive with evidence and the jury box to the right, which would soon be filled with people to judge the defendant. The room smelled musty, and the fans whirred overhead.

I sucked in a deep breath and continued to the defense table. I was ready. This was my arena. This is where I felt most comfortable.

Caleb Rutledge was escorted in fifteen minutes later, looking fresh in a new black suit. Bruce had pulled a few strings to ensure he was clean-shaven and had a new haircut. His shirt was pressed, and the collar was firm. His tie was red, his shirt was dark blue, and his black shoes were polished. He appeared respectable and trustworthy.

The prosecution had come back with a better deal the day before the trial. They had offered twelve years for voluntary manslaughter. Bruce tried his hardest to push it down to ten, but Harley wouldn't budge. Caleb rejected the offer.

Harley and his team of three walked into the courtroom at 9:45 a.m. He looked confident—strong back, chin up, a stern gaze in his eyes. Stephen Freeman walked in at 9:55 a.m., taking a seat behind the prosecution.

The room stood for the entrance of Judge Gregory Grant at 10:05 a.m. He walked to his chair without any expression on his face.

The bailiff confirmed the defendant's name and the lawyers introduced themselves to the court. Judge Grant asked Caleb if he understood the charges against him, and after Caleb confirmed, the judge called for *voir dire*, the jury selection process, to begin.

To pick the right jury members, lawyers had to know what sort of case they wanted to present. For the State, it was a plain and simple case, and they needed people who thought like that. They needed people who wouldn't doubt what they were told. They needed people who trusted authority. They needed people who had

180

complete faith in the justice system. They needed strong men and women, people who would've done anything to protect an innocent angel like Millie Aiken.

For the defense, it was the opposite. We needed analytical jurors, people who could see the evidence before them and make an educated decision. We needed the free thinkers, the people who could see a hole in a story and pick it apart for themselves. People who had a healthy distrust for those in power. People who wouldn't be influenced by someone's title or position.

In selecting jury members, most lawyers avoided jurors with existing knowledge of the subjects at issue. They wanted a clean slate, people who would hear the evidence for the first time without bias or preconceptions. Both sides wanted to bring experts to the witness stand, people who were paid to present a side of the case, and they wanted the experts' information to be accepted without question. Anyone with more knowledge than the experts was instantly dismissed.

Bruce had worked with the prosecution to prepare the list of questions for the potential jury members. The potential jurors were presented with the fifteen-question document before the start of the day. Judge Grant reviewed the answers and dismissed several people.

Anyone who was related to either family was dismissed. Anyone who knew the families well was dismissed. Anyone who had business dealings with the families was dismissed. Anyone who shared their thoughts and opinions on the case was dismissed.

There were fifty-five people in the jury pool. Some looked like they wanted to be anywhere else. Others looked like this was the highlight of their year.

While the lawyers were studying the jury members, the jurors were doing the same to the lawyers. They studied the different sides, looking for signs of trustworthiness, truthfulness, and credibility.

Most jury members weren't concerned with the showmanship of a court case—they wanted steady, boring, authoritative lawyers. They wanted people they could trust. They wanted people who seemed in control and balanced. They wanted the truth.

As the groups of potential jurors were called forward, Harley and Bruce questioned their positions on a wide range of life circumstances. They were looking for little hints that might indicate how a person could vote in the upcoming trial. They asked the jurors if they had children, what their favorite televisions shows were, and how they liked to spend their free time. They asked about their political persuasion, what sort of live music they liked, what they did on the weekends. They asked if they had ever smoked weed. They asked if they enjoyed alcohol. They asked if the jurors liked to hunt. They asked if the jurors liked to read. They asked about their education, about their cooking habits, and if they were close with their families. They asked what they thought about the troops. They asked what they thought about the President. They asked what they thought about the South.

As the lists of potential jurors were presented, I searched their names for publicly available information on my laptop. Under Formal Opinion 466 of the American Bar Association, guidelines were set informing lawyers how much they could search for about potential jurors online. The opinion advised that lawyers were able to conduct passive research about the jurors, but it must be restricted to publicly available information. Lawyers were not to issue any social media requests to view information not available to the public, nor were they to communicate with the potential jurors directly or their family members. The internet search proved successful, and several potential jurors were eliminated after it was discovered they had commented online about the death of Millie Aiken.

The day was long, monotonous, and strenuous. At 4:55 p.m., moments before Judge Grant was about to send everyone home for the day, the jury pool was settled.

The selected jurors were mostly middle-aged, with two older and two younger. Some were married, some single, some divorced. There was a realtor, a truck mechanic, and a schoolteacher. There was a housewife with five children at school. A plumber, a retired road worker, and a librarian. There was a large male tour guide, who appeared a natural leader, and an overly confident financial planner in his twenties. There was a well-spoken bricklayer. The last two chosen were both bartenders, although they didn't know each other. Six women, six men. A solid group. The court also selected four alternates, and while they would listen to the evidence every day, they wouldn't participate in the jury deliberations unless a jury member was excused.

After the jury was selected, Judge Grant spoke to them at length about their roles and responsibilities, and then the clerk of the court led the jurors to swear their oath.

"Mister Foreman, Ladies and Gentlemen of the jury, please stand and raise your right hand to be sworn: You shall well and truly try, and true deliverance make, between the State of South Carolina, and the defendant at bar, whom you shall have in charge, and a true verdict give, according to the law and evidence. So help you God."

After they had confirmed their oath, Bruce filed a motion to move venues based on the make-up of the jury pool, but Judge Grant took little time in refusing it. He was satisfied with the *voir dire* process.

Bruce looked at me and nodded. We were ready. The action was about to begin.

CHAPTER 37

INDICTMENT

STATE OF SOUTH CAROLINA

COUNTY OF BEAUFORT

IN THE COURT OF GENERAL SESSIONS

INDICTMENT NO.: 2025-AB-05-155

STATE OF SOUTH CAROLINA, V. CALEB ANDREW RUTLEDGE, DEFENDANT

At a Court of General Sessions, convened on 15th of March, the Grand Jurors of Beaufort County present upon their oath:
Murder.

S.C. CODE SECTION 16-3-10. MURDER

That on or about 5th of March, the defendant, CALEB ANDREW RUTLEDGE, in Beaufort County, did murder with malice afore-thought. To wit: CALEB ANDREW RUTLEDGE did murder

MILLIE ANNE AIKEN per violation of Section 16-3-10 South Carolina Code of Laws (1976) as amended.

Against the peace and dignity of the State, and contrary to the statute in such case made and provided.

———

The following morning, the seats of the court were packed. People squeezed into the pews, squashing up against each other. The crowd was buzzing. There was a constant murmur. Electricity was in the air. The family and friends of Millie Aiken sat on one side of the courtroom, behind the prosecution, and Caleb's supporters on the other. The tension between the two groups was clear.

Violence was threatening to explode at any minute.

Judge Grant welcomed the parties to the court to begin day two, and invited the bailiff to call for the jurors. As the chosen twelve entered, some appeared tense, some appeared poised, and all appeared prepared.

Judge Grant explained the process of the court case, and the rules which govern the court. "Under the constitution and laws of South Carolina, you, the jurors, are the finders of the facts in this case. As the trial judge, it's my responsibility to preside over the case and to rule upon the admissibility of the evidence. However, I will not make comment on the case while you are in the room. During this trial, you must listen to the testimony of each witness, consider the exhibits presented to you, and then make a decision based on what you have heard or seen in this courtroom. It would be a violation of the court's instructions, and highly improper, for you to consider anything you hear from other people, hear on television, or read in the newspapers. You cannot bring outside bias into the courtroom."

While the jurors were the "triers of fact" in the trial, the judge was the "trier of law." It was his responsibility to ensure a fair trial. He would decide on the evidence presented and the appropriate legal guidance to be given to the jury. He was to ensure a fair and just courtroom, and whether evidence presented stepped outside the strict rules of law.

Judge Grant spoke at length to the jurors about the trial and procedures. When they confirmed their understanding of the process, he then spoke to them about the opening statements. "The opening statements are not evidence. The purpose of the opening statements is to provide you with a roadmap for what the lawyers think the evidence will show you. You should not form your opinion during the opening statements. These statements are merely an overview of what the State and the defense will present over the coming days and weeks."

Judge Grant then invited Assistant Solicitor Andrew Harley to begin.

———

"Ladies and gentlemen of the jury, welcome to the Beaufort County Courthouse. Today, and over the coming weeks, you have a big job to do. The responsibility for justice is on you. I am Assistant Solicitor Andrew Harley, and these are my assistants, Thomas Western, and Jackie Hill. Together, as a team, we'll work toward justice for this horrific murder.

"But let's start at the start. This is a story about intimate-partner abuse. This is a story about domestic violence. This is a story about the devastating effect domestic violence has on our close-knit community.

"This is a story about the abuse one young girl suffered at the hands of her boyfriend.

"Millie Anne Aiken died on the night of March 5th. That is fact. Plain and simple.

"What we know is she was struck across the face and then fell to the floor. As she fell, she hit her head on the side of the kitchen bench. This impact, this devastating impact, cracked open her skull behind her ear.

"She was unconscious, but not yet dead.

"Did anyone help her? No. Did anyone try to assist her? No. Did anyone call 911 at the time of the incident? No.

"Millie Aiken was left to die, cold and alone on the tiled floor of her kitchen. Over the next twenty-five minutes, maybe less, maybe more, between 9 p.m. and 9:30 p.m., Millie Aiken bled out.

"This beautiful young lady, this happy, fun, and charming young lady, died on the tiled floor of her own kitchen.

"Before her death, Millie Aiken broke up with her then boy-friend Caleb Rutledge. They had been together since they were fifteen, five or six years. We know this break-up made Caleb Rutledge angry.

"Caleb Rutledge arrived at Millie Aiken's home in Lady's Island after 9 p.m. on the night of March 5th. Was anything said between them? We don't know. Was there a fight, or did Millie Aiken say something that triggered Caleb Rutledge? We don't know. What motivated Caleb Rutledge to lash out? We don't know.

"What we know is that Caleb Rutledge slapped her across the face. He slapped her so hard that she fell and cracked her head on the edge of the kitchen table.

"We know Caleb then left the Aiken residence and travelled to a gas station to refuel his car. It was during this trip to the gas station that the attendant saw a red stain that looked like blood on Caleb's hand.

"During this trial, we'll present witnesses to you, and these witnesses will form the evidence in the case.

"You will hear from the gas station attendant who will testify she saw Caleb Rutledge with a red mark that looked like blood on his hand as he paid for gas. On the night of March 5th, at 9:25 p.m., he entered the gas station. The attendant asked Mr. Rutledge what the mark was, and he confirmed it was blood. The attendant will testify the blood looked like it was a smear on his hand. She offered to provide him with a bandage, but he refused.

"You will hear from the owner of a business whose surveillance footage captured Caleb Rutledge's car driving toward the Aiken residence at 9 p.m. on the night of March 5th.

"You will hear from a person Caleb Rutledge had been sleeping with, and she will testify that Caleb Rutledge was angry about the break-up with Millie Aiken.

"You will hear from a corporal of the Beaufort County Sheriff's Department. She will tell you about her investigation into this case, and guide you through the steps she took to ensure they arrested the right person. She will also tell you there were two items of Mr. Rutledge's left at the scene of the crime—his jacket, which was hanging over a nearby chair, and his cap, which was resting on top of that jacket.

"You will hear from Miss Aiken's mother, Naomi Aiken, about how she found the body. She will also testify that she does not remember seeing the jacket and cap the day before.

"You will hear from a communications expert, and she will testify about the aggressive nature of the messages sent by Caleb Rutledge to Millie Aiken before her death. She will also testify that Miss Aiken had invited Mr. Rutledge to her home around the time of death.

"You will hear from expert witnesses, and these witnesses will explain the forensic evidence in more detail. These experts will explain exactly how Millie Aiken died, they will explain the DNA evidence found at the scene of the crime, and they will explain the most likely position of the attacker when they slapped her.

"You will also hear from character witnesses, who will testify about Caleb Rutledge's unresolved anger after the death of his mother.

"You will hear from friends of Millie Aiken, and they will testify they saw Caleb Rutledge physically handle Millie Aiken in a possible assault.

"During this trial, you will hear a lot of information, and some details may upset you. I implore you not to look away when the going gets tough. I ask that you study the evidence, take it all in, and form a decision based on all the details that are presented to you.

"If you do that, if you listen to the evidence presented, there is only one decision you can make.

"At the end of this trial, I will stand before you again and ask you to find Caleb Rutledge guilty of the murder of Millie Aiken.

"Thank you for your service to the court."

———

The stakes were high in every murder trial.

Assistant Solicitor Andrew Harley delivered his opening well. He was more expressive than I'd ever seen him. The crowd rose and fell with him and were hooked on his version of the story. The jury seemed impressed, watching him as he moved around the front of the room.

A murder trial, especially one with media interest, was a lawyer's chance to flex their muscle, to show the world their talents. It was a chance to stand on the big stage, to be the main player, to have the eyes of the world on their performance.

Before the State took any case to trial, before they even considered jury selection, they had to be almost certain of their case. The solicitors didn't throw a dart at a board and hope it would land. They had to be almost certain the jury would find in their favor. If not, the case wasn't worth the effort, time, and cost. To lose a case at trial was a significant waste of public money, and could destroy reputations.

In the vast majority of cases, the defendant accepted a deal long before the trial. That was why prosecutors across the country won around 95 percent of their cases.

With his lack of experience in a murder trial, Bruce had asked me to deliver the opening statement. I was happy to take the reins. When invited by Judge Grant, I stood and moved to the lectern to begin.

———

"Ladies and gentlemen, Your Honor, thank you for giving me the chance to stand here and defend justice. My name is Dean Lincoln, and along with my colleague Bruce Hawthorn, we are the attorneys representing Mr. Caleb Rutledge.

"I'm glad Assistant Solicitor Andrew Harley talked about justice, because that's what this trial is about—justice.

"And let's be clear on what justice is. Justice is not blind vengeance. Justice is not blind retaliation. Justice is not blind punishment. Justice, and all its related terms, is about convicting the right person for the crime.

"Mr. Caleb Rutledge is not the right person.

"You will see that during this trial, because there are so many holes in the prosecution's case that you cannot reasonably convict Mr. Rutledge.

"I need you to remember that the burden of evidence is on the State. This court does not require Mr. Rutledge to prove his innocence. This court does not require Mr. Rutledge to prove anything.

This court requires the State to establish guilt by legally obtained evidence and they must do so beyond a reasonable doubt.

"What is a reasonable doubt? This means the evidence and arguments presented by the State must establish the defendant's guilt so clearly, and in such a well-defined way, that it would be accepted as fact by any rational person.

"It's not enough to merely 'believe' what the State has presented; you must be certain of the facts. Belief cannot be used in this courtroom—you must be certain. Gut instincts cannot be used in this courtroom—you must be certain. Bias cannot enter into this courtroom—you must be certain of the facts.

"When listening to the evidence presented by the State, you must have a skeptical mindset. You must view each piece of evidence with cynicism and suspicion. Then, you will see the truth.

"When you hear the evidence the State has, when you see the case they present to you, you will notice there are many gaps in their story.

"There are pieces of information that aren't filled in. There are holes in this case. And it's in those holes that you will find the truth.

"The case you will hear from the State is based on circumstantial evidence. Circumstantial evidence requires an interpretation to connect it to an outcome. The evidence of the State is based on *an interpretation*, nothing more. As we go through this case, you will see this interpretation is wrong.

"There's no direct evidence that proves Mr. Caleb Rutledge was at the Aiken residence that night. There's no direct witness that places Mr. Caleb Rutledge at the scene that night. And there's no direct evidence that Mr. Caleb Rutledge slapped Miss Millie Aiken. None.

"There's no direct evidence, none at all, that Mr. Caleb Rutledge was involved in the death of Miss Millie Aiken.

"During the case, you will hear from expert forensic analysts, and they will tell you that the Sheriff's Department did not conduct a thorough investigation into this crime.

"There were suspects not even listed on any of the police documents. There were suspects who were not interviewed. There were suspects who were not even spoken to.

"Expert witnesses will testify that Mr. Rutledge's DNA was in the kitchen because he was dating Miss Aiken and had been present in the house in days prior. Expert witnesses will testify that the evidence the prosecution has presented is incomplete. They will testify that there are holes in the forensic analysis of the evidence. Expert cell phone witnesses will testify that the cell phone data used by the Sheriff's Department is not accurate enough to determine that a person was at a particular place at a specific time. Expert medical witnesses will testify it's unlikely that Mr. Rutledge slapped Miss Aiken. And character witnesses will testify it's very unlikely Mr. Rutledge ever attacked Miss Aiken.

"There's a lot of uncertainty in this case. There are a lot of holes in the evidence.

"At the end of this trial, you will have many reasonable doubts.

"There's no justice in convicting an innocent man. There's no justice in punishing someone who is not responsible for the crime.

"Throughout this trial, the burden of proof remains on the State, and when they fail to meet that obligation, you must find Mr. Rutledge not guilty.

"When this case draws to a close, when all is said and done, I will stand before you again and point out how the State has failed to present enough evidence to convict Mr. Rutledge beyond a reasonable doubt.

"At that point, you'll use your common sense to make a decision. Your decision must be not guilty.

"Thank you for your service to our great justice system."

CHAPTER 38

After the frenzied excitement of the opening statements, the court hushed as the prosecution called their first witness. But there was still restlessness in the gallery. People were unable to sit still, moving in their seats, trying to control their rage, anger, and distress. Whispers flowed through the crowd. Nervousness was in the air.

"The State calls Corporal Jody Fletcher."

Harley's voice echoed through the full chamber. The doors at the back of the room opened. Corporal Jody Fletcher stepped inside.

Fletcher walked to the stand with a rigid back and a solemn expression. She wore a black pant suit with a white shirt and black heels. Her crisp image presented a confident woman to the jury, one who was sure about her ability to do her job. Fletcher went through the gate to the witness stand and was sworn in as routine dictated. She was the perfect first witness for the prosecution—strong, intelligent, and a true leader.

The primacy and recency bias were perceptive favoritisms that resulted in a stronger recall of information presented early or late in a list. Acknowledging this, a strong first witness was vital to any prosecution case, and a strong closing witness was equally as important.

"Corporal Fletcher, I understand you're a very busy person and I wish to thank you for taking the time to testify in court today," Harley opened with as he stood behind his desk. "Can you please begin with your name and profession?"

"My name is Jody Fletcher, and I've been serving as a member of the Beaufort County Sheriff's Department for more than two decades and have been employed as a corporal for the past five years. I work as an investigator with the Northern Investigations Division. I'm proud to say I've dedicated my life to serving this beautiful county, and I'm also proud to say my father was a deputy sheriff here, and my grandfather was a sheriff. My eldest son is currently training for the Marines, and I'm proud that our family has dedicated itself to serving this great country."

"Thank you for your family's service," Harley acknowledged. Almost every jury member nodded. They already had complete faith in the corporal, and by proxy, they had faith in the prosecution. "And can you please explain to the court your connection to this case?"

"I was the lead investigator into Millie Aiken's homicide. I investigated the scene, looked for the evidence, led the team of crime analysts, built the case, and then made the arrest of Mr. Caleb Rutledge."

"And why wasn't this case handled by the Beaufort Police Department?"

"It was outside city limits on Lady's Island, and anything outside city limits is handled by the Beaufort County Sheriff's Department. During the investigation, we had assistance from the Beaufort Police Department and the South Carolina Law Enforcement Division, or SLED, as they're more commonly known."

"Have you previously investigated murder cases?"

"Unfortunately, I have. In my two decades as an employee of the Sheriff's Department, I've led more than fifteen murder investigations. All of the cases are heartbreaking, and all the cases are terrible, but this one hurt me particularly so."

"And why is that?"

"I knew the family of Millie Aiken, and she had served me coffee many times over the years. Within the first day of taking the case, I declared my conflict of interest. After consideration, it was decided I was still the right person to lead the investigation. It was with honor and respect that I investigated this difficult case for the Aiken family."

"You found this particularly hard?"

"I hate intimate-partner violence. Nothing makes me angrier than domestic-abuse cases. When little boys like—"

"Objection," I called out before Fletcher could finish the sentence. "The next sentence is about to be an accusation from an authoritative figure. There's no way the witness should be allowed to finish that sentence."

"Sustained." Judge Grant turned to the witness. "Please keep to the facts, Corporal Fletcher. We can't have any name-calling in the courtroom."

Fletcher glared at me, drew a long breath, then turned back to Harley. "What I tried to say was that domestic-violence cases can be overwhelming for law enforcement officers because they are so personal."

"And were you the first person to find Miss Aiken's body?"

"No. Unfortunately, that was her mother, Naomi Aiken." Fletcher shifted in her seat and then leaned forward. She drew a deep breath and then sighed. "It must've been a horrible experience for her. She came home one night after a long dinner in Beaufort and walked into the kitchen. She arrived shortly before midnight and found the body of her daughter on the floor. She did all she could and dialed 911. Listening to her 911 call is horrifying."

"And we'll listen to that at a later time," Harley commented. "Were you the first law enforcement officer on the scene?"

"I was."

"Can you please explain to the court what happened when you arrived?"

"The 911 dispatcher had notified me and had also sent out the EMTs to the scene. We arrived within seconds of each other. I was working at the time and was driving nearby when the call went out. I immediately turned for the Aiken home when I heard the call."

"What did you find when you arrived?"

She grimaced and shook her head again, fighting back the tears.

"Take your time," Harley said. He picked up a box of tissues from his desk and placed it on the edge of the witness stand. "We have tissues here if you need them."

Fletcher nodded, sucked in another deep breath, and continued. "The EMTs and I entered the property together and we found Millie's mother, Naomi, holding Millie by the head and howling in pain. The sound of her howling still gives me chills. I've never heard anything like it. It was genuinely horrifying." She took a tissue and dabbed at her eyes. "I secured the scene, checking for any danger, before I consoled Naomi. The EMTs tried to attend to Millie, but Naomi wouldn't let go of her. After a few moments of trying to convince Naomi that the EMTs were there to help her, she released Millie and fell into my arms. The EMTs tried to attend to Millie, but it was obvious to us that she was deceased. At this point, Naomi was covered in Millie's blood, and there was blood on the floor and on the kitchen bench. It was a shocking scene."

Harley let the pause sit in the room. Nobody moved. Nobody even whispered a word. There was not a single sound from the packed gallery.

Once Harley was sure the intensity of the scene had been burned into the jurors' minds, he continued. "Why do you think Naomi wouldn't let go of her daughter?"

Behind him, a woman burst into tears. I turned. It was an older person seated with the Aiken family. She was dressed in black and holding her head in her hands. Two friends placed their arms around her shoulder, and when she wouldn't stop crying, they led her out of the room.

Once the courtroom doors had closed behind her, Harley again let the silence sit for a moment before he continued. "Corporal Fletcher." He paused and tapped his hand on the desk. "Corporal Fletcher, why do you think Naomi Aiken wouldn't let go of her daughter when you arrived?"

"Naomi was in shock. She kept crying out her daughter's name for a long time after that. It was such a distressing tone, and it was so hard to forget. I don't think I'll ever forget the pain in her voice. It was . . . it was the worst sound in the world."

"Who were the next people to arrive at the scene?"

"Corporal Miriam Bester arrived next, followed by more police staff. Around an hour later, the father, Robert, arrived and he began to care for Naomi. He had been working in Charleston, but rushed back home as soon as he heard the news. He was distressed when he saw the body of his daughter, but he didn't touch her. The EMTs declared her deceased and we established a crime scene. A member of the Sheriff's Department's Crime Scene Unit arrived, and I advised one of the officers to take photos of the body and the surrounding area, and after that, I advised the EMTs to cover the body with a cloth before anyone else saw her."

"Was Naomi Aiken considered a suspect?"

"At that point in the investigation, we were unsure what had happened and whether the mother was involved or whether it was a terrible accident. We had to treat it as a crime scene because we didn't want to miss anything."

"And are these the photos of the scene you found?"

Harley pointed to the court monitor at the side of the room. It came to life with photos of the deceased. Harley's assistant used her laptop to scroll through the images of Millie Aiken's bloodied, lifeless body. Several jurors recoiled in horror at seeing pools of dark red blood over the tiled floor. Millie's face was spotted with blood, and there was bruising over her cheek and eye socket. Her skin was pale and looked cold. Her eyes were open, but vacant. There was a cut on her cheek.

"Those are the photos, yes," Fletcher confirmed, and swallowed hard.

Once the assistant had scrolled through twenty-five photos, Harley turned back to his witness. "Was it at this point you decided it was a homicide investigation, rather than a terrible accident?"

"It was defined as a homicide investigation once the deputy coroner made that decision. I'm unsure exactly when that happened, but it was early in the investigation. It was clear to us that Millie had bruising around her left eye that was consistent with a heavy blow. You could see in the photos that her face was purple, and you could tell it was a heavy hit on the opposite side of the face to where her skull had cracked. We asked the mother if Millie had a bruise there earlier in the day, and she advised that she did not. Once we started to piece together the scene, it became clearer she had been struck and then she fell and hit her head on the side of the kitchen table."

"And what led you to Mr. Rutledge as the lead suspect?"

"When we accessed Millie's phone, we saw she had invited Mr. Rutledge to her home around the time of death. We found a jacket and a cap at the scene, and Naomi Aiken advised us that those items belonged to Mr. Rutledge. When we also talked to witnesses who saw Mr. Rutledge heading toward the Aiken house around the time of death, he became a prime suspect."

"Did any of the crime scene analysts take fingerprint samples from the crime scene?"

"They did."

"And did any of those samples match Mr. Rutledge's fingerprints?"

"Yes. We found Mr. Rutledge's fingerprints on the fridge and on the kitchen counter."

"What were your next steps in the thorough investigation?"

For the next two hours and twenty-five minutes, Fletcher led the court through the steps of her investigation. Prompted by questions from Harley, the corporal spoke about how she had examined the scene, talked to nearby neighbors, and discussed the case with the deputy coroner. She talked about the officers who worked under her instruction on the case. Harley used Fletcher to introduce several pieces of evidence into the court, including photos of the table where Millie had hit her head. Fletcher talked about the photos taken by the police photographer and about the witness statements provided. She talked about Millie's cell phone and how the messages between her and Caleb were the last ones she sent. She talked about how Millie's mother couldn't remember seeing Caleb's jacket or cap there the previous day. Harley repeated the term "thorough investigation" several times, trying to convince the jury that the investigation had been accurate and complete.

During her testimony, Fletcher tried to remain stoic but had to stop to compose herself several times. The jury members felt that emotion.

"Thank you, Corporal Fletcher." Once Harley was sure the facts of the case were established, he turned the witness over to the defense. "No further questions."

Bruce and I had decided on a clear strategy for questioning the witnesses during the case. He would cross-examine the likeable witnesses and I would cross-examine the data-driven ones. As a local, Bruce had a softer touch than I did, and his local knowledge would go a long way in helping break down the testimonies.

Although Corporal Fletcher's testimony was heavy on the facts, it was her personable demeanor that warmed the jury. When invited to begin his cross-examination, Bruce stood and buttoned up his suit jacket. He walked to the lectern and looked at his notes. He nodded to himself and then looked at the jury. When one of the jurors nodded to him, he began.

"Firstly, Corporal Fletcher, thank you for your family's service to our county, state, and country," Bruce said. "It is with great respect for you personally and professionally that I question you today."

"Thank you, Bruce."

Bruce nodded. It was a good opening line, one that showed the jury he was a respectful local.

"Corporal Fletcher, did you conduct a search of the whole house?"

"We did."

"And did you find any other items that belonged to Mr. Rutledge during the search?"

"We found another jacket and a pair of shoes that belonged to Mr. Rutledge in Millie Aiken's bedroom cupboard. We asked the parents who the clothes belonged to, and they confirmed the jacket and shoes belonged to Mr. Rutledge."

"So, it wasn't unusual for Mr. Rutledge to have clothes at this residence?"

"No, not from what we gathered from the parents."

"Were there unidentified fingerprints found at the crime scene?"

"In the kitchen, there were five unidentified fingerprint samples, however these were in high-use areas such as the kitchen bench and the fridge door."

"And this is where you found Mr. Rutledge's fingerprints?"

"That's correct."

"Do you find it unusual that someone who was dating the deceased had fingerprints on the kitchen counter or the fridge door?"

"No. That would be normal, considering they had been together many years."

"Do the fingerprints prove he was there on the night of March 5th?"

"The fingerprints prove he was there at some time in the past."

"Some time in the past," Bruce noted, tapping his finger on the lectern. "Corporal Fletcher, do you think your relationship with the deceased's family clouded your investigation at all?"

"No. Not at all."

"And do you consider your investigation to have been thorough?"

"Yes."

Bruce nodded and looked at his notes. He grimaced slightly, indicating to the jury he was about to ask several hard-hitting questions. "And can you please tell the court if you missed anything during the initial investigation?"

"No investigation covers everything, especially in cases like this."

"Were you aware Miss Aiken and Mr. Rutledge were no longer dating?"

"We weren't aware of that during the early stages of the investigation. Later, on review, there were indications in their text messages that they were breaking up, but when those messages were taken out of context, we didn't establish that."

"Did you establish that at any point in the investigation?"

"Not the Sheriff's Department's investigation, no, but it was later discovered by the State's prosecution team."

"By which point you had already made the arrest, correct?"

"Correct."

"During your 'thorough' investigation, were you aware Mr. Rutledge had begun seeing Miss Ava Healy?"

"Objection," Harley called out. "Relevance. The defense is trying to establish a culpable third-party when there was no reference to this during the opening statement. The rules of this court state that if a third party is going to be presented as a defense, then it must be established during the opening statement."

"Your Honor," Bruce retorted. "The prosecution has established this investigation was thorough. In fact, I noted the solicitor used the term 'thorough investigation' several times during the questioning of this witness. We're trying to establish if that is fact."

"I see your point," Judge Grant noted. "The objection is overruled. The witness may answer the question."

"I'm sorry." Fletcher looked up to the judge. "What was the question?"

Bruce looked at his notes, and continued, "Corporal Fletcher, I asked if, during your 'thorough' investigation, you were aware that Mr. Rutledge had begun seeing Miss Ava Healy?"

"No, we were not aware of that until later."

"Were you aware Miss Healy was sleeping with Mr. Rutledge?"

"No."

Bruce ran his hand along the edge of the lectern five times before he continued. "During your 'thorough' investigation, did you find out that Miss Healy didn't get along with Miss Aiken?"

"Not during our investigation."

"And during your 'thorough' investigation, did you take any fingerprint or DNA samples from Miss Healy?"

202

"No."

"During your 'thorough' investigation, were you aware Miss Healy lived only half a mile away from Miss Aiken?"

"No."

"During your 'thorough' investigation, did you question Miss Healy about her whereabouts that night?"

"No."

"Did you question Miss Healy at all during your 'thorough' investigation?"

Fletcher sat up straighter. "No."

"So, during your 'thorough' investigation, you didn't find there was another party who was close to the scene of the crime, had the motive for an attack, and could've left fingerprints or DNA at the scene of the crime?"

Fletcher glared at Bruce with a stare that would've given a lesser man a heart attack.

"Corporal Fletcher?" Judge Grant leaned across. "Can you please answer the question?"

"No, we did not question Miss Healy during our investigation."

Bruce looked at the jury. "It appears your office didn't investigate much."

"We investigated—"

"That wasn't a question, Corporal Fletcher." Bruce cut her off. "But this is—how did you complete a 'thorough investigation' if you didn't investigate all the suspects related to this case?"

The corporal's mouth hung open for a long moment as she thought about the right response.

"I thought so." Bruce didn't allow her time to answer. He closed the folder in front of him. "No further questions."

A solid start to our case, but still a long way to go.

CHAPTER 39

Harley called the 911 dispatch operator next.

The first part of her testimony was expected—yes, she had received the call from Naomi Aiken. Yes, she sent law enforcement and EMTs to the address. Yes, she ensured the call was recorded. While her testimony was straightforward and no frills, her presence allowed Harley to play the evidence in question, and the call had its desired effect on the jury.

The 911 call from Naomi Aiken was horrifying.

Naomi Aiken screamed for her daughter, howling in pain with a tone of voice that could only come from a place of deep anguish. When the recording was finished, there was not a dry eye in the court. Two of the jurors were sobbing. Once the dispatcher's testimony was completed, Judge Grant called for a recess so the court could refocus.

The court resettled after a fifteen-minute break, but the sadness in the room lingered.

When invited by the judge, Harley called his next witness.

"The State calls Dr. Joan Goulds."

Beaufort County Deputy Coroner Dr. Joan Goulds walked to the stand with a stern look on her face. She looked like she hadn't smiled in years. She was dressed in a brown pencil skirt with a white top. Her glasses were thick, and her hair was tied back tightly.

"Dr. Goulds, thank you for joining us in court today," Harley began, staying seated behind his desk. "Can you please begin by telling the court your experience?"

"My name is Dr. Joan Goulds, and I've been employed as a deputy coroner with the Beaufort County Coroner's Office for the last five years. I'm a proud member of the South Carolina Coroner's Association, and I've previously served as a military medical doctor."

"Thank you for your service, Dr. Goulds. Can you please tell the court about your involvement in this case?"

"At the Coroner's Office, we conduct independent investigations into certain types of deaths within our county limits. During these investigations, we look to define the cause of death and define it as either natural, accident, suicide, homicide, or sometimes undetermined."

"And your determination in this case?"

"Homicide."

"Dr. Goulds, did you examine the body of Miss Aiken?"

"Yes, along with the assistance of consulting physician Dr. Marie Colston."

"And is this your report here?" Harley held up the report for everyone to see.

"It is."

Harley submitted the coroner's report into evidence and then continued, "And can you please tell the court what you found in your report?"

"The report states Miss Aiken died as a result of intracranial hemorrhage caused by blunt force trauma to the side of the head causing a basilar skull fracture. She had damage to the temporal bone and the occipital bone on the right side of her skull."

"An intracranial hemorrhage. Can you please explain that term further?"

"A simple way to describe it is as a brain bleed. This is common after a fall or a traumatic injury, as happened in this instance. The blood vessels are broken and the blood collects, or pools, within the brain. This causes pressure within the brain and prevents oxygen from reaching the brain cells and brain tissue."

"Have you seen this type of injury before?"

"As a coroner, I've seen a lot of blunt force trauma to the head that has resulted in death. This can happen from bike accidents, motor vehicle accidents, being shot, being struck with a blunt object, but most commonly, it happens with falls, particularly in the elderly."

"Where did this blunt force trauma take place on the head?"

"To the right side of the head, behind the ear. This part of the skull is vulnerable, but it appeared extra vulnerable in Miss Aiken. During the autopsy, it was discovered she had damage to the temporal bone from a previous injury, and while the injury did completely heal, the bone still appeared weak."

"Was there any indication what the injury was from?"

"We questioned her parents and they stated she'd been in a vehicle accident at age fifteen, and this is what caused the injury. This was confirmed when we checked her medical records."

"And it was an intra . . ." Harley paused and pretended to think about the answer, but it was a tactic to focus the jury's attention on the detail. "Sorry, Doctor, what was the cause of death again?"

"Objection," Bruce called out. "Asked and answered."

"Your Honor." Harley looked across at the defense table. "The death of Miss Aiken is complex, and I'd like the jury to be sure of what caused her death."

Bruce scoffed in disapproval.

"Overruled," Judge Grant said. "Because of the complex nature of the meaning, you may answer the question, Dr. Goulds."

Dr. Goulds nodded. "The cause of death was an intracranial hemorrhage caused by blunt force trauma to the temporal and occipital bones."

"Intracranial hemorrhage caused by blunt force trauma to the temporal and occipital bones," Harley repeated. "Was there any sign of what caused this blunt force trauma?"

"The impact was consistent with a rounded object, such as the edge of the kitchen bench. I didn't attend the crime scene; however, the Sheriff's Department took crime scene photographs, and you can see there's blood on the edge of the kitchen bench. This is consistent with the deceased's injuries."

"And how long did it take her to pass away after this injury?"

"Over fifteen to thirty minutes, and it's likely she was unconscious during that time."

"Miss Millie Aiken lay on the ground, bleeding out, dying on the floor of her kitchen. She—"

"Objection," I interrupted. "Mr. Harley is testifying."

Judge Grant looked at me. He shrugged. "Sustained. Please move on to a question, Mr. Harley."

"Certainly, Your Honor." Harley looked at me and then back to the witness. "Dr. Goulds, is it possible she moved at all after the injury that caused her death?"

"No. It didn't appear that she had moved at all."

"And what time of death did you record?"

"Speaking to witnesses, we know she was alive at 6 p.m. and deceased when found by her mother before midnight. Using the standard formula of hours since death equals 98.6 degrees minus corpse core temperature, divided by 1.5, we were able to accurately determine the time of death. Factoring in the warm temperature of the night, we determined that this was most likely between 9 p.m. and 10 p.m. on March 5th, and she was likely to have been struck fifteen to thirty minutes before that time."

"Between 9 p.m. and 10 p.m.," Harley repeated. "Did Miss Aiken have any other injuries?"

"She did. She had bruising to the left side of her face, around the cheekbone and eye socket, and we determined it was very recent before her death. Given that the bruising was not there when she spoke to her mother that evening at 6 p.m., and assessing the placement of the body, we determined the strike most likely caused her fall, although we cannot be 100 percent certain."

"Do you know what caused this injury to the left side of her face?"

"Due to the shape of the bruise, it was most likely a slap or a strike with a hand or a flat instrument."

For the following hour and five minutes, Dr. Goulds answered many questions about the report. Harley asked about the brutality of the scene, highlighting the terrible nature of what had happened to the victim, and the injuries she sustained. The jurors were interested during the first section of the testimony, but as it ran into the afternoon slump, around 3.30 p.m., they began to lose focus.

When Harley had finished his questioning, Judge Grant looked at the jury and then at his watch. He decided to continue. "Your witness, defense."

"Thank you, Your Honor." I reached for a file on my desk, opened it, and removed a piece of paper. I spoke as soon as I stood, not waiting to arrive at the lectern. "Dr. Goulds, did you conduct a toxicology report on the deceased?"

"Yes, although I didn't personally do it. The toxicology report was provided by the South Carolina State Law Enforcement Division Forensic Services Laboratory."

"And what was found in the toxicology report?"

"The deceased had alcohol in her system. Her blood alcohol reading was at 0.05, which is usually associated with a low level of intoxication."

"How does alcohol interact with the body's ability to move?"

"Because alcohol is a depressant, it can result in drowsiness, motor skill impairment, delayed responsiveness, and poor decision-making abilities."

"Motor skill impairment," I reiterated, and looked at the jury. "Is it possible that Miss Aiken was intoxicated, lost her balance, and fell?"

"That's possible, but it doesn't explain the recent bruise on her left cheek."

"Is there anything in your investigation that directly indicated Mr. Rutledge committed the murder?"

"No." Goulds shook her head. "Although that isn't what my report is for. My report is for the analysis of the deceased and her injuries."

"And is there anything in your report that directly indicates Miss Aiken was hit by her ex-boyfriend?"

"Not in the report, no."

"Was there anything in your report to directly indicate Miss Aiken was attacked by someone she knew?"

"No."

"Was there anything in your report that proves Mr. Rutledge struck Miss Aiken?"

"No."

"Was there anything in your report that proves Mr. Rutledge was present at the time of death?"

"No."

"Was there anything in your report that proves Mr. Rutledge murdered her?"

"No."

I nodded. "Thank you, Dr. Goulds. No further questions."

Judge Grant called an end to the day. After the jury members shuffled out, the court was humming with murmured conversations.

The atmosphere was heating up, and I was sure it would explode soon.

CHAPTER 40

Jack Appleby was called to the stand to start day three.

An almost perfectly round man with a grin always near to laughter, he was a joyful spirit. His suit looked twenty years old. There was a button missing on the left cuff. The hem had been restitched on the left arm, and the gold color didn't match the rest of the hemming. I wondered what had happened to the left sleeve, and reasoned it was probably a scuffle at a wedding or a funeral. I couldn't think of another reason the man would wear a suit.

"Thank you for coming to court today, Mr. Appleby," Harley began. "Can you please state your name and occupation for the court?"

"Jack John Appleby. I'm the owner of the Marine Repair Store on Little Capers Road on Lady's Island."

"How far is your repair store from the Aikens' residence?"

"About half a mile."

"And the Rutledge residence?"

"About half a mile back in the other direction."

"So, between the two," Harley noted. "Do you have security footage around your repair store?"

"We do. We had a few break-ins around five years back, so we added an extensive security network that monitors everything around the shop and the sheds near the edge of the property. We had a few people try to break in since then, and the security footage helped capture them."

"Was the footage working on the night of March 5th?"

"Yes."

Harley waited for him to continue and when he didn't, Harley said, "And can you please tell the court if any of the security footage picked up movement on the night of March 5th?"

"Oh, right," Jack said. "The security footage is activated when there's movement nearby, and it picks up anyone driving up or down Little Capers Road. The security footage activated to show a white Ford pickup driving up the road at 9:05 p.m."

"Is this the footage here?"

Harley pointed to the monitor, and it came to life. His assistant typed into her laptop, and the black and white footage played. It was focused on the driveway entrance to the property and showed all the cars driving past. The assistant paused the footage at 9:05 p.m. to show Caleb's car driving in the direction of the Aiken house.

Harley paused the video on a still frame that captured Caleb's license plate number. It was as clear as day. Two of the jury members made a note on their notepads, while several others nodded.

"And I assume this works every time a car passes?"

"That's correct."

For the next twenty-five minutes, Harley questioned Appleby about the footage in an attempt to reinforce the importance of it. Once he was sure the jury wouldn't forget this vital piece of evidence, he finished his questioning.

Judge Grant asked the defense for a cross-examination and Bruce stood almost immediately. "Mr. Appleby, have you met Mr. Caleb Rutledge before?"

"I have."

"And would you call him a good guy?"

"Objection," Harley stated in a flat tone. "Leading the witness."

"Withdrawn," Bruce replied quickly. "Mr. Appleby, how would you describe Mr. Rutledge?"

It's often said that a lawyer should never ask a question he doesn't know the answer to, and Bruce lived by that notion. Jack had fixed Bruce's boat on numerous occasions, and they often talked about life, loves, and everything in between. While not stated in the witness statement or in the deposition, Bruce knew Caleb had volunteered to help fix boats in the Marine Repair Store during his teens.

"I couldn't speak more highly of Caleb, Bruce," Appleby replied. "He used to come around and help out in fixing some of the boats brought to the shop."

"For free?"

"Yeah. He lived up the road and used to ride his bike past all the time. One day, when he was about fifteen, I saw him looking at one of the boats and I invited him in. He'd lost his mother a few years earlier, and I knew her. Great woman. So, for about a year, Caleb came to help out in the store, and I taught him how to fix the outboard motors. He was a great help, and I love teaching people about boats."

"Did you ever pay him?"

"No. I tried to pay him once for helping clean one of the boats, but he refused it." Jack sat up straighter. "He was a really good kid."

"And had you ever seen him become violent?"

"Never. He was a kind kid with a good heart."

Bruce turned to look at Harley, who had disappointment written on his face. The State's witness had turned into an unintentional character witness for the defense.

"Thank you, Jack," Bruce concluded when he saw a head nod in the jury box. "No further questions."

CHAPTER 41

Miss Ava Healy was a problem, for both the prosecution and the defense.

Her evidence for Caleb's whereabouts that night was solid for the prosecution. However, her personality was challenging to deal with.

From her witness statement to her deposition, her story had changed. Even during the deposition, she had changed the details. She was willing to say anything to keep herself out of trouble. Bruce had asked about her at the restaurant she worked at, and the staff all confirmed they wouldn't trust her.

Harley knew it was a risk bringing her to the stand, he knew she could say the wrong thing at the wrong time, but her evidence was compelling. He took a chance and called her to testify.

"Miss Healy," Harley began as the witness struggled to find a comfortable position in the stand. "Can you please describe where you were on March 5th?"

"I was out at a bar, Tommy O'Toole's, and had some bites to eat with a work colleague. I came home around 7 p.m." Ava's fingers were fidgeting as she spoke. "And then I sent Caleb a message."

"What did your message to Caleb say?"

"I told him I was home alone, and invited him over."

"Did Caleb respond to that?"

"Almost immediately. He only lived two doors down, so it was easy for him to come over. He messaged back and said he'd be there in five minutes."

"And did he come over?"

"Yes."

"At what time?"

"Five, maybe ten minutes later, like he said. He was there almost straight away."

"And what did he do while at your place?"

"We, um . . ." She shrugged and looked at her hands. "We had sex."

"Were you boyfriend and girlfriend?"

"No. We were doing things casually."

Harley nodded. "Were you aware Mr. Rutledge was dating Millie Aiken?"

"They'd broken up. Caleb told me that Millie wanted to see other people after she had a fling with a guy in Bluffton, and Caleb agreed. He sent me a message one day and we hooked up after that. It was a bit of fun between us. Nothing serious."

"And when was the first time you were intimate together?"

"Two weeks before that day."

"And how many times had you been intimate with Mr. Rutledge during those two weeks?"

"Five or six times."

Harley nodded again. "Was Miss Aiken aware you were sleeping with Mr. Rutledge?"

"I don't think so."

"Was anyone aware of it?"

"Caleb asked me to keep it quiet. Because I'd only been in town for a year, I didn't know many people. I didn't tell anyone we got together."

"Did Mr. Rutledge talk about Miss Aiken at all?"

"Yes." Ava was avoiding eye contact with the defense table. "We were talking about officially dating, and he said, 'It would be easier if Millie wasn't around.'"

"Those were his exact words, 'It would be easier if Millie wasn't around'?"

"That's right."

"And what do you think he meant by that statement?"

"Objection," I stated. "The prosecutor is asking the witness to speculate."

"Sustained," Judge Grant responded. "Move on, Mr. Harley."

Harley looked at his notes, and continued. "On the night of March 5th, what time did Mr. Rutledge leave your place?"

"I'm not sure of the exact time, but it was around 9 p.m."

"After he left your house, did Mr. Rutledge say where he was going?"

"Yes." She sighed. "He said he was going to talk to Millie." Ava paused for a moment and appeared to be thinking about her answer. "Caleb called her earlier that night. He told her he wanted to talk to her."

Harley paused, surprised by the answer. This hadn't been mentioned in any of her witness statements.

I could also feel the surprise in Caleb next to me.

"She's lying," he whispered. "I didn't do that."

I held my hand out to calm Caleb down.

"Thank you, Miss Healy," Harley finished, trying to avoid any further questioning. "Nothing further."

Bruce looked at me and I nodded. We'd both heard the statement from Ava, and we both knew what it meant. Bruce waited a few moments before he began questioning. He was testing the witness, asserting his power, showing his dominance in the courtroom. Ava was uncomfortable in the silence. She squirmed in her chair, anxious to finish her testimony.

215

"Miss Healy." Bruce's voice was firm. "Were you drinking that night?"

"Not really."

"Not really?" Bruce raised his eyebrows. He walked back to his desk and typed several lines into his laptop. A photo appeared on the screen to the left of the room. "Miss Healy, can you please explain what you're holding in these pictures?"

Ava looked at the screen. A gleam of sweat appeared on her brow.

Bruce tapped several more keys, scrolling through the photos.

"Miss Healy, these are the photos you posted on your social media page that afternoon. In the short time frame of two hours, we can see from these three photos that there are different drinks in your hand on each occasion. One photo shows you holding a can of beer, the next a cocktail, and the third is another beer, but this time in a glass. Would you like to reconsider your answer, since you're lying to this court?"

"Objection." Harley rose to his feet. "That's a direct accusation."

"Be careful with your questions, Mr. Hawthorn," Judge Grant stated. "But the witness may answer the question."

"Alright. I had three drinks. So what? I wasn't drunk. I'm fine with it."

"You weren't drunk? That's good to know." Bruce walked back to the lectern. "Do you recall what Mr. Rutledge was wearing?"

"Yeah. He was wearing a blue T-shirt and black jeans."

"Did he have a jacket?"

"Not that I saw."

"How about a cap?"

"No, I didn't see him with one."

"Interesting. He wasn't wearing a jacket or cap that night," Bruce noted. "You testified you heard Caleb call Miss Aiken on his cell phone. Is that correct?"

"That's what I said."

"And are you sure you heard the phone call?"

"Yes."

"And are you sure it was on that night? March 5th?"

"Yes. That's what I said."

"Did you overhear anything that was said during this phone call?"

Bruce was setting the trap. I knew it, Bruce knew it, and even Harley knew it. Harley leaned forward, rested his elbow on the table and rubbed his forehead. I heard his sigh from the other side of the room. He couldn't do anything about it.

"I heard bits and pieces."

"And what was said during this phone call?"

"He sounded angry with her. I mean, I didn't hear it all."

"Interesting." Bruce tapped his hand on the lectern. "And you're sure this was on the night of March 5th?"

"Yes."

"Miss Healy, are you aware that phone calls leave a record?"

She remained motionless for a long moment before she shrugged. "Um, yeah. Of course."

"And are you aware the police searched both Miss Aiken's phone records, and Mr. Rutledge's phone records?"

She didn't answer.

"Miss Healy?"

"Ah, no. I didn't know that."

"And are you aware those cell phone records did not record any call between Mr. Rutledge and Miss Aiken that night?"

"Ah." She looked around the courtroom and settled her eyes on the door at the far side of the room. She was looking for an escape. "No. I didn't know that."

"With that knowledge, do you still testify you heard Mr. Rutledge call Miss Aiken that night?"

She sat up straighter and swallowed. The sweat on her brow grew thicker. "Maybe I got my nights mixed up."

"So he called her on a different night, did he?"

"Yeah, that must be it."

"And are you aware that during the previous two weeks, no cell phone call occurred between Mr. Rutledge and Miss Aiken? They communicated via text message only. Were you aware of that, Miss Healy?"

"Ah . . . no. I didn't know that."

"Do you care to explain what you're testifying about then?"

She wiped her brow. Her breathing had quickened. "Maybe . . . maybe I was thinking about someone else."

"Maybe you were thinking about someone else?!" Bruce slapped his fist on the lectern, shocking the whole courtroom. "Miss Healy, this is a court of law, not a schoolyard. This is a place for the truth, and only the truth. This isn't a place to spread rumors and lies."

The tears welled in her eyes. "I'm sorry. I got mixed up."

"Miss Healy, is it true you lied to this court to make Mr. Rutledge look guilty?"

"No," she whispered. "I just . . . I got confused."

"Confused?! You stated you heard him call her that night! You stated you weren't confused! Why did you lie to this court?"

"Objection," Harley stated. "Badgering the witness. The witness stated she was confused, and there is nothing more to question."

"Confused?" Bruce said, and looked at the judge. "This witness is lying to this court, and the prosecution is seeking to protect those lies."

"Overruled," Judge Grant agreed. "You may continue, Mr. Hawthorn."

"Miss Healy." Bruce settled his voice and stared at the young woman. "Why did you state Mr. Rutledge called Miss Aiken that night?"

"I just . . ." She shrugged and wiped the tears from her eyes with the back of her sleeve. "I wanted justice for Millie. That's all. I just . . . I don't know. I—"

"Motion to strike this witness's testimony from the record." Bruce interrupted her answer and turned to Judge Grant. "This so-called eyewitness has admitted to lying under oath today. We move to dismiss this witness and her entire testimony under Section 16-9-10 of the South Carolina Code of Laws; Perjury and subornation of perjury. It's clear the witness is deliberately committing perjury and is lying about what happened that night to prejudice the case against the defendant."

"Your Honor," Harley argued, "we strongly object to the motion on the basis that she was with the defendant on the night of the murder. She merely got confused. That confusion is not a meaningful mistake."

"The truth is meaningful," Bruce retorted. "She's admitted to lying on the stand."

"Your Honor—"

Judge Grant held up his hand to stop Harley protesting any further. "Miss Healy, do you admit you lied to this court to try and influence the jury's decision?"

"Not on purpose. I just . . ." She drew a breath as she considered her answer. "I want justice for Millie."

Judge Grant grunted in disappointment. "The motion to strike the witness testimony is granted. Miss Healy, you may leave the stand. However, you will be charged with perjury under Section 16-9-10 of the South Carolina Code of Laws. No witness is allowed to willfully and blatantly lie to the court."

Judge Grant turned to the jury as Miss Healy stepped off the witness stand.

Two of its members were shaking their heads, staring at Miss Healy, trying to process what was happening. Judge Grant spoke at length to the jury about how they couldn't consider any part of Miss Healy's testimony to form their decision.

Once the judge was satisfied they all understood, he declared a recess for lunch.

After Caleb was guided out by the bailiff, Bruce turned to me.

He spoke in whispers, and when I suggested a new motion, he agreed. For the next hour, we sat at the defense table, preparing the motion, typing line after line, checking documents and precedents, desperate to have it finished before Judge Grant returned.

As soon as the judge walked back into the room, Bruce stood with the printed motion in his hands. He looked at the prosecution and then at me. I nodded. Bruce nodded. He was ready to attack.

"The defense submits a motion for a mistrial." Bruce handed the piece of paper to the bailiff, who then passed it to the judge. "The false and misleading testimony by the prosecution's witness has unduly and unfairly influenced this trial. This trial needs to be fair and just and yet, we have the prosecution producing witnesses who are clearly stating untrue prejudicial statements. The rights of the defendant have been violated. The prosecution is presenting a case that's deliberately misleading the jury with false testimony."

"Your Honor, that's an outrageous statement!" Harley leaped to his feet, shocked at the accusation. "The prosecution had no prior knowledge that the witness would lie to the court, as evidenced by the deposition and witness statement presented to the defense. Her statement on the stand was as much a surprise to us as it was to them."

"And despite the surprise, the prosecution did nothing to correct the statement," Bruce argued. "Their inaction was a deliberate choice as they took no action to correct the misleading and untruthful evidence."

"Your Honor, a mistrial must only be declared if the jury has been unduly influenced, and the denial of due process must be clear. This witness lied without our knowledge, and that lie was discovered during the testimony, and as you stated to the jury, the steps have been taken to correct this unfortunate error. You've instructed the jury to disregard the entire testimony. No further action is needed."

"The prosecution has established they'll continue to present false, misleading, and untruthful evidence in this trial," Bruce argued. "You cannot allow this trial to continue."

Judge Grant waited until the dueling lawyers had finished before he responded. Once there was calm in the room, he took a deep breath. He read the motion in front of him and nodded several times. "This is quite the argument, Mr. Hawthorn. The court will recess until tomorrow while I consider this motion."

Judge Grant stood without another word and exited the room. Confused mutterings resonated all around as the gallery was ushered out. Harley didn't acknowledge Bruce as he left. Bruce looked at me and smiled. We had a chance.

CHAPTER 42

The following morning, the buzz continued in the air around the courthouse. The whispers were snaking through the community—could the judge dismiss the case early?

As I walked toward the court, five men dressed in jeans and T-shirts walked toward me. They didn't move. I deviated from my line, but my shoulder connected with one of them. It was a solid bump. I stopped and turned to look at them. The five men also stopped.

"If you want to create trouble, then continue that behavior," I stated, staring at the man who had bumped me.

He didn't respond, but another of them stepped forward and pointed his finger at me. He stated, "We don't want dirty city slickers like you around here."

Our stare-down lasted a few moments before I turned away. They didn't follow me.

With consistent media coverage, the intensity around the case was high. When the doors to the courtroom opened, the gallery quickly filled. There were members of the media among the crowd, identified by the lanyards around their necks. They had their notebooks and cell phones ready to record. With the extra attention, the Sheriff's Department assigned additional staff to the courtroom. The five staff stood at the front of the room, not a smile between them. With all the people in the room, the smell was stale, and the air conditioners were struggling in the heat.

Judge Grant delivered his decision on the motion. "After careful consideration of the argument, I have decided to dismiss the motion for a mistrial. However, I will warn the prosecution, again, to be careful with the witnesses they call or the trial may be jeopardized."

A murmur rose in the crowd and Judge Grant called them to order. Bruce nodded. It was expected.

The intensity of Ava Healy's lies had left the court unsettled, and when Harley called his next witness, the buzz was still in the air.

"The State calls Dr. Anna Dawson."

Dr. Dawson came to the stand looking the picture of professionalism. Not a strand of black hair was out of place, not a single crease in her suit. Her make-up was perfect, and her expression was composed. Harley waited patiently as the bailiff took her through the procedure, then began by thanking her for her time and asking about her profession. Dr. Dawson stated that she worked for the South Carolina State Law Enforcement Division Forensic Services Laboratory, before explaining that her role was to forensically test any materials that were given to her by the Sheriff's Department, including the hairs found on the jacket and cap in the kitchen.

Harley led Dr. Dawson through her detailed report about DNA found in hair follicles.

She described how hair analysis is conducted by evaluating the hair structure and using the DNA from the cells attached to the root of the hair. She explained there was no DNA in the hair itself; however, they were able to extract DNA from the follicle. They had five samples from the cap and jacket. Those samples matched the DNA samples taken from Caleb Rutledge after his arrest. Her testimony was bland, with no frills or fireworks, exaggerated expressions, or drama. Just straight facts and details.

The chairs for the jury members were just comfortable enough, and deliberately so. They were comfortable enough to sit in for eight hours, but not comfortable enough to sleep in during a tedious and boring testimony.

Although the dry testimony couldn't prove Caleb's guilt, it established the jacket and cap belonged to Caleb, and his DNA was present at the scene. The prosecution had to establish, without a reasonable doubt, that he was present at some time before her death.

Once the fifteen-minute testimony was completed, Judge Grant asked the defense if they had any questions. I remained seated to begin questioning. "Thank you for testifying, Dr. Dawson. As an expert in DNA analysis, can you please tell the court how long DNA can remain on an item?"

"Unfortunately, there's no scientific way to determine exactly how long a DNA sample can last, as its lifespan depends on many factors such as temperature of the environment, exposure to sunlight, or exposure to human contact. In general, DNA on a hair follicle, if stored correctly, could last many decades, centuries, or in some cases, even longer. However, given the environment where the hair follicles were found, and relative humidity of the area, I would suggest this DNA could last anywhere up to several years."

"Several years? So, the presence of Mr. Rutledge's DNA at the scene indicates he was there sometime in the last few years?"

"It indicates the jacket and cap had been used by Mr. Rutledge at some time in the past, yes."

"And did you test the items found in Miss Aiken's cupboard for DNA samples as well?"

"No, we didn't. With information from the parents of the deceased, we established that those clothes belonged to Mr. Rutledge."

"So, it wasn't unusual for Mr. Rutledge to have clothes at the Aiken residence?"

"That's what the parents told us, yes."

"And so, what you're testifying about, right now, is that the DNA evidence establishes that Caleb Rutledge was there sometime during the past few years?"

"I guess so, yes. That's correct."

"Thank you, Dr. Dawson," I finished. "No further questions."

CHAPTER 43

Psychologist Dr. Mary Gibson walked to the stand full of confidence.

Another doctor, another fancy title. Harley was hoping to build a mountain of small facts from authoritative figures who could convince the jury of Caleb's guilt.

Dr. Gibson sat in the witness box without even the slightest of smiles. Her hands were clasped together and resting on her lap. Her red hair was tied back without flair. Her suit was nice, but not lavish. Her glasses were modern, but not flashy. She was an expert, appearing plain and boring to allow her report to do the talking. Despite her lack of expression, she had an unquestionable magnetism. Her sense of superiority looked like confidence to the jury.

Dr. Gibson was a graduate of Yale. She was well published. She had presented lectures all over the country. She'd testified in hundreds of cases. She was a well-credentialed expert on her subject. But she was also a salesperson, a person who was selling theories to any prosecution that wanted to purchase her expertise.

I was surprised the prosecution was using her. Either they hadn't done their homework, or they expected we wouldn't.

"Thank you for taking the time to talk with us today, Dr. Gibson," Harley began, still sitting behind his desk, with his laptop open in front of him, but to the side. He began by confirming Dr.

Gibson's lengthy qualifications, as this was essential in establishing her ability to discuss the case as an expert. While an eyewitness is limited to discussing what they saw or did, an expert witness can give an opinion on forensic evidence in the case. "Can you please tell the court your occupation and experience?"

"I'm a forensic analyst, specializing in cell phone communications. I've spent many years studying the emotions behind messaging and how that has developed over the years. I've presented lectures in major colleges across the country, including at Harvard and UCLA, and have been published in many scientific journals."

Bruce groaned next to me. There really was a job for everything out there.

"And have you testified in cases before?" Harley continued.

"Many times. In fact, more than a hundred cases across the country."

"Have you reviewed the text messages Mr. Rutledge sent Miss Aiken before her death?"

"I have. I was supplied a list of messages between them from the Sheriff's Department, and I reviewed them from the previous five months. From that, I prepared a report."

"And is this the report here?"

Harley stood and walked the report to the witness stand. She took it and scanned her eyes over it. "It is."

"Can you please read the text message Miss Aiken sent to Mr. Rutledge at 8:15 p.m. on the night of March 5th?"

"She wrote, '*You can come over to my place now, if you want to talk.*'"

"And what did Mr. Rutledge reply?"

"At 8:25 p.m., he replied, '*Maybe. I'm busy rn.*'"

"What does 'rn' mean?"

"In text speak, it means 'right now.'"

"And were there any other text messages after that exchange?"

"No. They were the final text messages sent between them."

Harley nodded. "Did you analyze any other text messages between them?"

"I did."

"And in your expert opinion, were any of these messages aggressive?"

"Yes, obviously so." She adjusted her glasses. "There are some quite threatening messages from Mr. Rutledge to Miss Aiken."

"And can you read the most threatening messages sent from Mr. Rutledge to Miss Aiken?"

"These are the five most threatening messages I read." She adjusted her glasses again, cleared her throat, and read the messages from the report. "On March 3rd, Mr. Rutledge sent a message that said, *'If you tell anyone about this, it'll hurt us both,'* before he sent, *'Please don't tell anyone yet. I don't want to hurt you.'*"

"I don't want to hurt you," Harley repeated. "Go on, Ms. Gibson. What were the other aggressive messages?"

"On the 2nd of March, he also sent a message that said, *'I don't want to hurt you,'* and *'I hate it when I hurt you like that.'*"

"Any others that really stand out?"

"On the morning of March 5th, at 10:05 a.m., he sent, *'Please don't make me hurt you.'*"

"Please don't make me hurt you," Harley shook his head. "Please don't make me hurt you. And that message was sent on the day she died?"

"That's correct."

"Please don't make me hurt you." Harley shook his head again, and when one jury member responded with the same action, he continued. "How did Miss Aiken respond to these types of messages?"

"She didn't. She ignored him. She didn't respond to any of those five messages."

"Does it strike you as odd that Mr. Caleb Rutledge used text messages to convey his feelings?"

"Objection," Bruce said. "Conjecture."

"She's an expert in her field, Your Honor. Dr. Gibson can comment on whether she found this odd."

He didn't need to explain further as Judge Grant waved for Harley to stop. "Overruled. You may answer the question, Dr. Gibson."

"Yes, it was surprising because most young adults tend to use apps to message, such as social media apps."

"Why do you think this was different?"

"When conversations turn serious, younger adults tend to text message."

"Threatening messages, perhaps?"

"In some instances, yes."

"Can you please explain the assessment you made of Miss Aiken's responses?"

"Miss Aiken displayed significant avoidant behavior to Mr. Rutledge's messages. She displayed textbook anxiety behaviors. Avoiding messages is a classic fear or anxiety response."

"A classic fear or anxiety response. Interesting. Can you please tell us how you assessed the messages between Miss Aiken and Mr. Rutledge in more detail?"

For the next fifty minutes, Harley took Gibson through the worst of the messages between Caleb and Millie. She talked in depth about the messages he had sent, and how Millie's avoidant behaviors displayed her anxiety. She talked about how emotions are heightened in young adults, and how some struggle to understand, or control, their emotions. She talked about how the messages indicated the couple was going through a long break-up. And finally, she talked about how Caleb's messages could be considered threatening.

229

When Harley was satisfied the court understood that Caleb was threatening Millie, Judge Grant opened the floor to me. I read through my notes and moved to the lectern at the side of the room.

"Dr. Gibson," I began. "You've done a lot of talking about this report. Obviously, you've observed a lot of behaviors from Miss Aiken. Had you met her before her death?"

"No, I had not. I studied her messages."

"You state Miss Aiken's messages displayed elements of anxiety?"

"Yes."

"Did you observe that behavior in her?"

"No, I didn't. My job, as an expert in this field, was to analyze the messages she sent. Nothing more."

"So, you didn't witness any of these behaviors?"

"Objection," Harley called out. "The witness has already conceded the information she has presented is the result of analyzing the messages, not witnessing any of these behaviors in person. Dr. Gibson is an expert witness, and her expertise is well established."

"Agreed," Judge Grant responded. "The objection is sustained. Mr. Lincoln, we've established the environment in which the report was made, so please move on with your questioning."

I nodded and turned a page on my legal pad. "Dr. Gibson, in all your assessments of messages, in all your testimonies, have you ever testified on behalf of a male victim?"

"No." She shook her head. "Not that I can recall."

"And how many assessments have you performed?"

"More than a hundred."

"More than a hundred," I repeated. "And not one of those reports was for a male victim?"

"That's correct."

"Interesting," I noted. "Dr. Gibson, do you remember testifying in a case for Mrs. Jane Gaze?"

230

She sat up straighter. She knew where this was going. "The name rings a bell."

"Rings a bell," I said. "Were you aware that after you presented your report to the court, as you have here, and you testified in that case, as you're doing now, the person Mrs. Gaze accused of assault was found guilty?"

"I was aware of the outcome of the trial, yes."

"And were you aware the conviction has since been overturned on appeal?"

"Objection. I fail to see how this is relevant," Harley called out.

"Your Honor," I said, "the prosecution has presented this person as a credible witness. As such, the defense has the right to question her on issues of credibility."

"The objection is overruled." Judge Grant turned to the witness. "You may answer the question."

"Yes, I was aware the case was overturned on appeal."

"The man convicted in that case pleaded not guilty and said Mrs. Gaze was lying to exact revenge on him because he had rejected her advances at work. After you wrote your report for that case, the one you presented to the court, the one you talked about to the jury, did you think she was lying?"

The witness shook her head.

"Dr. Gibson?" I pressed. "Did you think she was lying?"

"No."

"Were you aware that Mrs. Gaze had been charged with perjury for lying to the police, the court, and the jury?"

She nodded again.

"Please answer the question verbally. Were you aware that Mrs. Gaze had been charged with perjury for making up an allegation of sexual harassment?"

"Yes." Her tone was firm. "I was aware of that."

"And were you aware Mrs. Gaze admitted you removed fifteen messages from your messaging report that was tabled to the court because you thought they would weaken your case?"

Her mouth hung open. "That's . . . that's not exactly what happened."

"Then please tell the court why you removed fifteen messages from your report. Messages that may have influenced the jury's decision?"

"I talked with the police and the prosecution, and we didn't believe the messages were relevant. Those fifteen messages were from five years earlier. She threatened him and said she would make a false report to the police unless he took over her shift at work. The prosecution deemed they weren't relevant to the current case."

"Was the man representing himself in court?"

"That's correct."

I shook my head. "Did you make him aware you had removed those messages from the report?"

"No, but—"

"No? You removed fifteen messages, messages that could've influenced the jury's decision, and you didn't make him, or the jury, aware of that fact?"

"Well . . . yes and no."

"Were you aware those fifteen messages were used by a lawyer to overturn his conviction?"

She drew a breath. "I was aware of that, yes."

I paused for a long moment. "So, if there were messages that cleared a person of a crime, you would hide those messages from the court. Is that correct?"

The witness looked to the prosecution. The shock was written on their faces as well.

"Dr. Gibson?" I pressed.

"I don't see how that's relevant to this case."

"It's relevant to your credibility. Please answer the question."

"There were extenuating factors in that case."

"Please answer the question."

"None of that is relevant to this case. Every message between Mr. Rutledge and Miss Aiken is lodged in that report." Her breathing quickened. Her reputation was on the line. "I do what's right for the court."

"Even if it convicts an innocent man." I shook my head in disappointment. "No further questions."

CHAPTER 44

Despite the small wins for the defense, the evidence continued to pile up as the days passed.

The State called expert witness after expert witness to talk about the crime scene. A forensic expert testified about the blood spatter patterns in the kitchen, followed by a crime scene expert who declared Millie could not have slipped, as there had been nothing on the ground to slip on. Another specialist witness testified that the only blood found at the scene belonged to Millie Aiken. Another testified about the state of the kitchen and how things weren't out of place, and with nothing stolen, it indicated Millie Aiken knew her attacker. Another expert testified about the fingerprint analysis they had conducted.

When the jury appeared convinced by the experts, Harley moved on to the character witnesses. Friends of Millie talked about how Caleb had an aggressive streak, and how she was fearful of him when he was angry. Another testified that Caleb acted worse when he had a few drinks. Another testified about their relationship and how Millie didn't want to hurt Caleb. The witnesses painted a picture of a fragile relationship that had fallen apart.

The State called numerous witnesses who stated they saw Caleb push Millie once at a party two years earlier. He was drunk, she was drunk, and the push was small. It wasn't a good look, and it was a horrible action. The prosecution kept focusing on that evidence, implying they didn't know what else had happened behind closed doors.

Bruce and I spent the warm evenings in the office working on trial strategies, brainstorming ideas, and studying the witness statements. We searched for holes in the testimonies, we searched for character flaws in the witnesses, and we searched for anything that could cast doubt on the case.

Another week of the trial pushed past, and with every day, Caleb looked more and more guilty.

Bruce lodged several motions, slowing the case down, but Judge Grant dismissed them with regularity.

The parade of witnesses was beginning to convince the jury of Caleb's guilt, with one jury member nodding whenever a witness indicated it could've been Caleb. The prosecution was presenting their case well.

In a discussion after a day in court, Caleb argued that he wanted to take the stand, but Bruce shut the idea down, explaining that the jury wouldn't be interested in the gaps in the prosecution's case; instead they would ask themselves one question—do I believe this guy is telling the truth? After an hour-long discussion, Caleb agreed it wouldn't be a good idea.

The state-wide media continued their interest in the story. The case appeared on podcasts and in longform media articles, and at one point, there was even a reporter from New York in the courtroom. There was talk of a true-crime series and one producer had approached Caleb directly. He referred them to us, and Bruce told them he didn't have time to play games with the media.

Everyone in the city of Beaufort was talking about the case. Anytime I walked into a café or restaurant, conversations stopped. People looked at me, wondering what I was thinking. Nobody said anything to me, but I could tell they were thinking about it. I heard whispers of Caleb's name, whispers of *guilty*, but never once did anyone confront me. That wasn't the Southern way.

Emma and I came home one evening to find Terry Wallace in our driveway again. He'd received a call from a concerned neighbor who had seen someone lurking around the house. When Wallace arrived, he had found a smashed window on the left side. The assailant had climbed through it and tossed all our belongings out of the cupboards before leaving. Emma checked all our valuables and said nothing had been taken. She tried to remain calm, but she was spooked. A stranger had been in our house. They'd been through our possessions. And they had no intention of taking anything.

Wallace dusted for fingerprints, but there were none. He suggested putting cameras on each entrance and along the sides of the house. I ordered the cameras that evening. Emma didn't sleep much in the nights that followed. She woke after every strong gust of wind, and struggled to go back to sleep. Even the bird calls scared her. I tried my best to reassure her, tried to tell her everything would be okay, but even I was starting to wonder how far the attackers would take it.

I met Bruce and Kayla in the conference room of our office after week three had finished. Bruce looked beaten, and Kayla looked worried. The bags under Bruce's eyes were heavy, and he was starting to slouch. "He does that when he's tired," Kayla explained. Bruce spoke about the stress, about the pressure, and about the case. He didn't think we could win.

And for once, I was starting to agree with him.

CHAPTER 45

There was an order to how people sat in church.

Nobody dared break the unwritten rules of the pews. Mrs. Smith and her family sat in the front rows, hanging off every word spoken by the pastor. The Green family sat behind them, taking up two full rows with three generations of God-fearing people, filling up the left side of the church. The visitors and strangers were to sit at the back, welcomed with open arms, but many years away from proceeding forward up the pews. Grandma Lincoln and her family were to the right of the church, sitting in the fifth row from the front, close enough to listen intently, and far enough away to have a little nap if required.

I once read a theory that religion had more influence in the South because people were more imaginative and they had more time on their hands in which they could visualize a future in the eternal firepit of hell. I wasn't sure if that was true, but it explained a lot.

For me, almost as an outsider looking in, it was the sense of community that kept the church going. It was one of the great failures of the modern city, one of the great failures of modernity that nothing had replaced the church—a place where all were welcomed, be they rich, poor, or somewhere in between, where hands were shaken, where people were greeted with respect, where the village thrived. A place where the community gathered each week, where families were brought up, where young people seemed to be playing with toys one year and learning to drive the next. The community of the church was a safety net, with the sense that, even if everything fell apart, there would be smiles to be seen on Sunday.

Of course, church was not always like that. Some of the worst people I had ever met were also some of the most religious. Some of them acted as if one good morning in church exonerated their weekly sins of corruption, mistreatment, and abuse.

For the sake of my mother-in-law, my grandparents, and at the insistence of Emma, I attended church on Sunday morning, dressed in my Sunday best. It was nice. I walked out feeling lighter, like the world was a beautiful place, inspired by a great sermon, but I didn't think I would make it a weekly event. The rivers, I reasoned, were my church, where I felt the heartbeat of something bigger, of something greater than I could comprehend.

After church, I drove Granddad Lincoln to his secret fishing spot, around an hour south of Beaufort. He refused to let me put the coordinates in the GPS or in the maps. He didn't want 'the computers' knowing about this spot. Only he knew about it, he said.

Fishing was one of the best pastimes in South Carolina. It was like golf—the purpose of the activity wasn't to be the best, it wasn't to outperform everyone else; it was to enjoy the moment, to disappear into the calmness, to let it all go, and just be. I still had a long way to go to understand that way of life, but Granddad Lincoln had acquired those skills long ago.

There seemed to be an agreement between him and the river— it would continue to flow gently while he continued to appreciate its wonder. This part of the river smelled like the ocean—full of salty goodness.

"Have you seen Paul Freeman again?" Granddad Lincoln asked me after our moments of quiet reflection.

I shook my head. "I told him to walk the other way if he sees me coming."

Granddad Lincoln smiled. "You can't hate the Freeman family."

"Really?" I was perplexed by the statement. "Why not?"

"What you wish for others, you'll find in yourself." Granddad Lincoln stared out to the water. "If you wish hate for others, you'll find it within yourself. If you wish pain for others, you'll find that. But if you wish love, joy, and happiness, then you'll find that in your heart."

"How can you wish happiness for them?"

"Because I'm old enough to know how to direct my anger." He smiled. "I'd snap his neck if he stood next to me, but I'd hope he was happy while I did it."

I chuckled. "I'm surprised his father hasn't run for state or federal politics."

"No chance." Granddad Lincoln cast another line into the water. "Stephen would be a small fish in a big pond. Here, he gets to be someone. Besides, who would he run for? He'd need his own party to handle his ego."

"So true." I laughed. "George Washington was against the idea of political parties. He hated the idea of them. Even back then, he saw how a two-party system would divide the country and told everyone they'd do more harm than good."

"Is that right?"

"It is. Even in the 1700s, he saw how the parties would become political engines that would become a detriment to democracy. He said parties enabled cunning, ambitious, and unprincipled men to make decisions for themselves before the country."

"Drain the swamp, eh?"

"The question is who's doing the draining."

He looked at me. "Don't tell me they made you a Democrat up there?"

"I'm sticking with George Washington—we should vote for policies, not parties. We shouldn't treat parties like football teams. Sometimes one side gets it right, sometimes the other side gets it right. We need to be objective enough to see that."

"Vote for policies, not parties. I like that." He nodded. "But I'm surprised they didn't brainwash you into becoming woke up there."

"Being woke is about awareness of social issues, especially in relation to inequality and discrimination."

Granddad Lincoln waved my comment away and over the next fifteen minutes, he made several more comments about how the North corrupted good Southern morals.

It was an art form to hate the North, and it was an art form most Southerners were very skilled at. There were always fears that offspring would head North and become the dreaded "woke," that the indignant swagger of righteousness that abounded in every Northern city would make its way South, that the loss of manners was creeping down the country. None of it was true, of course, but it gave Southerners an identity, something to hold on to and be proud of.

We pulled the lines after an unsuccessful hour of fishing, thankful to be spending time together.

"I think it's time for you to reproduce so I can meet my great-grandkids," Granddad Lincoln said. "It'd be a good place for them to grow up around here."

I let the silence sit between us before I spoke again. "We've tried."

"That's my boy." He laughed. "Keep trying."

I didn't smile. I turned to him. "No, I mean Emma has gotten pregnant, but we've lost the baby twice."

Granddad Lincoln didn't say anything, and he didn't need to. He reached out and grabbed my shoulder. He gripped it tight and it told me everything I needed to hear.

The language of not speaking was one his generation was well versed in.

CHAPTER 46

I went to the office in the afternoon, and Bruce and Kayla were already there. There were two empty coffee cups on Bruce's desk. He was preparing details for the week ahead, but mostly he was trying to figure out how to convince Caleb to take the deal.

Bruce explained that he'd had a brick thrown through the front window of his house the night before. He said he stormed out of the house with his gun, but the vandals were already leaving the street in their car. Kayla suggested it might be kids letting off some steam, that it all might be a coincidence, but she didn't sound convinced. Bruce said he waited on his front porch all night for them to return, but he didn't see another sign of them. I could see the tiredness in his eyes.

"Sean Benning called with a lead on Isaiah's location," Bruce said as he finished another cup of coffee. "He found someone who knows someone who knows something." He reached over his desk and handed me a piece of paper. "Here's the address. I've got things covered here for now. You should follow the lead and see if you can convince him to come back before his next court appearance. If he skips it, or if anyone discovers he's missing, he'll end up in prison for a lot longer."

"Benning found someone who knows someone who knows something?" I questioned. It seemed like a long bow to draw. "That seems a bit vague."

"That's how things are done around here."

I looked at the address and considered what needed to be done for the week ahead. I had enough time to make the drive. With Bruce's approval, I drove an hour south to Pooler, Georgia, a city on the outskirts of Savannah. I loved Savannah and all the area surrounding it. The place had history, it had mystery, and it had an amazing art school that was constantly displaying modern pieces. It was always interesting to catch a glimpse into how the next generation would lead the art world.

Benning had said money was coming into the Clyburn household, and it was most likely Isaiah had picked up work with a cousin and was sending money back to support Lana. The theory seemed to fit. Isaiah didn't want to leave Lana unsupported, and he thought running across the state border was his best option.

When I reached Pooler, I followed the GPS to the address Sean had provided in the neighborhood of Williams. Tucked in amongst the trees, the single-level homes were tidy, but small. None had fences. The road was bumpy, patched with concrete, and wide enough for only one car.

I arrived at the address and drove past, checking out the place. It had overgrown grass, overflowing trash cans, and five cars parked around the home. Two were parked on the front lawn. I rolled past, turned around, and parked farther down the road, under the shade of a sprawling elm tree. I watched the house, waiting patiently for any movement.

An older sedan, with paint faded by the hot sun, pulled up and parked on the road. A younger male stepped out and hurried into the house, checking over his shoulder. He didn't bother to close the door of the sedan. Another young male met him at the front door, and they exchanged a handshake. After a quick exchange, the man returned to his car and drove off.

I sighed. It was a drug house. And that meant there would be weapons on site.

I couldn't go in there dressed in a shirt and trousers and ask for Isaiah. Even without a tie, I still looked like a lawyer. Or the young men inside could mistake me for a plain-clothes cop, and could panic and even shoot me on sight. No, I had to wait.

Fifteen minutes later, I watched one of the young men leave the house and walk up the street. I checked the maps on my cell phone and saw there was a convenience store five minutes up the road. That would be my chance to talk with him.

I drove from my parking spot and toward the shop, parking the SUV a few spots down from the entrance. The young man arrived a moment later and entered the store. It had bars on its windows and doors. The sign above the entrance, at least twenty-five years old, proudly declared the store sold 'Grocery. Beer. Whiskey. Lotto.' All of life's essentials.

I reached across my car and removed my Glock 19 from the glove box. I slipped it into my belt, and when I stepped out of the car, I put on my suit jacket, despite the muggy heat.

A minute later, the young man stepped out of the store with a Coke in one hand and a bag full of chips in the other.

"Hey, pal." I stepped forward.

He glared at me. "I didn't do nothing."

"I'm not a cop." I raised my hands to ease his apprehension. "But I need to talk to you."

"I don't know nothing." He turned and started walking away.

"It'd be worth a twenty," I said. Money always talked in places like this.

The young man stopped and turned back to me. He walked toward me with a limp, or perhaps it was an attempt to have some swagger. "Why don't I just take the twenty?" he said, eyeing me up and down.

I pulled back my jacket and showed my Glock.

He stepped back and nodded in approval. "Alright. Alright. Don't get excited, my man."

I reached into my pocket, took out my wallet, and removed a twenty-dollar bill. He licked his lips, but I slipped the bill back into my pocket. "You've got to talk first."

"What about?" He sniffed and looked around. "I ain't selling anyone out. That's not who I am."

"You're not selling anyone out," I explained. "I'm a lawyer who represents Isaiah Clyburn. I want to know where he is."

"Isaiah? Yeah, I know him."

"And?"

He nodded toward my pocket.

I took the note back out, folded it up, and held it out to him. "And?"

He snatched the money and then looked up and down the street. "And he was trying to keep a low profile, you know? He was staying with us but working at a job site. He was someone's cousin, but he got word people are looking for him, so he skipped again."

"Do you know where he went?"

"Jacksonville, Florida. He's got another cousin there who he can work for. Construction, or something."

I nodded and the man walked away with an exaggerated limp, continuing to check the street.

Jacksonville was another two hours away, and I didn't have the time to spare.

Isaiah Clyburn's case would need to wait.

CHAPTER 47

By Sunday evening, I was back in the office, sitting on the other side of Bruce's desk and discussing the week ahead. Bruce had ideas about how to discredit the witnesses, and they seemed solid, but not groundbreaking.

Sean Benning called around 7 p.m. I stepped outside into the humid air and took the call.

"You were right about Jacksonville," he said. "Your tip-off that he was working for a cousin appears correct. His cousin is running a new build down there. I've got the information on the job site and the address for you."

I drew a deep breath and wiped my brow. I squinted as I looked at the sunset. "Do you think he'll stay there for a while?"

"I can't guarantee it, but I think so. He wants to send money back to his parents to keep them afloat. It'd be hard for him to keep moving and getting jobs. If nobody harasses him, then I don't think he's going anywhere. Do you want me to go down and confirm it?"

"No, that might spook him again." I flapped my shirt, trying to cool down. There was always more than one case, always more than one place to focus on. "We're in the middle of the murder trial right now, and Caleb looks like he's losing. Isaiah's case will need to wait until this one is over."

"You got it."

I hung up and returned inside to the comfort of the air-conditioned office. Kayla arrived with baked goods. Biscuits, this time. She had baked them that afternoon with her niece, she said. Bruce and I happily ate them, thanking her for such delicious goodness.

"So, what are we looking at this week?" Kayla sat down opposite Bruce's desk.

"It's most likely they'll call their pseudo-science guy tomorrow," I explained. "But he's a gun for hire and will say anything to please anyone."

"We should have enough to discredit him," Bruce added, wiping the crumbs from his mouth. "But it's the remaining witnesses that worry me."

"And who are they?" Kayla asked.

"The big guns," I said. "They're the heavy-hitting ones, the two who will convince the jury to punish Caleb."

"And the jury is already being swayed," Bruce said. "I can see it in their eyes. All the evidence is stacking up, and they're starting to think Caleb is guilty. If a vote was taken today, I'm sure he'd be spending the next thirty years behind bars."

"Have you considered putting him on the stand to explain the missing eighteen minutes?" Kayla dusted a loose crumb off the edge of Bruce's desk. "That seems to be the key. If you let him speak, he could tell the jury he pulled over and smoked a joint before he went to the gas station."

Bruce ran through an inner argument, squinting his eyes, pressing his fingers together, lips tightening, before he nodded, as if he were in agreement with an invisible counsel. "He's not credible. It'll just look like he's making it up."

"And the issue with putting a defendant on the stand is the jury ignores everything else," I explained. "They won't see the holes in the evidence, they won't see the gaps in the prosecution's case, and they won't raise questions about reasonable doubt. If a defendant sits on the stand, the question for the jurors becomes, 'Do I trust this guy?'"

"And I hate to say it, but Caleb is the son of one very dishonest guy. Everyone in town knows Gerald isn't trustworthy." Bruce shook his head and leaned back in his seat. He put his hands behind his head and sighed. "And under cross-examination, you can bet Harley will pull his family history into it. He'd already have the questions prepared, waiting to pounce. There'd be a long list of indiscretions that Harley could indirectly tie to Caleb, and then Caleb will look like a fraud. The jury wouldn't trust a word he said, and then it's over."

A silence fell over us for a while, each of us contemplating the guilty verdict, before Kayla turned to me. "Do you think he's innocent?"

"It doesn't matter. We need to do the best for him."

"But do you? In your heart, your gut instinct, do you think he's innocent?"

I nodded.

She turned to Bruce and raised her eyebrows. "And do you?"

Bruce nodded as well.

"Then we need to find a way to win this case," Kayla said. "It doesn't matter how, but you've got to win it. You can't let an innocent kid be convicted."

CHAPTER 48

Fighting crime was big business throughout the country.

On both sides of the law, jobs were plentiful. Law and order kept the economy going. Law enforcement, attorneys, specialist technicians, therapists, medical examiners, forensic analysts, administration, management; the justice system kept so many people employed. Without criminals, without the jobs their actions created, the economy would go backward.

And the ones who really benefited from the justice system were the pseudo-experts. The people who could talk the talk and convince anyone to buy into their theory. They flew around the country, paid out of the prosecution's budget, testifying to anyone who would listen.

Matthew Wang appeared to be an energetic man. Standing at five-ten and 155 pounds, he walked with big steps, almost bouncing along the floor until he reached the witness stand. Dressed in black trousers and a blue shirt, he looked like an everyday office worker, nondescript and apparently trustworthy.

"Mr. Wang, can you please tell the court your profession?" Harley began.

"Hello everyone. It's a pleasure to be here." Wang leaned forward to speak into the microphone at the front of the witness box. "My name is Matthew Wang, and I'm a forensic engineer employed by a consultancy company called Forensic Behaviors. We're based out of Florida; however, we travel the country to provide expert opinions on forensic analysis."

"And how many trials have you testified in?"

"This is the fifty-fifth testimony I've provided."

"Impressive." Harley nodded for the sake of the jury. "And did you provide a forensic analysis of the direction of the slap that hit Miss Aiken?"

"That's correct. The circuit solicitor requested our company to review the evidence and the file on her death and provide a report."

"And is this the report you provided?" Harley held up a thick file for the jury to see.

"It is."

While the file was thick, it was mostly to show the circuit solicitor it was money well spent. I had read through the two hundred and fifty pages, and had only found one page of relevant information. The rest were filled with buzz words disguised as an expert opinion.

"Mr. Wang, in your professional opinion, what do you know about how Miss Aiken was struck?"

"With the information and data available, we developed a computer model for how the incident took place. We analyzed the height of the kitchen bench, the height of Miss Aiken, where she fell, the bruising on her face, and what type of force was required to make her fall."

"And is this one of the diagrams your computer analysis generated?" Harley pointed to the screen at the side of the room, and a diagram appeared on the court monitor.

It was an outline of two bodies, with lines and angles and numbers dotted over the picture.

"That is one of the diagrams, yes."

"Can you please explain what this diagram shows?"

"Of course. From our analysis of the crime scene, we can work backward with the information that we have. Given the height of the victim and where she fell, we calculated where she was standing when she was struck by the slap. Then, we entered the minimum force required to leave a bruise on her face, and we ran a program to determine the attacker's height."

"And what did you find?"

"We found the height of the attacker was most likely five foot ten."

"Five foot ten?" Harley turned to look at Caleb. "Mr. Wang, are you aware of how tall Mr. Rutledge is?"

"Yes. In the report, it's noted Mr. Rutledge is five foot ten."

One of the gallery members gasped. Judge Grant looked at them, ready to call them out, but no further noises came.

Harley waited a moment before he continued. "Mr. Wang, why have you used this angle for the direction of the slap?"

"Given the victim's height, where she was struck, and where she hit her head, it's most likely the slap came down from an angle above the shoulder."

For the next twenty-five minutes, Harley continued to question Wang about his findings in the report. It didn't state much more than that the attacker was five foot ten, but Wang did his best to pad out the answers and prove to the prosecution his testimony was worthwhile.

"Thank you for your expertise, Mr. Wang," Harley finished. "No further questions."

Harley sat down behind his desk and looked across at us. I shook my head, sighed, and then stood. I carried a folder to the lectern, waited a moment, sighed again, and then looked at the witness.

"Mr. Wang." I sighed again. "Do you consider your report accurate?"

"Of course."

"Can you please tell the court if all humans have the same arm length?"

"No, they don't." He squinted. "Men and women are known to have differences in average arm length."

"Is that right?" I said. "So, do all men have the same arm length?"

"We know there are variations in arm length relative to height." He scoffed at my question. "Can you imagine someone who was five-seven with the arms of someone seven foot? It'd look very strange."

I nodded. "But then, of course, all men of the same height have the same arm length. Is that right?"

"No," he scoffed again. "Of course not. There are variations across people of the same height."

"Is that right?" I repeated, and tapped my hand on the file in front of me. "Then please help me, Mr. Wang, because I've read your report, and it hinges entirely on one statistical data point—the length of the arm. Your report states the person who attacked Miss Aiken has an arm length of 73 centimeters. Is that correct?"

He looked at me blankly.

"Mr. Wang?"

"Um, I'm not sure. I don't remember the data point we used."

"You're not sure?" I questioned. "Well, that's okay, because I have the report here." I walked back to the defense table, picked up a copy of the report and handed it to the witness. "Can you please read the section I've highlighted on page fifteen, and tell the court if the report is based on your assessment the attacker has an arm length of 73 centimeters?"

"Uh, yes." Wang looked over the report. "That's correct. We use centimeters in medical measurements, not inches. And it's important to note we used arm length in the report, not arm span, which is the measurement of wingspan. We—"

"Thank you, Mr. Wang," I interrupted before he could continue. "The average arm length of someone five foot ten is 75 centimeters. Can you please explain why the report is based on a lower arm length of 73 centimeters?"

"That's what we calculated for the scene."

I shook my head. "In your report, it states, 'The diagram uses a factor of the arm length at 73 centimeters.' There's no evidence as to why you would use this arm length. So, can you tell me what would happen to the diagram if the arm span was increased to 75 centimeters?"

"I'm not sure."

"You're not sure?" I said. "That's okay, Mr. Wang. Because using the calculations detailed in this report, we created a different diagram." I walked back to the defense table and picked up another piece of paper. I walked it to the witness and handed it to him. "Would this diagram be correct if the arm length was 75 centimeters?"

"I'm not sure. I'd need to study it."

"Take your time."

"I would, um . . ." He stumbled over his words. "I would need to take it back to the team to analyze."

"There's no need. We've done the analysis for you." I handed him another piece of paper. "It was checked by Dr. Stephen Cole, a math professor at USCB. Can you please tell the court what the end result is?"

"This isn't my report."

"Are you doubting Dr. Cole's calculations?"

"No, I haven't had the chance to analyze this report."

"Okay. Given that if you change the arm length to 75 centimeters, the height of the person is estimated to go to five foot eleven, do you agree your calculation only works if they had 73-centimeter length arms?"

"I guess so."

"You don't need to guess. The information is right there."

"Ah, sure. Yes."

"So we're clear, the calculations are only accurate if the attacker had an arm measuring 73 centimeters in length?"

"I guess."

"Objection." I looked to Judge Grant. "Non-responsive."

"Sustained," Judge Grant agreed. "Please answer the question directly, Mr. Wang."

"Okay. Um . . ." Wang moved in his chair and tugged on his jacket. "Um, yes. The calculations are based on the fact the person had 73-centimeter length arms."

"Would the person's height be different based on the arm length?"

"Well, what we need to understand is—"

"Please answer the question, Mr. Wang."

Wang took a deep breath and sighed. "Yes. The person would be a different height if the calculations used different arm lengths."

"And how tall would the person be if you used the average arm length of 75 centimeters?"

"I guess . . . taller than five ten."

"You don't need to guess—the information is in front of you."

He looked at the piece of paper. "Ah . . . if the arm length was 75 centimeters . . . the person could've been five foot eleven."

"And if the arm length was 70 centimeters?"

"I'm not sure."

"Again, the information is on the report provided by Dr. Cole. Can you please read it out to the court?"

"Ah . . . okay." He took another deep breath. "The person could've been five-five."

"Five foot five?" I responded. "Would that be Miss Ava Healy's height?"

"I'm not sure how tall she is."

"She's listed as five foot five on her driver's license."

"Then, yes, I guess it would match her height."

"You guess it would match her height if you changed the arm length in your report . . ." I repeated, locking eyes with juror number five. "Thank you, Mr. Wang. No further questions."

I sat back down and nodded to Bruce. We had proven the witness's report was nothing more than junk science, but it didn't matter.

The prosecution's star witnesses, the ones that pulled on the heartstrings, the ones that pieced the puzzle together, were still to come.

CHAPTER 49

The rest of the fourth week of the trial passed in a blur of expert witnesses and forensic specialists.

Bruce said he spent most nights with his gun next to his bed, listening to every car that drove past his house, waiting for the vandals to return. He hadn't slept properly in a week, and it was starting to show on his face. Emma was the same. No matter what she tried, she couldn't get to sleep. She couldn't bear the thought of someone else breaking into our home. The surveillance cameras had arrived, and I set them up as soon as I got them out of the box. It calmed Emma's worries a little, but she was still spooked. Before bed every night, I checked that my Glock was loaded. I didn't know how far these people were going to go. I needed to be ready for anything.

Harley was trying to stretch the case until Friday, when he would bring in the two witnesses who sealed the deal. He wanted the jury to leave for the weekend with the star witnesses' testimonies in their heads.

On Friday morning, Bruce and I knew what was coming.

The Aiken family and all their supporters were gathered in the foyer when we arrived. They were there as support, to show their care for their friend—Naomi Aiken. An inconsolable mother, a shattered soul, and someone who could tear out the heartstrings of the jury. The gallery was packed when the court was called to order to start the day.

When asked by Judge Grant, Harley stood, swallowed, and looked behind him. Millie's father gave Harley a nod, and then Harley turned back to the judge. "The State calls Mrs. Naomi Aiken."

A hush settled over the packed gallery as the doors opened.

Mrs. Naomi Aiken, heartbroken by the loss of her angel, stepped through the doors. She stared at the floor, not making eye contact with anyone as she walked past. Her jacket was black, her skirt was black, and her shoes were black. She was in mourning, consumed by grief and sadness. Her beautiful girl had been taken far too soon.

Mrs. Aiken stepped into the witness stand, quietly swore her oath, and sat down. Harley picked up the tissue box and walked it to the stand, resting it on the edge. Harley returned to the lectern and drew a deep breath.

"Thank you for coming to court today." Harley began with a soft tone. "We understand how extremely difficult this must be for you."

Naomi nodded her response, already trying to hold back tears.

"Mrs. Aiken, can you please tell the court your relationship with the deceased?"

"I'm her mother."

"And were you the person who found her body on the night of March 5th?"

"Yes."

"And when was the last time you saw your daughter alive?"

She swallowed hard. She blinked several times and then reached for a tissue. "It was that evening, on March 5th, when I left for dinner. If I'd known what would happen, I never would've left . . ." She burst into tears, holding her head in her hands. The sounds of her sobs echoed around the packed but silent room. Nobody knew what to do. She was alone on the stand. "I'm sorry," she sobbed.

"No, please don't be sorry," Harley said. "Take all the time you need. We understand how hard this is for you."

Several members of the jury dabbed their eyes with tissues. Naomi's heartbreak was real, and it was radiating through the room. Even I could feel it.

"The last time I saw her"—Naomi took a deep breath, exhaled heavily, and settled herself—"the last time I saw her was on March 5th. I went out to dinner, told her I'd be home late, and I wished her a good night."

"And was your husband, Mr. Robert Aiken, home?"

"No. He was working a few jobs in Charleston and was staying up there for a few nights. It was easier than driving back and forth every day."

"So, Millie was home alone?"

"That's right." Naomi dabbed at her eyes again. "She was alone."

"And what time did you arrive home?"

"Before midnight," she whispered. "I—"

She cried again. It was painful to watch. Nobody wanted to see her relive that moment. Not me, not the jury, and certainly not her family members.

After half a minute, Naomi did several breathing exercises, avoiding eye contact with anyone, and composed herself. "I came home right before midnight."

Harley paused, allowing her time to settle, before he continued. "And when you left the house, do you remember seeing Mr. Rutledge's jacket and cap on the dining room table?"

"No, I don't. I'm sure it wasn't there when I left."

For the next fifty minutes, Harley questioned Naomi Aiken, having to stop several times. There were no consoling hugs, no handholding, and no escape from her agony.

When the jury members appeared to be emotionally shattered, Harley nodded. "Thank you, Mrs. Aiken. No further questions."

Bruce stood behind the desk. "Mrs. Aiken, as we discussed personally before, I'm so sorry for the loss of your daughter."

"Thank you, Bruce."

"Mrs. Aiken." Bruce kept his voice low and soft, trying not to offend her. "Is it possible Mr. Rutledge had left his jacket there in the previous weeks, and Millie moved it that evening?"

"Yes, that's possible. Caleb had some things in Millie's cupboard."

"Thank you, Mrs. Aiken." Bruce nodded and looked to Judge Grant. "No further questions."

CHAPTER 50

Kelly-Ann Walter walked to the stand full of calm confidence.

A mother of two in her thirties, a volunteer at the children's elementary school, and, most importantly for this case, an attendant at the gas station on Lady's Island, Kelly-Ann was dressed well in jeans, a white blouse, brown boots, and blue earrings. Her auburn hair was tied back. Her make-up was minimal. She was educated. Well spoken. And worst of all for us, she was likable.

During the deposition, she was honest and upfront. She had nothing to hide. She had nothing to fear. She calmly, and with a sense of authority, told us what she had seen. There were no holes in her witness statement and no way to pull her apart.

She was the perfect final witness for the prosecution.

"Thank you for attending court today, Mrs. Walter," Harley began. "Can you please tell the court your name and occupation?"

"My name is Mrs. Kelly-Ann Walter, and I'm an attendant at the gas station on Fairfield Road on Lady's Island." She smiled at the jury. The jury members smiled back. "I'm a mother of two young boys, aged five and eight, and I've been happily married for over ten years. My husband works as a mechanic around the corner from the gas station and we live a simple, but very happy, life."

"Thank you, Mrs. Walter," Harley said. "Can you please describe to the court where you were on the night of March 5th?"

"I was at work."

"And can you describe what you saw at work, around 9:25 p.m.?"

"When I was working, Caleb Rutledge came into the gas station at 9:25 p.m. I know it was this time because that's the time his receipt notes he paid for gas. Also, there's video footage of his truck pulling into the gas station at that time."

"Did anything seem out of the ordinary when he paid for gas?"

"Absolutely. He came up to the counter to pay, but I noticed he had a smear of blood that ran from his hand over his wrist and on to his forearm. I asked him if he was okay."

"And what was his response?"

"He seemed to be distracted. He said he hadn't noticed the blood. I offered to give him a bandage and he said he didn't even know where the blood was from."

One jury member gasped. That wasn't good for us.

"Did he take the bandage?"

"No, but I gave him a tissue to wipe it up. He paid for the gas, took the tissue, and continued on his way."

Harley nodded, then checked his notes. "Mrs. Walter, when Mr. Rutledge entered the store, how did he seem?"

"Objection to the word 'seem,'" I called out. "It asks the witness to speculate."

"Withdrawn," Harley said. "Did the blood stain appear new?"

"Objection to the word 'appear.' Again, it's speculation. This trial should be about the facts, not speculation."

"Sustained," Judge Grant agreed.

Harley frowned, a little frustrated, but even with the objections, even with the disruption to his rhythm, the facts were still clear. Caleb Rutledge had arrived at the gas station with an unknown blood smear on his hand and arm.

Harley nodded for a long moment and then offered, "Thank you, Mrs. Walter. No further questions."

Bruce pointed at his notepad. *I've got nothing*, his note read. I nodded. I felt the same.

Bruce drew a breath, and then offered, "We have no questions, Your Honor."

As Kelly-Ann Walter stepped out of the witness box, Harley stood. He looked at his team, and they nodded.

"Your Honor," Harley announced. "The State rests."

CHAPTER 51

Bruce threw his pen onto the table.

It bounced and rolled a few feet before it fell to the floor. The Saturday morning sunshine was streaming through the tall window of our office.

Bruce had lodged a motion for a directed verdict at the end of the prosecution's case, but it was nothing more than a formality. He told Judge Grant the State had failed to prove the charges against Caleb Rutledge. Judge Grant had considered the motion for a whole five minutes before it was declined.

"The ridiculous thing is I think the kid might be innocent," Bruce grunted as his heavy frame leaned back in the seat. The seat struggled under his weight. "If only he hadn't stopped to smoke the joint. If he hadn't, there wouldn't be a case."

"They've proven he was near the scene, but that's about it," Kayla said as she sat down. "That's not enough to convict someone, surely?"

"Given the circumstances, the unexplained blood smear, and the text messages between Caleb and Millie, I think it is," Bruce replied. "Right now, Caleb Rutledge looks guilty."

"The jury is thinking the same thing," I said as I sipped from a mug of coffee. "They've bought into the prosecution's story."

"Any more thoughts on our tactics?" Bruce walked around the table and picked up his pen. "Maybe we should consider putting him on the stand? If we think a guilty verdict is a done deal, his testimony might be the last hope."

"I don't like it," I said. "But if the case doesn't improve, it might be our only choice. There are positives to his testimony—he can explain why he stopped at the edge of Fairfield Road, and how he cut his hand. We can present photos of his truck with the sharp bit of metal and show the court pictures of where he pulled over."

"Still, without a witness to confirm he was there, he looks like he's making it up. And Harley will tear him apart in cross-examination." Bruce shook his head and then looked at me. "How do you feel about Chester Washington?"

I sighed. "It's a long shot, but maybe we can attack him on the stand and make him say something stupid."

"I like it," Bruce said. "If nothing is going our way in five days' time, we call him to the stand."

"What do we do before then?" Kayla asked.

"We go heavy on the lack of forensic evidence early, and I'll lead that section," I said. "I'll focus on how all the evidence presented by the prosecution doesn't mean anything, and I've got the expert witnesses lined up to say there were lots of holes in the prosecution's case."

"Then I'll bring in the character witnesses," Bruce confirmed. "We've got a few people lined up, although some of them have withdrawn their support, which is understandable after all this media coverage. The Aiken family is well liked and not many people want to offend them by testifying for Caleb."

"We need to be willing to pivot at any moment," I added. "If we get anything that might be a chance, we need to run with it."

"Agreed," Bruce noted.

We spent the next five hours discussing tactics. We discussed the witness list, the order in which we should call them, and the questions we'd put. We discussed the questions the prosecution was likely to ask in cross-examination, and how we should prepare the witnesses. Bruce made a joke about Caleb's future in prison, but it wasn't funny. Kayla and I offered him a small smile but kept our minds on the task at hand.

After we'd eaten lunch around the boardroom table, my cell phone buzzed. It was Sean Benning. I answered.

"Tell me it's good news."

"It's not," he replied.

I drew a deep breath and said, "Go on."

"I've had one of my contacts asking around the work site, and word is Isaiah thinks someone is watching him. The contact followed him, and saw Isaiah packing up his things. He got spooked. Maybe it was my guy that spooked him, but the bottom line is he's on the move again. You either question him now, or we might not find him next time. I don't have any contacts farther south than Jacksonville."

I looked at my watch. Jacksonville was more than three hours away.

"Send me the address. I'll drive down now," I said. "I'm not losing two cases in one week."

CHAPTER 52

I weaved in and out of weekend traffic on I-95.

Massive RVs cruised up the middle lane, driving without a care in the world, semis kept to the right, and I flew down the left lane, speeding toward my destination. The congestion became heavy in some areas, especially around the turnoff for the Savannah/Hilton Head Airport, but for the most part the drive was clear.

I arrived at the address Benning had supplied a little after 5 p.m. It looked like another single-story drug house—older cars parked on the front lawn, garden unkept, peeling paint on the house. I parked on the strip outside, grabbed my Glock 19, and tucked it into my belt. I had no time for games.

Either I found Isaiah or that was it. If he didn't return to Beaufort, he would have to face the consequences of skipping bail. If he chose to run, his fate was out of my control.

As the sun started to cast long shadows, I strode to the front door. It opened before I got there. A young man with baggy jeans and an oversized T-shirt stood in the doorway. One hand held something under his white shirt, but I couldn't see it. I assumed it was a handgun.

He stared at me. "You a cop?"

"Not a cop." I raised my hands, lifting them enough to expose my weapon. "I want to talk to Isaiah."

"Ain't nobody here by that name."

"I'm sure there is. Tell him Dean Lincoln wants to talk to him."

"Who?"

"Dean Lincoln," I explained. "That's me."

He looked me up and down. "If you ain't a cop, what are you then?"

"Someone who wants to help him out."

The young man looked behind him and then back at me. "I told ya, ain't nobody here by that name."

"See that car there"—I pointed over my shoulder back to my SUV—"I'm going to wait outside for fifteen minutes. I need you to tell Isaiah that I want to talk, that's all. I'm not here to take him anywhere. I just want to talk."

"Whatever, man." The young man swung the door shut.

I lowered my hands and walked back to my SUV. I leaned against the hood. One of the curtains in the house moved, and I saw a face look at me. It could've been Isaiah, but I wasn't sure.

If he didn't come out, I was satisfied I'd done all I could. His bail conditions specified he couldn't leave South Carolina, but officially, if I couldn't find him, then I'd done all I could. If he didn't make it to his next court appearance, that was on him.

A patrol car drove down the street, and the cops stared at me with a confused look on their faces. They weren't used to seeing a man like me in this neighborhood. I gave them a wave, and they shook their heads before continuing without any questions.

After the patrol car had rolled past, the front door of the home opened. It was Isaiah.

He walked out with his head down and hands tucked into the pockets of his sweater. He was wearing a cap and it was hard to see his face.

"You've broken your bail conditions by crossing state lines," I said as he approached. "That's not a good look."

He stopped a few feet away. He looked sober, something that was hard to do in a drug house. "How'd you find me?"

"I've been looking for you."

"It was you looking for me?"

"That's right."

"I thought it was someone else."

"Who?"

He shrugged and took off his cap. His hands looked scarred from hard work.

"You're working?" I asked him.

"At a job site run by my cousin. Got to keep some money coming in for Lana," he said. "Are you here to drag me back there?"

"I'm not dragging you anywhere." I shook my head. "Anything you choose to do is your own decision. I want to talk and make sure you're okay."

"I'm okay."

"You won't be if you miss your next court appearance," I said. "You'll be facing a range of extra charges if you don't come back to South Carolina. I know you don't want to do prison time, but we've a real chance to win this case at trial."

"You think I ran because of the court case? That's not why."

"Then why did you run?"

He bit his lip and shook his head. I could tell he wanted to tell me, but something was holding him back.

"Isaiah?" I pressed. "Who are you running from?"

"I'm not running from the law," he said. "I'm running from Gerald Rutledge."

"Gerald Rutledge?" I squinted. "Why?"

"Because that man is a killer."

CHAPTER 53

"Dean." Bruce answered my call as I raced back to Beaufort. "It's after 7 p.m. on a Saturday night. Why on earth are you calling me? A bit old for bedtime stories, aren't you?"

"We're on," I said. "We've got an angle and we've got a case."

"What is it?"

"Meet me in the office at 9 p.m. and I'll explain everything."

Bruce agreed and I called Sean Benning. He agreed to meet in the office as well.

Isaiah was driving back to South Carolina in his car but wouldn't leave until morning. I trusted he would return.

My drive back was quicker than the drive down. We had a lead, we had a chance, but we only had a day to understand how it fitted into our case. As I sped back, my mind was running at a hundred miles an hour.

Before I knew it, I was back in Beaufort.

"What on earth is going on?" Bruce asked as I stepped through the front door of the office.

"Put the coffee machine on," I said. "We need to focus."

Saturday night passed in a blur.

I arrived home at 4:05 a.m. and was back in the office at 10 a.m. Bruce and Sean were the same.

Kayla joined us on Sunday morning. We had a steady supply of coffee, donuts, and takeout coming through the door for most of the day.

Together, we watched the footage from the Marine Repair Store on the night of March 5th. We called numerous people and confirmed our leads. I called John Pearson, from Pearson and Sons farm. I spoke to everyone I knew to see if they had anything to point me in the right direction. I scoured the internet. I searched our files. I checked every document I could think of.

By the time we left the office that night, it had already turned into Monday morning. I could've worked longer but we needed to sleep.

The first witness for the defense was going to be explosive.

CHAPTER 54

"The defense calls Mr. Gerald Rutledge to the stand."

Gerald Rutledge had been prepared as a character witness for his stepson. He had lodged a witness statement to say he saw his son that morning and didn't know his whereabouts that night; he claimed he'd arrived home after dinner at around 9:30 p.m. and Caleb arrived home a few minutes after him. On paper, he was a solid witness, but nothing special. I could see the confusion on Harley's face as Gerald walked past him to the witness stand.

Gerald looked confident, arrogant almost. He wore black pants and a white shirt with the sleeves rolled up. His silver watch looked expensive, as did his brown shoes. His hair was combed back, and his tanned complexion made it look like he'd spent the past month outside.

I looked out to the crowd. They'd packed in again. They wanted to see how the defense case was presented. Stephen Freeman was seated behind the prosecution's desk. He eyed me suspiciously.

Gerald Rutledge was sworn in by the bailiff and the defense case began.

"Thank you for coming to court today, Mr. Rutledge." I stood behind the lectern with a file open in front of me. I looked at Bruce. He nodded. "Can you please tell the court how you know the defendant?"

"Caleb is my stepson. When he was five, I officially adopted him when I married his mother, and he changed his name to Rutledge. His mother passed away when he was ten and he's been living with me ever since."

"And is it just the two of you in the house on Little Capers Road?"

"That's it. It's a nice place and we've expanded over the years. We've got a pool and a large shed for my three cars. I could afford to live on Old Point or by the water, but I prefer it on Lady's Island. It's quieter over there."

"Three cars?" I pretended to be surprised. "And what sort of cars are they?"

"I have my Mercedes sedan, which I drive the most, but I also own a Ford F-150, and a 1970 Dodge Challenger, which is my pride and joy. I love that thing."

"That's great," I quipped. "And are you employed?"

"I'm retired from work, but I used to own a produce farm out past Ridgeland. I still sit on the board for the Beaufort Branch of the South Carolina Farm Agency. We're a lobby group for local, state and federal politicians, and we make sure we look after our members. There's been a lot of financial growth in farming through Beaufort over the last five years, and it's created a lot of jobs for the area. I'm very proud of the positive changes we've made for the farmers of South Carolina, and I'm very proud of the success we've had in Beaufort County."

There was no doubt about it—Gerald Rutledge was a smooth talker.

"There's a lot of potential growth in sweet-potato farming for Beaufort. Is that correct?"

"Objection. Relevance," Harley called out. "This is all very nice, but is there even a point to this line of questioning?"

"Your Honor," I retorted, "we're making our way to the point of the questioning. If you allow us a little leeway, we'll make sure we get there quickly."

"The objection is overruled for now," Judge Grant stated. "But do get to the point, Mr. Lincoln."

"Thank you, Your Honor." I turned back to face Gerald. "Mr. Gerald Rutledge, can you confirm there's potential for a lot of growth in sweet-potato farming for Beaufort County over the next few years?"

"That's right," Gerald agreed, starting to become apprehensive. "The interstate quarantine ban on sweet potatoes was lifted in 2017, and a lot more growers added to their crops and increased profit. The ban was put back in place in 2018, but now we're only a few months away from it being lifted again. Sweet potatoes grow very well in Beaufort County, and it'd be great to show them off to the world."

"And what was the quarantine ban for?"

"Weevils that were detected in the sweet-potato crop." Gerald slowed his speech pattern, and his apprehension was becoming clear. "But I have to agree with the prosecution. I'm not sure what this has to do with Caleb and Millie?"

"And of course"—I ignored his question—"if weevils were detected in Beaufort County, that would devastate the farming growth, would it not?"

"It would."

"And the result would be millions of dollars in lost revenue?"

"Most likely. People, including myself, have invested heavily into the ban being lifted. But again, I fail to see how this is relevant?"

"It is relevant," I stated. "Any loss of revenue would affect your job on the board of the South Carolina Farm Agency, would it not?"

"I don't know about that."

"But if weevils were found here, it would affect your recent investments in farming in this area?"

"Maybe."

"So, it would be in your best interest to ensure no weevils were found in Beaufort County?"

"It would be in the best interest of the people of this county, and in the best interest of the people who run the farms." Gerald's voice became firmer. He glared at Harley. Harley nodded his response.

"And what would you do if one of the farmers came to you and said they'd found weevils in the sweet potatoes on one of their farms?"

"Objection." Harley stood. "Is there any relevance to this at all? Where is this questioning going?"

"Sustained. We've given you leeway, Mr. Lincoln, but I fail to see the point of the questioning."

"I'll move on now, Your Honor," I said. "Mr. Gerald Rutledge, how well did you know Millie Aiken?"

"Quite well." Gerald's tone had become defensive. He leaned back in his chair and crossed his arms over his chest. "She'd been dating my stepson for five or six years. She was always around the house, at least once a week. So yeah, I knew her quite well."

"And did she know your business dealings quite well?"

"I'm not sure what you're asking."

"I'm asking, when did Millie Aiken discover that you instructed someone to burn the crop of sweet potatoes on the Pearson and Sons farm to rid it of weevils?"

The shock washed over Gerald's face.

"Objection!" Harley's voice was exasperated. "Accusation. What is this?"

"Your Honor, this question goes to the heart of why Millie Aiken died, and if you will allow me to continue, we'll present evidence to show as much."

"Overruled. You may answer the question."

"Whoa," Gerald stated. "I didn't come here to be accused of anything. I'm a character witness for my stepson."

"You're on the witness stand, Mr. Rutledge." Judge Grant leaned closer. "You will answer the questions put to you, or you'll be held in contempt of court."

"Mr. Rutledge." My voice grew louder. "When did Millie Aiken discover that you instructed someone to burn the crop of sweet potatoes on the Pearson and Sons farm to rid it of weevils?"

"I don't know what you're talking about."

"Interesting," I noted. I turned a piece of paper over on the lectern. "Mr. Rutledge, you stated earlier that you were at your home that night. Is that correct?"

"Around 9:30 p.m., yes. Before that, I was in town. At dinner."

"Can you please look at the court monitor and tell us what car you see driving past the Marine Repair Store at 9:20 p.m. on March 5th?"

Bruce typed several lines into his laptop, and the court monitor came to life. It showed a still shot of Gerald Rutledge's Mercedes driving down Little Capers Road.

"I guess that's my car. I was heading home."

"And where had you been before that time?"

"Ah." Gerald shrugged. "I was coming back from dinner in town. I said that already."

"From the direction of Millie Aiken's house?"

"No." He shook his head. "No. That's the way back from town."

"It's also the way back from the Aiken house. Is that correct?"

"Ah, no. I didn't go there." He kept on shaking his head. "I didn't go there."

"Mr. Rutledge." My voice rose again. "Is it true that on the night of March 5th, you received a call from John Pearson, the owner of Pearson and Sons farm, and he informed you Millie Aiken was writing a longform article about the weevils found on his farm and how it was covered up by a fire on his crop?"

"No, no."

"Mr. Rutledge." I held a piece of paper in the air. "Are you aware that calls are logged? We have Mr. Pearson's cell phone record here. It states you had a five-minute discussion with him that started at 9:03 p.m. and ended at 9:08 p.m."

"Ah . . . maybe. Maybe he called me that night. I don't remember."

"Minutes after that call is recorded, your car is seen driving away from the Aiken household. Can you explain that?"

"There's nothing to explain. I was driving home."

"Did you confront Millie Aiken about the news article she was writing on the night of March 5th?"

"No, no, no."

"Did you tell Millie Aiken not to write the article when you spoke to her on the night of March 5th?"

"I didn't speak to her."

"Did Millie Aiken refuse to stop writing the article, and is that why you slapped her?"

"Objection! Accusation!" Harley stood.

"Sustained," Judge Grant grunted. "Mr. Lincoln, there will be no accusations of the witness."

"I withdraw the question, Your Honor." I returned to the defense table, and Bruce handed me another file. I nodded to him and then to Caleb, whose mouth was hanging open in shock. I went back to the lectern and opened the file. "Mr. Rutledge, were you aware that the GPS data on your new Mercedes records everywhere you go?"

Gerald sat up straighter. "No, I wasn't aware of that."

"And we've lodged a subpoena with Mercedes to share that information with the court. Do you know what that GPS data will show for your movements on the night of March 5th?"

He sat back. His face went pale.

"Will that GPS data show you left dinner after a phone call from John Pearson and arrived outside the Aiken residence before 9:20 p.m. on the night of March 5th?"

"I don't . . ." He shook his head. "I don't know what it'll show."

I stared at Gerald for a long moment. Several jurors looked stunned. I turned to look at the Aiken family and they were glaring at Gerald. "No further questions."

CHAPTER 55

"What do you mean?" I stood and paced the back of the conference room, rubbing my brow. "You heard him—he knows the GPS data from the Mercedes will show he pulled up at the Aiken household after 9 p.m."

"Maybe it will, maybe it won't," Andrew Harley stated. He was sitting on the other side of the conference room, flanked by his two assistants on one side and Stephen Freeman on the other. "We don't know what it'll show."

The beige-colored, plainly designed meeting room did nothing to ease the tension between us. The smell of coffee was strong in the room, but I would've much preferred the smell of whiskey, given the situation.

Bruce leaned forward on the white table. "You have to admit, Andrew, this doesn't look good for Gerald."

"It doesn't prove anything," Freeman added.

"You're kidding, right?" I was exasperated. "How can you not see this? Gerald took John Pearson's call, and then went to convince Millie not to write the article. When she didn't agree, he slapped her, and she fell. In a panic, he raced away from the scene."

"It's a good theory, but what would you have me do?" Harley shook his head. "Ask for a five-week recess until the evidence comes back?"

"Yes!" I threw my hands in the air.

"None of it proves Caleb wasn't there," Freeman stated. "We don't know if there was more than one person involved."

"What do you mean?"

"Right now, we're working with the theory they both were involved," Harley explained. "There's an eighteen-minute window where Caleb could've been doing anything. Maybe he went to see Millie, slapped her, killed her, called his father, and his father raced to the scene. Maybe they were both in this weevils theory together. We don't know, and right now, we still think Caleb is guilty."

"You've seen the phone records. Caleb didn't call anyone."

"He could've messaged him via a social media app. That wouldn't have come up on the phone records."

"You're letting a killer walk away!"

"There was a blood smear on Caleb's hand, Dean!" Harley cried. "We know he was arguing with Millie. We know there's an unexplained eighteen-minute window! He's involved—the only question now is whether he was the only one. We're not withdrawing this case. We're still chasing the right man for this murder."

"Unless, of course"—Freeman smiled—"the young man wants to tell the truth and explain to the court what really happened when he and his father were at the Aiken household."

"Do you have an offer if he does that?" Bruce questioned.

I raised my eyebrows. Bruce was always looking for the deal, always looking to strike out.

"If he confesses and tells us the truth about what happened," Harley said. "Ten years involuntary manslaughter."

CHAPTER 56

"Really?" Caleb stared at the roof, leaning back, head resting on the top of the chair. "My stepfather killed Millie?"

"That's what it looks like," I said as I moved around the table in the courthouse meeting room. "As soon as Gerald Rutledge found out about the weevils in the sweet-potato crop at Pearson and Sons, he paid someone to burn it all."

"Why?"

"Because the discovery of weevils would mean more quarantine bans for the county," Bruce explained. "It would've meant a lot of farmers would've lost a lot of money. My bet is Gerald invested in those farms and would lose a considerable amount of money himself if more weevils were found."

"The person burned the barn as a cover for the crops. The barn was a distraction," I continued. "Being an investigative journalist, Millie found out about the weevils and the cover-up and threatened to expose them with an explosive article. It would've been her big break. But Gerald went around to tell her not to write it. Once they met face to face, he slapped her."

"And framed me . . ." Caleb stood, looking more energized than I'd seen him in weeks.

"I don't think he did it intentionally," Bruce added. "But he was never going to take the fall for you."

Caleb walked around the small room, tapping his fist against the wall. He mumbled to himself before turning back to us.

"I knew the stupid old man never liked me." He leaned his hands on the table and dropped his head. "I can't believe he did it."

"The prosecution is working with the theory that you were both there."

"What? That's ridiculous."

"And they've got a new deal—ten years if you confess you and your father were there together."

"No! That's crazy." He swung around to look at us. "What about the GPS data? Surely it proves he did it?"

"The Sheriff's Department will issue a request for the GPS data from the car company, but it could take months to deliver," Bruce explained. "Mercedes are really good with requests but it's a long process to get the information. And even then, we're not sure exactly what it'll show. Right now, all we have is a theory."

"Why can't you call the car company to the stand?"

"Things don't work like that, Caleb," I told him. "They can take time to respond to the subpoena, and they will. They have an extraordinary amount of data to sift through before they can give an accurate answer."

"But he's guilty!"

"We don't need to prove his guilt," Bruce said. "We need to prove there's reasonable doubt it was you, and right now, that's what we have. Our case is in a much stronger position thanks to his testimony."

"I'll kill him." Caleb's face turned serious. "If he killed Millie, I'll kill him."

"No." I tried to settle him down. "There'll be none of that."

"But he killed Millie!"

"I know, but we should allow the authorities to handle it."

Caleb slumped back into his chair and put his face in his hands.

We were in front. We were in a good position. But the case was still a long way from over.

CHAPTER 57

Confusion had spread through the courthouse.

When we returned to the courtroom after lunch, the buzz of anticipation was almost deafening. I heard whispers as I entered and it was all the same: "Why hasn't the State withdrawn the case? They must still think Caleb's guilty."

We called our next witness. Keith McMillian was the lead editor at the *Gazette*. He was a broad-shouldered man with the look of someone in power and control. He confirmed Millie Aiken was working on a longform article about the damage to the sweet-potato crop, and the possibility it had been burned to cover up the presence of weevils. McMillian said if he'd thought Millie was in danger, he would've told her to stop. He was shocked when he heard the article might've led to her death. Harley objected to the statement, but McMillian merely said what everyone was thinking.

John Pearson came to the stand next. He confirmed Millie Aiken had been to his property that day to talk to him about possible weevils in the crop. He told the court he called Gerald Rutledge at around 9 p.m. and told him he was worried about the article. Upon our advice, when asked by Harley about the weevils, John Pearson exercised his rights under the Fifth Amendment, preventing him from answering questions that could lead to self-incrimination.

His story, and his grief about being involved in Millie's death, were convincing.

For the rest of the week, we presented witness after witness who created reasonable doubt as to Caleb's guilt. We presented forensic experts, character witnesses, and crime scene specialists. We called blood spatter analysts, technological experts, and DNA specialists. We cast doubt on the fingerprints, we cast doubt on the DNA, and we cast doubt on the placement of the jacket and cap. We continued to focus on the lack of a thorough investigation and highlighted all the ways the investigation had failed to be completed. As the week closed, the nods from the jury members became more frequent, and the prosecution team looked more dejected.

Despite our consistent calls and pressure, we didn't hear back from the car company about the GPS data. It would take weeks to go through the information, they told us repeatedly. It wasn't as simple as searching for something online. It was encoded data, and there were trillions of lines to go through.

Gerald Rutledge had gone to ground. The rumor was he had fled to Florida and was ready to board a plane to South America the second a contact called him to say the prosecution was going to charge him. I imagined Stephen Freeman had his finger on the pulse and was ready to protect his old friend.

By 9:55 a.m. on Friday morning, our case was finalized.

"The defense rests, Your Honor."

CHAPTER 58

Caleb sat at the end of the white table in the courthouse meeting room, arms folded across his chest. "But he did it, right?"

"That's what we think, and we hope the jury thinks the same way," Bruce said. He looked at me and then back at Caleb. "The prosecution has offered one last deal—two years if you confess now."

"Two years?"

"That's right."

"Should I take it?" Caleb looked at me.

I shook my head. "They've offered a good deal because they don't want to risk it with the jury."

Bruce nodded. "Even I think we're close, Caleb."

I agreed. "Our closing statement is going to be focused on the fact there's reasonable doubt you were involved in her death." I checked my watch. "It's time to go back in."

Bruce looked at Caleb. "I need an answer on the deal."

Caleb stood. "I want to leave it up to the jury."

We left the meeting room, and Harley was waiting for us outside the door. Bruce told him the deal had been rejected, and Harley scurried back into the courtroom.

The gallery seats in the courtroom filled quickly after the recess. The tension was high.

Judge Grant wasted no time in calling for closing statements. Harley stood, walked to the lectern, and made one last plea for a guilty verdict.

"Ladies and gentlemen of the jury, good people of Beaufort County, thank you for taking the time to listen to this case. This process has been long, at times boring and arduous; however, you must not forget why you're sitting in the jury box.

"You're here to make a judgment on a person's guilt based on the evidence presented to you.

"And because of that, I need you to remember one fact—a young lady died as the result of a slap.

"That's a fact.

"Millie Aiken died as a result of a slap.

"It's been shown Caleb Rutledge was going in that direction at the time of the murder. It's been shown Caleb Rutledge's DNA and fingerprints were found in her kitchen. It's been shown Caleb Rutledge had an unexplained smear of blood on his hand after her time of death. It's been shown there are eighteen minutes where Caleb Rutledge isn't accounted for.

"We know, *we know*, that was enough time to drive to the Aiken household, slap her, and then leave.

"The missing eighteen minutes, and the blood smear. That's what you need to remember.

"You've heard from the defense a theory that maybe there was someone else present at the time of the murder. Maybe that's true— but their theory doesn't prove Caleb was not also present. If you're to believe the defense theory, all they're saying is there was more than one person present.

"The application of the law in this case is simple—if you find beyond a reasonable doubt that Mr. Rutledge murdered Miss Aiken, then you must return a guilty verdict.

"And it's plain and simple—Mr. Rutledge is the only person who had the motive, the means, and the desire to murder Miss Aiken. The cold, hard truth is Caleb Rutledge murdered his former girlfriend and should be found criminally responsible for his actions.

"This is a chance to hold someone accountable for their actions and punish a murderer. This is your chance to show the world that the residents of Beaufort County will not allow a murderer to get away with such a terrible crime.

"The only reasonable conclusion you can draw after this trial is that Mr. Caleb Rutledge is guilty.

"Thank you for your service to the court."

Harley walked back to his seat, avoiding eye contact with us. I made several notes on my closing statement and then stood, moving behind the lectern to begin my statement.

The State's case rested on circumstantial evidence, and that had been the focus of Harley's statement.

It was now my turn to highlight all the holes in their theory.

"Caleb Rutledge is not guilty.

"After the weeks we've spent together in this courtroom, that should be clear to you now. You cannot ignore the facts.

"There's no evidence Caleb Rutledge was in the Aiken household on the night of March 5th. There's no evidence he met with Miss Aiken that night. And there's no evidence he caused Miss Aiken's death.

"Let me repeat that for you so it's clear—there's no evidence, *no evidence*, that Mr. Caleb Rutledge caused Miss Aiken's death. None. Not one piece of evidence proves he murdered her.

"We know the Sheriff's Department didn't complete a thorough investigation into this crime.

"We know there were other suspects in this case, and they weren't considered.

"We know there's evidence that wasn't investigated.

"We know there's a reasonable doubt Mr. Caleb Rutledge caused this death.

"And that's the critical point—there's a reasonable doubt Mr. Caleb Rutledge caused this death.

"When making your decision for this case, you need to consider the evidence presented to you, not the stories around it. You need to consider the lack of proof, the lack of evidence, and the lack of a thorough investigation, not some ill-informed theory.

"It's reasonable to have doubts about this case.

"We know someone slapped Miss Aiken that night. We know she fell and hit her head. We know there were others with the motive and ability to cause this death. We know those people weren't even part of the Sheriff's Department's investigation.

"Study the case, study the holes in the case, and you can only come to one reasonable result—there's reasonable doubt Caleb Rutledge caused this death.

"If you believe there's not enough evidence, you must find the defendant not guilty.

"If you believe you have reasonable doubt over the evidence presented, you must find the defendant not guilty.

"And if you believe someone else murdered Miss Aiken, you must find the defendant not guilty.

"Thank you for your service to the justice system."

CHAPTER 59

By day five of jury deliberation, my nerves were almost uncontrollable.

I couldn't focus on anything else. What was taking them so long? Had we done enough? How come they didn't have a verdict yet? The jury had returned to court five times for clarification on legal issues and evidence. Nothing they said gave us any indication as to which way they were leaning.

The worst part of any trial is waiting for the verdict. It's a patience game. And for someone with little patience, like me, it's torture. It's when others are in control, when I have zero power, when I have no choice but to sit back and wait.

I called Terry Wallace of the Beaufort Police Department. He confirmed everyone was keeping an eye out for Gerald Rutledge. Wallace acknowledged the theory that Gerald had fled to Florida, waiting for further instructions from his contacts, was most likely correct. He would be hoping the GPS car data wouldn't prove anything conclusively, Wallace said. Wallace also noted Gerald had fled with nothing, and it was likely he'd make a quiet return to his home before fleeing to another country. Perhaps even drive his beloved 1970 Dodge Challenger south.

The Sheriff's Department confirmed they wouldn't open an investigation into Gerald until the GPS data was returned. They worked with evidence, not theories.

"Can't stop thinking about it?" Bruce said as he smashed another drive down the middle of the fairway. "You've got to learn to let it go, my friend. Focus on the drive instead."

I had agreed to another round of golf with Bruce in an effort to ease my growing tension. It wasn't working.

In golf, the mind serves as the disciple of the body. Nothing interferes with the flow of the game more than a golfer who obsesses about every small action. At some point, you need to clear your mind and hit the ball. You line up, take a practice swing, line up again, and then hit it hard.

But today, my mind was still controlling things. "I don't see how they haven't made a decision yet."

"You don't get it, do you?" Bruce watched his ball roll off in the distance after a solid tee shot. "This is a community where decisions have impacts. People aren't faceless entities here. Everything we do affects someone else we know. The people in the courtroom want to get it right for the community and if it takes weeks, then that's what they'll do."

"They must know Gerald Rutledge is guilty."

"Maybe," Bruce said. "Or maybe they think they were both there. We don't know what they're thinking."

"Think he'll come back?"

"He'll be in contact with Stephen Freeman, and Freeman will let him know if there's enough evidence to charge him or not. If there is, Gerald will go straight to South America. If not, he'll lay low for a while and come back once it's all blown over."

I tried to focus on the golf and by hole five, it was starting to work. I was hitting the ball well, sweetly, and somehow, it seemed to be going straight.

We hit a few more balls, spending the day in the sun. I lined up for my next drive, but Bruce kept talking.

"You know, I've had a good morning," he said. "My wife apologized to me for the first time ever."

"Is that right?"

"Yeah, she said she was sorry she ever met me, but I'm taking it as an apology."

I chuckled as I tried to focus.

"And she told me I've grown as a person." He shrugged. "Well, she said I've gotten fatter, but same thing."

I laughed heartily and stepped away from the tee, unable to hit the ball. I looked at him. "I had an interesting morning as well."

"What happened?"

"I surprised our regular delivery guy by showing up at the door naked." I lined up my drive again. "I don't know which shocked him more—my naked body or the fact I knew where he lived."

Bruce laughed, and I laughed with him. I smashed the drive down the fairway, and I had to admit Bruce was right—there was something about being in the open air, sweating, and laughing, and talking, and losing ourselves in the moment. As I putted the ball into the hole, hitting my third par of the day, the stress of the jury decision was left behind.

After a morning on the greens, Bruce rolled the last putt into the hole.

"It's a draw," he said.

"A draw?" I smiled, knowing I'd beaten him by at least five strokes.

"Yeah. I gave you a five-stroke penalty for hitting it too far down the fairway."

"Too far?" I shook my head.

"I make the rules out here, pal. We've—" Bruce said, stopping as his cell phone rang.

He checked the number. "Kayla," he said. I remained silent while he talked to her. He looked at me. "They've got a verdict."

It was time to hear the jury's decision.

CHAPTER 60

The foyer of the Beaufort County Courthouse was buzzing with people talking, arguing, and gossiping, but the hum quietened as Bruce and I walked through.

I could sense their eyes on me. We were in the beating heart of the action, in the middle of the controversy, part of the biggest drama in town for the past year. We pushed through the crowd and when we reached the top of the stairs, I stopped and looked around. When Bruce joined me, he patted me on the back.

"Caleb has had the best possible defense," he said. "Whatever they decide, we did our best."

I drew a long breath and nodded.

Waiting at the end of the hallway, outside the courtroom, was Stephen Freeman, looking as arrogant and in control as ever, a smirk stretched across his face.

"Decision time," he noted. "I hope this is a lesson for you, Dean. It's time for you to learn how politics work around here."

"They haven't delivered a decision yet."

"No, but after this much deliberation, it can only go one way." Freeman grinned, then looked at his phone in his hand. It was buzzing loudly. "You couldn't save Caleb." He laughed and turned away to answer the call. I looked at his chin. It was open and defenseless. I wanted to land a clean left hook on it, to knock him out cold, but it would've served no purpose.

Bruce and I walked to the front of the courtroom. Caleb was already waiting for us, sweat covering his brow. He was wearing his best suit and had sprayed on too much cologne. He was twitching. He didn't say anything as we approached. I gave him a nod and he gave me one back.

The nerves were filling my stomach. Had we done enough? The question plagued me as we waited.

The courtroom began to fill behind us, and the tension in the air was palpable. There was a buzz, a jolt of excitement that was tempered by the threat of looming failure.

Harley arrived and talked to the Aiken family, who had taken up their seats in the front row. Behind them sat their friends. All the seats were filled.

At 5:05 p.m., the bailiff stood and brought the murmurs to a close. Everyone rose for the entry of Judge Grant. He shuffled into the room and took his seat. There was a murmur as everyone else sat back down.

Judge Grant instructed the bailiff to bring in the jury. The door to the right of the room opened and the jurors entered in single file. None made eye contact.

"Has the jury reached a verdict?" Judge Grant asked.

The man sitting in the front right seat rose and spoke. His voice was loud. "We have, Your Honor."

Bruce and I stood and instructed Caleb to do the same. The bailiff stepped forward, took the piece of paper, and walked it back to the judge. Once Judge Grant read the note, he looked back at the foreman. "And what say you?"

The court held its collective breath.

"In the charge of murder, we, the jury, find the defendant not guilty."

CHAPTER 61

I celebrated long into the night with Bruce, Kayla, and Caleb at the Bay Street Barbeque restaurant. Emma joined us for a while, as did my grandparents. Many of Caleb's friends arrived, jovial in their support. There were a lot of hugs, a lot of high-fives, and a lot of slaps on the back.

Caleb drank a lot. At one point, he told me how much he loved me, embracing me in a tight hug. He said I was the real father figure in his life, and that he wanted to grow up to be just like me. I knew it was the alcohol talking, but it was good to hear how much he appreciated my hard work.

As the night wore on, Caleb's happiness became tempered. He was happy he had survived the charges, happy he had survived the court case, but the weight of Millie's death was becoming clearer. In the detention center, life had felt different for him, detached from reality, but back on the streets, back in the real world, the truth was setting in—his childhood sweetheart was gone.

After 10 p.m., Caleb and his friends moved onto Ernest's, a dive bar known for its late-night antics. Knowing my limits, I left Caleb and his friends at that point.

Still, I awoke the next morning with a brutal hangover.

Emma looked after me. While I was still in bed, she gave me two Advil, several glasses of sweet tea, and then told me to stop being so soft and toughen up. By midday, I was beginning to feel normal again.

With my fifth glass of sweet tea of the day, I sat on the front porch, enjoying a Saturday without the murder trial hanging over my head. Emma joined me, and we chatted about life in Beaufort for a while. She spoke about her mother, and how positive she was trying to be. She was a fighter, Emma said, and she wouldn't give up without a battle. I listened, letting my wife talk as much as she needed to. We waved hello to passing neighbors, before Emma went inside and returned with a novel. She offered to grab a book for me to read, but I declined, my head still heavy from the night before.

As the day drifted into mid-afternoon, my cell phone buzzed in my pocket. I looked at the number.

"Caleb?" I answered the call. "Are you okay?"

There was silence on the other end of the line. I figured either he'd be drinking today or would be too hungover to function. It must be a misdialed call.

But then a voice spoke.

"Mr. Lincoln, it's Caleb." He was slurring his words. I looked at the time. It was five in the afternoon. I wasn't sure if he'd stopped from the night before. "I want to thank you from the bottom of my heart for finding out who murdered Millie. You've brought the real truth out, and for that, you deserve a medal."

"Did you sleep last night, Caleb?"

"I had a couple of hours," he said. "But we're back celebrating at a friend's house. I owe you so much, Mr. Lincoln. If it was left up to Mr. Hawthorn, he would've signed my name on the first deal they presented."

"I don't deserve anything, Caleb. I'm—"

"Now, I'm going to kill him. Someone called me and said they saw his car driving toward our house. He's probably going back to get his things before he leaves for good, so I'll give him what he deserves."

"Caleb—"

"My stepfather has been horrible to me my whole life and I'm going to give him some of his own medicine."

"Caleb, settle down." I lowered my tone. "Don't do anything stupid."

"You know Stephen Freeman and Gerald are friends. Freeman is going to make sure nobody will touch Gerald. And the old man is going to get away with murdering Millie. He won't spend a day in prison for what he did."

"Caleb, stop."

I heard an engine fire up.

"Caleb!"

Caleb ended the call. I tried to call back, but there was no answer. I sprinted to my SUV. I had to get there first.

CHAPTER 62

I raced to Little Capers Road on Lady's Island.

I sped through the streets, screeching around corners, racing through red lights, and overtaking cars with aggression. I pulled up and parked on the grass in front of the Rutledge home. Caleb's truck was already there, parked on the front lawn, right behind Gerald's Mercedes. I grabbed my Glock and jumped out of my car.

Moving along the side of the property, I stayed in the shadows. I heard a voice. It was Caleb. He was yelling from the back yard.

Adrenaline pumped as I closed in on the target. The sound of a handgun exploded somewhere ahead of me.

I broke into a sprint without a second thought, racing toward the sound. Holding my Glock 19 down, I peered around the corner of the house.

Gerald was standing on the back porch with a handgun pointed into his yard. He'd fired into the air, trying to warn Caleb not to come any closer.

Next to a tree, fifteen yards away, Caleb was kneeling. He had a shotgun aimed at his stepfather and was swaying from side to side.

"I know what you did," Caleb's voice sneered. "You killed her."

"You can't shoot me, you idiot boy." Gerald waved his gun in the air. "Did you hear me?"

"Why did you need to kill her?"

"I didn't, you idiot boy!"

"Caleb." I came around the corner. "Put the gun down."

"No! He killed her! He killed Millie!"

"The kid won't do it anyway," Gerald scoffed. "He's too soft."

I took another step forward. Gerald looked at me, then looked at Caleb. "And of all people to call, you called the city lawyer. What's he going to do? File a motion on me to stop me driving away?"

"You killed her." Caleb's words were woozy. "Why did you do that?"

"Caleb," I called out, still crouched at the corner of the house. "Lower the weapon."

"The boy's useless," Gerald called back, waving his handgun around. "It was clear the first day I met him. A little weakling boy. He needs a good slap around the head."

"Is that what you told Millie?"

"Ha," Gerald scoffed again. He looked around the yard. "Alright. Sure. That's what I did. I slapped her because she wouldn't stop talking about the weevils. I couldn't let her print that story. I'd go broke if the news got out. I didn't mean to kill her, but it is what it is."

Caleb lowered his gun. "That's a confession. You won't get away with it now."

"Ha!" Gerald laughed. "You're dumber than you look. There's no way I'm going down for this. Who have I confessed to? A lawyer and his client. That's never going to stand up in court."

"But the GPS data will," I shouted back.

"I won't be around long enough for that," Gerald responded. "I'll be gone tonight."

Sirens echoed in the distance.

"What?" Gerald called out to Caleb. "You called the cops?"

"Not me," Caleb raised his shotgun again. "I wanted to sort this out—me and you."

"You won't do that. You're—"

A gunshot fired, and I took cover behind the house. Another shot fired. Then another. Both weapons had gone off.

When the gunshots stopped, I peered around the corner.

One of the men had fallen.

CHAPTER 63

Two days later, Bruce and I were sitting in the conference room of the Beaufort County Courthouse.

The meeting room was cold, thanks to an overactive air conditioner. I wasn't complaining. I rolled up my shirt sleeves and rested my forearms on the wooden table.

"And now we're back here, doing it all again." Harley slapped a file on the table as soon as he entered the room. His assistant gently closed the door behind him. "Your client is very lucky Gerald Rutledge is going to survive. Two bullets to the chest, but he'll be okay. He's currently out of surgery and recovering well. We're still going to charge Caleb with attempted murder."

"We'll call for a hearing under the Protection of Persons and Property Act," Bruce confirmed. "Gerald pulled a gun on his stepson and shot first, but Caleb was the only one to hit anything. It's self-defense."

"They were both at home," Harley groaned. "Because you're in your own residence, it doesn't give you the right to shoot someone else who lives there. He's still charged with attempted murder. You won't win the PPPA hearing when it's Gerald's home."

"But we'll win on self-defense," Bruce retorted. "You know it and I know it—Gerald shot first. Caleb had no duty to retreat, and he used the appropriate amount of force in self-defense."

"We'll see what the Sheriff's Department investigation returns." Harley looked at me. "It can't be your case. You'll be a witness."

"And I heard a handgun go off first."

Harley groaned again and tapped his finger on the table. "We'll see what the investigation uncovers," he repeated. "We'll see."

"Gerald was on the run," I stated. "He only came back because he got an inside word he was about to be charged for the murder of Millie Aiken. He wanted to be in and out before the arrest warrant was issued. He was collecting his things before getting on the next flight to South America. He planned to leave two days ago and never come back. He would've been gone if he wasn't stuck in a hospital bed."

Harley shook his head, trying to dismiss the theory, but I could tell it struck a nerve with him.

"I'm interested to know who gave him the inside word," I continued. "Was it you?"

"Ridiculous," Harley muttered, avoiding eye contact. "How ridiculous."

"Are you really going to charge Caleb with attempted murder?" Bruce questioned.

"For now," Harley conceded. "But like I said, we'll see what the rest of the investigation brings up. We may drop the charges when all is said and done. Given the circumstances, we won't oppose bail, so he'll be free to walk out of here tonight after the hearing."

Harley picked up the folder on the table and stood. He paused for a second, opened his mouth but then closed it again. He looked at his assistant and nodded toward the door. The assistant took the hint and left the room.

"I should let you know the Sheriff's Department called me fifteen minutes ago and said the GPS data came back. I can't tell you what the findings are because it's currently the subject of an investigation." He dropped his head in disappointment. "But we're about to charge Gerald Rutledge with the murder of Millie Aiken."

He didn't look at us. He stepped out of the room and closed the door behind him.

Bruce began to laugh, his whole body bouncing up and down. He held his hands up in the air like he was crossing the line at the end of a marathon. He looked at me with a wide grin. "You did well, city boy."

"*We* did well," I said. We stood, shook hands solidly, and then embraced.

"Maybe I was wrong to push for the plea deal," he said. "Maybe I need to review my processes."

"You're admitting you were wrong?"

"Hey, I said, 'maybe.'" Bruce smiled. "But you've done well."

"I have no doubt they'll withdraw the case against Caleb after the investigation. I clearly heard a handgun fire first. There's no way Gerald can get out of this one."

"And with the murder charge for Millie Aiken, all of Gerald's friends will abandon him. There won't be a person in Beaufort who wants to be associated with him now," Bruce noted. "And you did well with Isaiah too."

I had received a message from Stacey Casey that morning. The State had agreed to the lower charge of arson, under Section 16-11-110, paragraph C, agreeing to a suspended sentence without any prison time. They wanted the case over and the story out of the headlines. It wasn't a good look for the State, and I leveraged that for Isaiah's case. I called him and he agreed to plead guilty for his actions and accept the deal. We still needed to sign the documents, but he wouldn't serve a day in prison, and he'd still be able to work and support his family.

Ethically, I also had to let the prosecution know that Isaiah had left the state borders, but I told them he had left for work, presenting them with payment receipts, and they let him off with a warning.

Isaiah was a good guy in a hard situation, and I was glad to be able to help him. He'd learned his lesson. And I didn't think he'd be burning down any more barns anytime soon.

"So, what's next?" Bruce asked.

"I'm sure the insurance company will investigate John Pearson and see if he was involved in the burning of the crops," I said. "He denied he knew what Gerald Rutledge was going to do when Pearson told him about the weevils, and came home one night to see the crop alight. I agreed to be Pearson's personal lawyer if they didn't accept his explanation."

"It's still all work with you." Bruce laughed. "I was hoping you'd say another round of golf."

With smiles on our faces, we walked to the foyer of the courthouse. It was as quiet as a library. It was empty except for one man, leaning by the far wall, staring at us with his hands in his pockets. The smile dropped from my face and I glared at him.

The man glared back.

"Leave him alone," Bruce said, placing a hand on my shoulder and guiding me away from a confrontation. "You've got to help me prepare for Caleb's bail hearing."

I stepped away, breaking eye contact with the man, but I knew it wouldn't be the last time I crossed paths with Stephen Freeman.

CHAPTER 64

Life in the Lowcountry had its own special beat.

On a quiet Sunday morning, Jane and my grandparents arrived at our home after they'd been to church. Jane, Grandma Lincoln, and Emma worked in the kitchen, preparing a pot roast for later that day, while Granddad Lincoln and I worked in the garden, pruning back several bushes.

When the time ticked past 1 p.m., we stopped for lunch and a game of cards. With little breeze about, we sat outside in the yard to play. I set up the table, Emma brought out the chairs, and Grandma Lincoln carried the sandwiches, sweets, and cookies.

Together, we ate, we laughed, and we challenged each other. We yelled when we thought someone was cheating, and expressed surprise when a game was close. I slapped my cards on the table when I thought I had won but I was always trumped by a smiling Emma. Granddad Lincoln punched me in the arm and told me I was a cheat. Grandma Lincoln remained focused, as if the card game was an intense battle for intellectual supremacy. When she hadn't won for a while, I held my cards back and let her take the win. The joy and smile on her face was worth the loss. We competed, we celebrated, and we connected. When the cards were done, with an unsurprisingly close finish, we carried everything back inside. Emma and I loaded the dishwasher, under the watchful eye of Grandma Lincoln. She had always wanted equality for men and women, and always made sure I did my share of the housework. With the dishwasher loaded, she checked on the pot roast, before she went to the living room to watch a reality television show with Emma and Jane. Granddad Lincoln had waited outside, sitting quietly under the buzz of the South. With two beers in hand, I joined him, handing him one.

"You did well in the murder case," Granddad Lincoln confirmed. "We're proud of you. You made a difference to that young man's life, and to this community. That means something, Dean."

I nodded my response, sitting down with a smile on my face.

"So, did you decide on the answer to my question?"

I squinted. "Which question?"

"Whether you want to be a worker who churns along in the big-city machine, or someone who leads real change in his community? Do you want individual success, or do you want to shape cultural change?"

I didn't answer, taking a sip of my beer instead.

The thought rolled around in my head for a while before Rhys's truck pulled up to the driveway.

Zoe and Ollie jumped out of the truck the second it stopped, running toward the house, eager to play a game of hide-and-go-seek with Emma. They raced inside and a moment later, they dragged Emma out of the house, each child holding one of her hands. When they made it to the yard, Emma started counting loudly with her hands covering her face. Zoe ran one way; Ollie went the other. I could still see both of them as Emma finished counting, their heads poking out of the bushes nearby. Emma looked around, spotted them, and then looked at me and smiled. She spent the next few minutes pretending to look for them until she surprised them with tickles.

The next round of the game started, and Jane called out for assistance in the kitchen. Granddad Lincoln went inside and helped prepare the meal.

"Thanks for having us over for dinner," Rhys said as he came out of the house with a beer. He leaned against the porch railing, watching the joy on his kids' faces as Emma found them, chased them, and tickled them again. "It takes a lot of pressure off preparing for the week ahead."

"Anytime," I responded. "Emma and Jane have spent most of the day preparing the pot roast. It gives them a reason to spend all day in the kitchen together. It's good for both of them."

When Jane called everyone inside to eat, Rhys reached out and rested a hand on my shoulder. I turned and saw the concerned look in his eyes. He needed to talk about something. Emma and the kids walked past us, and Emma stopped to give me a little kiss on the cheek. I told her we'd be ready in a minute. She looked at Rhys, saw his expression, and understood. She closed the door behind her as she went inside.

I turned and stood beside Rhys. I gave him a few moments to begin.

"I need to kill him, Dean," he whispered.

"Paul Freeman?"

Rhys nodded.

"You can't, Rhys. We've been through this. You can't touch him. Your children need you."

Rhys's grip tightened around the porch railing. His knuckles went white. "I can't stop thinking about him since he was released from prison. It's eating me alive. I can't sleep. I can't think straight. I can't do anything without seeing his face in my mind."

"Rhys—"

"I need to kill him, Dean. An eye for an eye. I need to honor my wife's memory."

"You can't, Rhys. You've got your kids to think about. They need you more than you need revenge."

He stared out at the yard for a long moment. "Then I need you to take them down, Dean," he said. "The whole corrupt Freeman family. I need you to crash the entire thing down on their heads. Either you do it within the law, or I'll do it my way."

I said nothing, watching as the sun began to touch the horizon.

"Promise me, Dean." Rhys turned to stare at me. "Promise me you'll take them down. Promise me you'll stop them."

We stood silent for a minute, before I nodded. "For Heather's memory, I'll stop them."

I made the statement with conviction, but Grandma Lincoln's statement from weeks earlier was echoing in my thoughts: *"How do you stop a family that controls everything?"*

ABOUT THE AUTHOR

Peter O'Mahoney is the author of the best-selling Joe Hennessy, Tex Hunter, and Jack Valentine thrillers. O'Mahoney was raised on a healthy dose of Perry Mason stories, and the pace and style of these books inspired him to write, and he hasn't stopped since. O'Mahoney loves to write fast-paced stories filled with exciting characters, thrilling legal cases, and mind-bending plot twists. His thrillers have entertained hundreds of thousands of readers around the world.

O'Mahoney is a criminologist, with a keen interest in law, and is an active member of the American Society of Criminology. When not writing or spending time with his family, O'Mahoney can be found in the surf, on the hiking trials, in the boxing gym, at home reading, or staring at a beautiful sunset in wonder.

Follow the Author on Amazon

If you enjoyed this book, follow Peter O'Mahoney on Amazon to be notified when the author releases a new book!
To do this, please follow these instructions:

Desktop:

1) Search for the author's name on Amazon or in the Amazon App.
2) Click on the author's name to arrive on their Amazon page.
3) Click the "Follow" button.

Mobile and Tablet:

1) Search for the author's name on Amazon or in the Amazon App.
2) Click on one of the author's books.
3) Click on the author's name to arrive on their Amazon page.
4) Click the "Follow" button.

Kindle eReader and Kindle App:

If you enjoyed this book on a Kindle eReader or in the Kindle App, you will find the author "Follow" button after the last page.